No Loyalty

Also by De'nesha Diamond

PARKER CRIME CHRONICLES
Conspiracy
Collusion

THE DIVA SERIES
Hustlin' Divas
Street Divas
Gangsta Divas
Boss Divas
King Divas
Queen Divas

ANTHOLOGIES
Heartbreaker (with Erick S. Gray and Nichelle Walker)
Heist and *Heist 2* (with Kiki Swinson)
A Gangster and a Gentleman (with Kiki Swinson)
Fistful of Benjamins (with Kiki Swinson)

Also by A'zayler

Passion of the Streets
Heart of the Hustle

Published by Kensington Publishing Corp.

No Loyalty

De'nesha
Diamond

A'zayler

KENSINGTON PUBLISHING CORP.
www.kensingtonbooks.com

DAFINA BOOKS are published by

Kensington Publishing Corp.
119 West 40th Street
New York, NY 10018

All Kensington titles, imprints, and distributed lines are available at special quantity discounts for bulk purchases for sales promotion, premiums, fundraising, and educational or institutional use.

Special book excerpts or customized printings can also be created to fit specific needs. For details, write or phone the office of the Kensington Sales Manager: Kensington Publishing Corp., 119 West 40th Street, New York, NY 10018. Attn. Sales Department. Phone: 1-800-221-2647.

Dafina and the Dafina logo Reg. U.S. Pat. & TM Off.

ISBN-13: 978-1-4967-1146-5
ISBN-10: 1-4967-1146-7
First Kensington Trade Paperback Printing: August 2018

eISBN-13: 978-1-4967-1148-9
eISBN-10: 1-4967-1148-3
First Kensington Electronic Edition: August 2018

10 9 8 7 6 5 4 3 2 1

Printed in the United States of America

DANGEROUS
LIAISONS

De'nesha Diamond

CHAPTER 1

2015

After weeks of record rainfall, the sun returned to southern California in time for the memorial service for Javid Ramsey. It was a good turnout of family and friends. Even Javid's estranged parents made an appearance. Of course, they sobbed on each other's shoulders and occasionally cornered the widow for details of their son's tragic end and why there was such a hurry to cremate the body.

Stone-faced and dry-eyed, Klaudya Ramsey gave no fucks about their fat tears and had no interest in assuaging their guilt for financially cutting off their son years ago—and for never welcoming her into the family when she married Javid.

Truth be told, Klaudya didn't even give a fuck about the ashes in the urn. In life, and especially in love, Klaudya had only asked for one thing: loyalty. Muthafuckas act like it's the hardest thing to give to their loved ones when it should be the easiest.

Lieutenant Erik Armstrong and his partner, Lieutenant Joe

Schneider, late to the service, blended in with the attending guests.

Armstrong kept his gaze centered on the dry-eyed widow while her eight-year-old twins, Mya and Mykell, looked like their beautiful mother's opposites, especially the boy. His small body trembled and shook with racking, silent sobs before the bronze urn.

Across from the grieving Ramseys stood another stone-faced observer, Nichelle Mathis—Klaudya's young mother. For more than a year, the mother and daughter had kept the Calabasas' grapevine buzzing. To Armstrong's chagrin, he'd played a part in it all. Only he believed he was helping an estranged mother and daughter heal their relationship, not setting up a death match between the two of them. If only he could have put two and two together much sooner—but it went back to the night of the first murder . . .

1995

The house looked like a war zone.

Veteran first responders mumbled to one another that they had never seen this level of carnage in their entire careers. In the center of the living room, a black male, wearing only a pair of silk boxers, lay sprawled across the floor with half of his skull splattered on the ceiling and walls. A bloody bat was clenched in his left hand.

"My God," Detective Erik Armstrong whispered, shaking his head. "The whole damn world has gone crazy."

"No shit, Sherlock," his partner, Detective Joe Schneider grumbled back, taking it all in.

The police and emergency responders held a brief debate about whether they needed to take the lone survivor, eight-year-old Klaudya Ramsey, to the hospital or straight to the police station. Soon after an ambulance arrived, they told her she needed to see a doctor.

Detective Armstrong cocked his head and smiled at the wide-eyed child. "Did you hear me, sweetheart?"

Klaudya couldn't unglue her lips to respond or stop the tears from streaming down her blood-splattered face.

The cop's concern dissolved into pity. "Poor thing. You're still in shock." He comforted the child. "Is there anyone we can call? A family member?"

Klaudya bunched her shoulders and sidestepped the cop's touch.

Armstrong took the hint and backed off.

It took forever for an extra ambulance to arrive. More people drifted in and out of the girl's face, asking questions. She stared, her bottom lip trembling while bodies of her family were carried out on stretchers.

At long last, her mother, Nichelle Mathis, was escorted out of the house. She held her head down with her hands cuffed behind her back.

Detective Armstrong pulled the child closer as they both watched her blood-covered mother marched toward a patrol car. At its back door, Nichelle locked gazes with her daughter.

Klaudya shivered. The ride to the hospital passed by in a blur. When a doctor and nurse came to see her behind a curtain, they wore matching plastic smiles and launched the same questions.

The questions slowed to a trickle.

"Nod or shake your head if you feel any pain," the doctor instructed before checking out her bruises. It was stupid because she was already in pain. Everywhere. But she refused to nod or shake her head.

By the time the doctor and nurse left her alone behind the curtain, their smiles were thin and flat. Later, she was taken to a strange place and led into a kid's room filled with toys. She was told to wait and that someone would be in in a minute to talk to her.

"Feel free to play with anything you want," a woman, whose name she'd already forgotten, said. Once the door closed, Klaudya sat trembling in the small room, covered in her father's blood. The bright toys clashed with slate gray walls, giving her conflicting vibes about how she was supposed to feel. She wished she could stop crying. How many times had her mother said that she wasn't a baby anymore? But it was hard, and she was scared.

Each tick on the clock matched the rhythm of her pounding eardrums. After two solid hours of it, Klaudya's head ached, and her eyelids were impossible to keep open. She'd nod off and jerk herself awake every other minute. Her next wave of tears was of frustration instead of anger. She wanted to go home and crawl into her bed.

Outside the door, she heard the police officers shuffle back and forth in the hallway. Maybe they forgot she was in there. It was possible, she reasoned. Adults always get busy and ignored her all the time. Klaudya wrestled with the decision about whether she should leave on her own. She knew where she lived. She'd taken the city bus home plenty of times. Only . . . she didn't . . . have any money. You can't do anything without money.

Her eyelids were like bricks again. She caved and laid her head on the table. Tonight's horror sped behind her closed lids. She could still see her father lunging.

Bang!

Klaudya woke with a jump.

A strange woman smiled at her. "I'm sorry. Did I startle you?" She closed the metal door behind her.

Lips zipped, Klaudya eyed the woman crossing over to the table.

When the woman settled into the chair across from her, she made her introduction. "I'm Mrs. Durham. You're Klaudya, right?"

Silence.

"Do you mind if I talk to you for a minute?"

Silence.

"Oookay." The woman held onto her smile. *"You're in shock and a bit confused about all the things going on right now—that's understandable. You're probably even scared, and that's okay, too."* She stretched out a hand, but Klaudya jerked away from her icy touch.

"Can I ask whether you remember what happened tonight?"

Silence.

"Do you remember anything at all?"

The image of her father's gun firing flashed in her head, but she said instead, *"Can I go home?"*

Mrs. Durham's ridiculous smile vanished, and her thin lips flatlined. *"I'm sorry, sweetheart. It may be a while before you can do that. But we're working on getting you placed somewhere safe. Everything is going to be all right."*

Tears pooled in Klaudya's eyes. *"But . . . but . . ."* She swallowed hard, but it was still hard to slow her breathing. *"What about Momma? She's coming with me, right?"*

"Aw, sweetie. I'm afraid not." Durham reached for the girl's hand and, again, Klaudya pulled farther away.

"I want my momma. Now!" Klaudya's bottom lip trembled.

Mrs. Durham shook her head. *"I'm afraid it may be a long time before that happens."*

"When can I see my daughter?" Nichelle asked the first officer entering the interrogation room.

"We'll get to that in due time." Armstrong settled wide-legged into the chair across from her while his partner stayed back and leaned against the door.

"She was scared and in shock when I left her. I have to talk to her and make her understand that everything is going to be all right. I'm going to take care of everything."

Armstrong's eyes narrowed as he watched her fret. She hadn't been processed and was still covered in her husband's blood. Her eyes were unusually wide.

"Calm down, Mrs. Mathis. Your daughter is in good hands. She is being well taken care of."

"But I will get to see her again, right? I can get one of the girls down at the club to bring her in for a visit, right? They do let you do that, right?"

"Mrs. Mathis, we need to go over what happened tonight. We need to know what happened to your husband and your son."

Tears streaked Nichelle's face as she opened and closed her mouth without a single word falling from her lips. Until that moment, she hadn't formulated what she was going to tell the police. Reality hadn't set in. Her daughter may have been in shock, but she was in denial. Nichelle needed a story and quick.

Armstrong cleared his throat and wrangled her thoughts back to the present. "You and your husband have quite the record of domestic violence. He'd call the police on you, and you call the police on him. He'd beat you up, and you'd beat him up. Which was it tonight, Mrs. Mathis? And who hurt little Kaedon?"

"That was an accident."

"But your husband wasn't an accident? Is that what you're saying?"

"What? No. He was . . . I was . . ." Her mouth kept moving even after the words stopped flowing.

Armstrong turned and glanced back at Schneider, who looked down at the woman and shook his head. Sighing, Armstrong turned back to their suspect and pushed her for an answer. "Tell us what happened to your husband, Mrs. Mathis?"

Another tear streaked down her face. "What happened? Shadiq . . . got exactly what he deserved."

At the end of the eulogy, Armstrong made a sign of the cross while the crowd's gazes crept toward him and his partner.

It was time.

They had a job to do. Together, the two lieutenants marched through the crowd.

"Nichelle Mathis?"

The flawless older beauty turned with her brows already arched inquisitively. "Yes?"

"We have a warrant for your arrest." Schneider flashed the warrant while Armstrong produced the handcuffs to the astonished woman.

"What?" Her beautiful caramel skin flushed.

"You have the right to remain silent . . ."

Nichelle stuttered indignantly as the funeral crowd halted in their tracks to stare.

Armstrong wasn't without sympathy as they led her back through the crowd. He did, however, make a sidelong glimpse at Klaudya. Her ice-cold expression had yet to change. No, that wasn't right. It had changed. A small smile tugged at the corners of her lips.

Not for the first time, Armstrong wondered whether they were arresting the right woman.

CHAPTER 2

Locked behind prison bars, Nichelle couldn't believe she was right back where she'd started. "This can't be happening," she repeated, raking her hands through her hair. How was she going to convince anyone she didn't do this?

Pacing, she couldn't stop the horrible images from running in her head. She was looking at life without the possibility of parole—*again . . .*

1996

Nichelle Mathis was going home. At least that was the energy she put into the universe for the last year and a half. No matter how many times it had been explained to her, she didn't grasp how this wasn't a simple open-and-shut case of self-defense. When the state's attorney had offered a three-year plea deal, she rejected it, confident her self-defense was well within the law. It was a risk. California had a fifteen-to-twenty minimum if she was convicted. This whole thing was ridiculous. Even more ridiculous, since she couldn't post bail, Nichelle had been behind bars since that awful night. Hell, Klaudya would be ten soon. In the pictures Klaudya's latest foster fam-

ily had sent Nichelle, she couldn't believe how big Klaudya was getting. She was missing out on a lot.

Nichelle wished Klaudya could be there today. She'd envision them walking out of the courtroom together and riding off into the sunset on the Metro to start her wreck of a life over. Everyone deserves a second chance. She clutched the silver cross around her neck and prayed.

The jury took fifteen minutes before informing the court they had reached a decision.

Fifteen minutes.

That couldn't be good.

I'm going home, she insisted, batting back a surge of negative thoughts from creeping into her head.

"Don't worry." Her lawyer rubbed her arm.

When her hand lingered too long, Nichelle cut a hard look at the attorney's hand until she removed it.

"Sorry." The lawyer retreated to her side of the invisible wall between them.

"All rise," the bailiff bellowed.

Nichelle climbed to her feet as the judge returned to the bench. Once she was back in her chair, the jury trooped into the courtroom. She scanned the twelve faces as they entered and settled into their chairs, but it was no good. Each one of them had an excellent poker face. She couldn't read a single one of them.

"Foreman, have you reached a verdict?" the judge asked.

"We have, your honor." The foreman stood and handed a slip of paper to the bailiff, who walked it over to the judge. The judge fiddled with his glasses before reading the paper and handing it back to the bailiff.

"All right," the judge said. "What say you?"

Nichelle held her breath.

The middle-aged, good-ole-boy foreman cleared his throat and read, "On the charge of manslaughter, we, the jury, find the defendant . . . guilty."

No! Nichelle's heart plunged to her toes. She couldn't have heard the man right. There had to be some mistake. Didn't they see the pictures of her beaten black and blue? Guilty? How in the hell did they find her guilty?

Her shocked gaze narrowed to thin slits on the foreman. However, he and the other white suburbanites kept their noses high and their gazes diverted from her distress. They knew this shit was fucked up. They didn't give a damn. She was another black bitch being shipped off to one of their numerous concrete plantations.

While the judge thanked the jury for their time and doing their civic duty, the jailers approached her table with instructions for her to put her hands behind her back.

Nichelle wanted to refuse but knew better. The judge dismissed the jury, and then he and her attorney negotiated a sentencing date while cold steel clamped around her wrists. The state's mandatory minimum charged back into her head. Her knees weakened. Had it not been for the jailer standing right behind her, she would've hit the floor.

"Nichelle Mathis," a prison guard's voice boomed.

Startled, Nichelle stopped pacing. "Yes."

"You got a visitor."

"I do? Who?"

"What the fuck do I look like, your personal secretary?" The woman's mud brown eyes leveled at Nichelle. It was the same look most guards had around there, and Nichelle knew better than to rock the boat.

Silently, the guard walked Nichelle from public holding to a private room, reserved for prisoner and attorney meetings. The only problem was she didn't have an attorney, and a new public defender hadn't been assigned to her. When she entered the room, however, there was only a mild shock at seeing Lieutenant Armstrong there, waiting.

Nichelle glared while she waited for the guard to handcuff her to the metal table. She didn't want to sit but relented and cut to the chase. "What the hell do you want?"

"A confession," he answered honestly.

"Well, you came to the wrong place."

"Figured as much," he acquiesced.

"Great." She stood. "Does that mean we're done here?"

Armstrong sighed and leaned his large frame back into his chair. "How about you help me help you?"

"You mean like the last time you helped?"

"Last time you confessed—and this time I believe there is more than what meets the eye in this case. It doesn't mean I believe you're innocent. You did, after all, steal your daughter's life. That in and of itself is a Maury Povich shit show."

"Javid's and Klaudya's marriage was over. She just didn't know it. Javid . . . needed a more *mature* woman at his side."

Armstrong stared. "What do you expect me to think when you say things like that?"

"I didn't kill him."

"But the gun was in your hand."

Nichelle stewed in her seat. "It wasn't me."

"We're not going to get anywhere if I have to play twenty questions," he said. "And just because I'm willing to lend you an ear doesn't mean my bosses are, too. So, if there's anything you can think of that could prove your innocence, speak now or forever hold your peace."

"I told you before. I don't know what happened. Most of that night is a complete blur."

Armstrong's brows sprung up. "We're going to play the amnesia game?"

She chewed her bottom lip. "It's Klaudya. She's behind this. I know it. She couldn't get rid of me, so she got rid of Javid."

Armstrong let the accusation hang in the air.

"You don't believe me." Nichelle tossed up her hands. "Great. They may as well give me the needle."

"Chill out. You know California doesn't have the death penalty. So, please. A little less drama goes a long way."

Nichelle rolled her eyes.

"Now what about proof?" he asked. "You got any?"

She shook her head. "If I did, I wouldn't be in here now, would I?"

"Fine. Do you know how I can get some?"

"I wish. There's gotta be some way to retrace Klaudya's steps after her release from jail."

"You mean after you put her in there?"

Nichelle glared back.

Armstrong grinned. "This is only going to work if you're one hundred percent honest with me."

Instead of answering the question, Nichelle pivoted. "All I know is she was released early, and no one knew about it. Someone picked her up from jail. It had to be this old friend of hers that used to work at the Kitty Kat with her. I heard she was the only one who'd visited her in jail."

"Does this friend have a name?"

"I don't know her government name, but people call her Sassy."

CHAPTER 3

Dressed head-to-toe in widow's black, Klaudya grew exhausted from everyone's condolences and fake hugs. Outside of her clique of girlfriends, Tabitha, Bethany, Emma, and Brandi, people were there fishing for more gossip to feed into the Calabasas grapevine. For more than a year, she and her mother, Nichelle, sat on the tip of everyone's tongues. But Klaudya was confident that this time her mother was out of her life for good.

Klaudya drifted from the house full of mourners toward the estate's back French doors and watched the twins play with the other children. At least Mya was. Mykell sat alone on a patio chair with his bottom lip nearly hitting his chin.

"It's going to be all right. Hang on," Klaudya whispered against the glass paneling.

A familiar voice spoke from behind her. "It's good to see that you're holding it together."

Klaudya stiffened but didn't turn around.

Emilio Vargas moved to her side and gazed out of the back door with her. "You have my deepest and sincerest sympathies."

Klaudya bit her lower lip and refrained from telling him what he could do with his sympathies.

"I wouldn't worry about the boy," Vargas added. "I lost my father about his age. I, too, was devastated. But I was resilient; most children are. You have to lead by example."

Klaudya turned toward him. "I appreciate the parental advice."

The corner of his lips twitched. "You know. I've always . . . admired you. Not only are you stunningly beautiful, but you also got spunk, and you're a survivor."

"Thanks. Now if you would excuse me, I need to attend to my other guests." She took one step, but he smoothly cut off her path. "Is there something else I can do for you?"

"As a matter of fact, there is." He glanced around. "Perhaps there is somewhere we can talk—alone?"

Klaudya frowned. "Now?"

"I promise. It will only take a few minutes."

"Sure. Why not?" She led him through the crowd of mourners and into her home office. It was awkward since it was across the hall from her husband's, and where his body had been discovered.

Vargas made himself at home by crossing to the minibar. "Drink?"

She frowned. "Pass. I gave up the stuff."

"Ah. Smart." He commenced making his own while asking, "I hope you don't mind?"

"Knock yourself out."

He lifted his glass. *"Salud!"*

Klaudya eyed him as he tossed back a shot of whiskey.

"I'll cut straight to the point."

"I'd appreciate that."

"As you know, your husband and I were in business together. I trusted him and his partner Ari with a shitload of my money. Do you know about that?"

"Sorry, but I don't know much about the financial industry. Any time Javid talked about the business, my eyes glazed over. If you're looking for another advisor, I wouldn't even know who to recommend."

"Humph. Referral. That's cute. No. You don't understand. I *trusted* your husband. And there have been some discrepancies."

She stared, incredulous. "You trusted him? Welcome to the club. I trusted him, too, before he fucked my mother, served me with divorce papers, and played house with her for a year while I sat in jail."

"That is unfortunate."

"You think? Look. I have no idea about any . . . discrepancies. I wasn't here. Whatever stupid shit my husband was involved in, I have no clue. His secrets died with him."

Vargas stared. "So you know nothing about his . . . business?"

She struggled to follow him. "Should I? I never worked for his firm. Why don't you go and talk to Ari? I know they liquidated the company while I was away, but if there's anyone else who knows the ins and outs of the business it would be him."

Vargas's smile returned. "I would love to talk to Arlington if I could find him. Any idea where he's slithered off to?"

"Sorry. He didn't send me a postcard."

Vargas's smile expanded. "It appears this time I'm barking up the wrong tree. Apparently, Javid kept plenty of secrets from you."

The statement hung in the air between them.

What the hell did he expect her to say? "I need to get back to my other guests. Whatever it was Javid did, I'm sorry. All I want to do now is sell this place, take my children, and go somewhere where we can start all over—preferably before their grandmother goes on trial for killing their father."

Vargas appeared as if he genuinely sympathized this time. "Guess I'll have to chalk it up as a lesson learned. Loyalty is a dying attribute."

"I've learned to be loyal only to myself."

Vargas caught her bitter tone. "Then you've learned the right lesson. Any idea where you'll go?"

"Not yet. Maybe I'll spin a globe and pick out a place blindfolded."

"You know Mexico has a lot to offer. Great place to start over and raise the kids."

"You're only saying that because your son is the president."

"He could always use another vote. He did cut it close the last time."

She laughed.

He set his drink on the bar. "I should go." He waltzed over to her. "Take care of yourself."

"You, too." He kissed her forehead and left her office with a wink.

Klaudya didn't relax again until he and his bodyguards left her home.

CHAPTER 4

Lieutenant Armstrong rolled through the alley of a nondescript strip mall in seedy East Los Angeles. Drugs and prostitution plagued the streets. The men cruising for a good time didn't give a fuck about age, health status, or whether the workers were there by choice or trafficked. Erik had seen it all when he was with vice. Johns who solicited sex with their kids strapped in child seats in the back. It wasn't unusual for undercover cops to wait until *after* services rendered before making an arrest.

The shit was mild compared to what he'd seen in his years on the force.

Lieutenants Armstrong and Schneider stopped next to a cluster of long-legged women in too-tight clothing and colorful wigs and rolled down the window.

One woman leaned into the car. "Whatcha doing here, sugar? You looking for a date?"

"Nah," the woman in a blue wig said, leaning in next to her. "How are you doing, Officer Friendly?"

Erik smiled. "Are we that obvious?"

"Like a bright neon sign." Blue flashed a gummy smile.

They shared a laugh before Erik got to the point. "I'm looking for Sassy. Has she been around?"

The women's laughter petered out.

"Never heard of her," Blue lied.

Erik cocked his head. "Do we need to take a trip downtown to jog your memory? It could take a long time."

"Now, why do you want to fuck up my numbers?" Her eyes narrowed.

"Or you can tell me where Sassy is."

After the women shared a consulting look, Blue spit out an address.

"See? That wasn't so hard. Was it?" Armstrong asked.

The women rolled their eyes and stepped back from the car.

Thirty minutes later, Lieutenant Armstrong marched up the steel steps of Roland's Billiard Hall to an upstairs apartment. He hammered on the door and waited.

And waited.

"C'mon, Sassy. I know you're in there," he shouted through the door. "I only want to ask you a few questions."

"I don't know nothing about nothing," Sassy's slurred words filtered back.

The lieutenant's patience wore thin. "C'mon, I know you know *something* about your friend Klaudya Ramsey."

Another long pause ensued before the locks were disengaged. Seconds later, the door cracked open, and one crystal blue eyeball peered out. "Klaudya?"

Armstrong nodded.

Sassy's eye narrowed. "What has she done now?"

"I was hoping you could help me with that."

"Me?"

"Yeah. When was the last time you saw Klaudya?"

The eye rolled skyward while a half laugh ignited a bad cough.

"Are you all right?" Erik asked, concerned. He gazed over Sassy's head. "Are you alone?"

"I'm fine—and that's none of your damn business." Sassy's clap-back lost its sting when another cough rattled around in her chest.

"Are you sure you're all right?"

Sassy attempted to answer but had to turn away and doubled over as if to dislodge both lungs through her throat.

Armstrong took advantage of the situation and pushed open the door. After he traipsed through the pigsty of an apartment, he found a clean glass and filled it with water. If Sassy was upset about the violation of privacy, she pushed that shit to the side and accepted the water. While she gulped, Armstrong took another look around.

"Nice place."

Sassy cut Armstrong a sharp look over the rim of her glass.

"Klaudya Ramsey?" Armstrong reminded her.

"Haven't seen her."

"But you picked her up when she was released from prison, right?"

"How do you know about that?"

Armstrong smiled. "I'm good at my job."

Sassy re-evaluated him. "Yeah, so what?"

"So tell me about it."

Sassy popped a squat on the corner of a messy queen-size bed. "There's nothing to tell. I picked her up. End of story."

Erik plastered on a fake smile. "You can do better than that. How was her mood? Where did you take her?"

"Why? What did she do?" she asked again.

Armstrong's smile tightened. "How about I ask the questions?"

Sassy shrugged and swallowed the rest of her water.

"Well?"

"Well, what?"

Armstrong walked past Sassy and headed toward a nightstand.

"Hey! What are you doing?"

Armstrong lifted Sassy's forgotten glass pipe and a tenfold of crack rocks.

"Sheeit!"

Armstrong smiled. "Tell me about the ride."

"It was like most days—shitty. Only on that day it was raining cats and dogs two weeks ago . . .

A steady downpour of thin, needle-shaped rain made it almost impossible for Klaudya to see as she walked out of the doors of the Twin Towers Correctional Facility. The painful sheet of rain took its pound of flesh while plastering her clothes to her body. But what did it matter? She had lost everything.

Her man.

Her children.

Her life.

She shouldn't have been surprised. There was no such thing as happily-ever-after for people like her from the place she was from: hell.

Klaudya closed her eyes and kept moving because it was against the law to loiter outside the prison. The last thing she wanted was to be thrown back into a cell. She hadn't made it to the curb before her sockless feet squished around in sneakers that felt like soggy bricks. When she stepped into Bauchet Street to cross toward the county sheriff's building, a car horn blasted.

Shielding her eyes, Klaudya recognized the approaching silver Camry. "Sassy?"

The car stopped, but not before a mini-tidal wave from its tires drenched half her body.

Sassy powered down the side window. "Sorry I'm late, girl. You know how bad L.A. traffic is, even without all this bullshit rain."

"Yeah, no problem," Klaudya mumbled, going for the car door.

Locked.

"Oops. Sorry." Sassy hit the powered locks while Klaudya counted to ten.

On the second attempt, the door opened.

"Wait," Sassy shouted while scrambling to move shit out of the seat before snatching a blanket from the back like she was performing a flamboyant magic trick. "There. Now, you can sit."

"Are you sure?"

"Well, no sense in you ruining my leather seats," Sassy volleyed the sarcasm back to her.

Klaudya sat on the musky blanket and closed the door. However, the rain pelted her inside until Sassy undid the child locks and powered up the window.

"There we go. Let's get you warmed up." Sassy beamed, fiddled with the car's heat, and pulled away from the curb.

Another car horn blared.

"Fuck off!" Sassy shouted and gave the middle finger before she saw it was a cop. "Oops."

Klaudya rolled her eyes.

Like always, Sassy's white-girl magic cast its spell, and the cop rode off without issuing a warning.

At the first traffic light, the heat blowing through the vents was like the Arctic winds, and the silence between them had grown as vast as its ocean.

"Girl, I know you're glad to be out." Sassy shook her head. "But I gotcha."

Klaudya held her tongue while her back molars sawed off a level of enamel; however, she had no choice but to eat the double-decker crow pie Sassy served, unless she wanted to dive out of the car and hope Noah was in the neighborhood with a second ark.

Sassy went on, "Let's face it. The way you'd rolled out of the Kitty Kat, acting all brand-new because you landed your ass a white G with jungle fever was fucked up. Betcha thought your ass was made for life, huh?"

In her head, Klaudya counted to ten.

Sassy's smile spread wider as she rubbed more salt into the wound. "Girl, I told you men were all the same. Color doesn't mean a damn thing. All dogs fuck from behind."

Klaudya grunted. Men weren't the only disloyal mutha-fuckas. Bitches were slicker with their shit. Her gaze sliced to-ward Sassy, but she kept her lips buttoned.

"Well," Sassy continued, "at least now you see who truly got your back." She pulled her eyes from the road to meet Klaudya's dead eyes. "I'm just saying," Sassy amended. "What goes up has to come back down. Right?"

Silence.

"And you crashed flat on your face."

"Sass . . ."

"Hmmm?"

"Shut the fuck up." Klaudya's venom shut off the rest of the asinine, one-sided conversation for three miles. "Look. You can drop me off at the next block," Klaudya said as they en-tered downtown. The streets were close to flooding.

Sassy's thin lips curled. "Are you sure? I don't mind—"

"Yes, I'm sure. Pull over to the curb."

"But—"

"Pull. The. Fuck. Over."

"All right. All right. No need to lose your shit." Sassy rolled to a stop as instructed.

Klaudya jerked on the door handle and swore a blue streak when the locked door refused to let her out.

"Hold on," Sassy said, frowning and hitting the power locks.

Shoving the door open, Klaudya scrambled out of the car, dropping pages from her stuffed notebook onto the wet side-walk.

"Nooo!" She lunged and snatched them back. "Fuck. Fuck. Fuck."

After watching Klaudya lose her shit for a few seconds,

Sass offered, "K, you don't have to walk in this shit storm. I can take you home."

"Thanks. But—"

"I can even keep my mouth shut if you want."

The offer was tempting. "I got it."

Sassy tossed up her hands. "Fine. I'm not begging a bitch to help her ass out."

Klaudya slammed the door.

Sassy rolled down the passenger's-side window. "Good luck putting your shitty life back together. Call me when you're ready to be a real bitch again." Sassy peeled from the curb and sent another mini tidal wave of pooling rainwater to drench Klaudya's ass again.

"Fuck!" Klaudya sputtered. A few self-pitying tears mingled with the sharp rain pelting her face. It was all right, though. She was still at least a foot from rock bottom. It was progress.

The pity party lasted a full thirty seconds before she shut that shit off and sloshed one foot in front of the other to her final destination: Home . . .

"And that's it. That was the last time I saw her," Sassy finished.

Lieutenant Armstrong frowned. "Where did she go?"

Sassy shrugged. "I don't babysit grown women. She wanted to walk in the rain like an idiot, so I let her walk. End of story."

Armstrong stared at Sassy until she erupted into another coughing fit, after which Erik dropped his gaze and sighed. He'd hoped this visit wouldn't lead to another brick wall—but it had. "All right." He removed a business card from his pocket. "If you remember anything else or . . . if you hear from Klaudya again, give me a call."

Sassy stared at the card.

Armstrong lifted a brow. "Is that a problem?"

"No." She snatched the card from the lieutenant's fingertips. "If I hear from her, you'll be the first person I call." She tossed the card to the side.

It was a lie, but Armstrong let it slide. "I'll see myself out."

Sassy rolled her eyes. "Are you sure you can manage?"

Back at the car, Lieutenant Armstrong climbed in behind the wheel.

"Well?" Schneider asked.

"Nothing. Sassy picked Klaudya up and dropped her off in the middle of downtown."

"She didn't say where?"

"Nope."

Schneider sighed while Armstrong started the car. "Where did you go, Klaudya? More importantly, what in the hell did you do?"

CHAPTER 5

The storm

Lightning flashed across the night sky, illuminating the Ramseys' haunted Calabasas house.

At least it was haunted to Javid. There wasn't a single nook or cranny in the estate that didn't stir old memories. Happy memories—like the day he and his wife, Klaudya, had completed building the home after two years and a dozen divorce threats. Strange how once they finished the project, they'd forgotten about all the pain and stress with lying contractors, greedy inspectors, and lazy laborers who believed budgets were guidelines and that money grew on trees.

However, christening the house had been fun.

Lots of fun.

It was the second-best week of their marriage, next to the honeymoon. Javid had been convinced the twins, Mya and Mykell, were conceived in the custom-made sauna room, but Klaudya insisted it had been on the chaise longue in her queen bedroom walk-in closet. Her confidence and certainty eventually convinced Javid as well. One doesn't argue with a woman's intuition . . . or more accurately, one didn't argue with Klaudya—period.

Javid turned away from the living room's bow window. A smile ghosted Javid's lips as his green gaze drifted toward his wife's picture, hanging from the opposing wall. A familiar ache throbbed in his chest and in his groin.

Klaudya's angelic face smiled back from a black-and-white portrait. She sat on a gold-toned Calacatta marble floor, swallowed in one of his white business shirts. Her long, tousled, black hair and sly Colgate smile completed her sexy, just-been-fucked look. If her smile and penetrating dark gaze didn't steal a man's heart, her long legs were guaranteed to quick-start every straight hot-blooded male's imagination. Javid's churned right now.

It had been more than a year since Klaudya had slept under this roof, and Javid doubted she would ever again. After all that time, he still didn't know how everything had gone off the rails. They were happy once—weren't they?

Javid stared into his wife's eyes until he saw shadows he'd never seen before: hints of a troubled soul. He edged closer and gazed beyond the reflected lights hitting the glass. It was there. Faint. But it was there. Why hadn't he noticed it before?

Thunder boomed.

"Aaaargh," six-year-old Mya and Mykell Ramsey screamed and raced into the living room.

Javid collapsed to the floor and shoved his fingers into his ears. "Ah. Ah. My ears!"

The children's squeals of fear morphed into peals of laughter at his shenanigans. It was a much better sound and warmed his heart, especially from Mya. She had a machine-gun laugh much like her mother's. It was as loud as it was infectious.

Noticing her father was wide open on the floor, Mya sprinted forward and was airborne when Javid saw he was in trouble. He'd barely gotten his fingers out of his ears before

Mya finished her somersault and stuck the landing in the center of his softening abs.

"Oomph!" Air whooshed out of Javid's lungs. A second later, pain, from the sixty-pound cannonball of a child, made stars and tweeting birds rotate his head like in a cartoon.

The twins were hysterical.

When Javid could breathe again, he sought revenge and transformed into the all-feared Tickle Monster. He attacked their bellies for all he was worth and until the children forgot about the brewing storm and filled the house with more laughter. Father, goofball, warrior, and hero, Javid was all the twins had left of their crumbling life foundation.

"Who wants cookies?" Nichelle sang, entering the room.

Almost all they have left, Javid corrected himself.

Beaming from ear-to-ear, Nichelle Mathis entered the family room with a smile the size of California.

"Me! Me! Me!" The twins bounced and waved their hands, hoping to be the first to receive their grandmother's delicious white chocolate cookies.

Even Javid's mouth watered for one. He'd developed a sugar addiction since his mother-in-law had moved in and taken the reins of running the house in Klaudya's absence. Often their housekeeper, Ruthie, complained of not having anything to do.

"Oooh. Look at those grubby hands," Nichelle chastised, smiling. "I know you guys aren't going to put those dirty hands on my nice tray of cookies without washing them first."

Disappointment rippled across the children's faces for a nanosecond before they bolted out of the living room, shoving each other out of the way to get to the downstairs half bathroom.

Laughing, Javid climbed to his feet. "Those cookies are like magic. I suspect they're how you get them to clean their rooms, too."

"I plead the fifth," Nichelle said, eyes sparkling.

Javid's chest ached. Klaudya's eyes used to sparkle the same way when she flirted with him. His cock throbbed at the memory, and the jovial mood shifted into awkward territory.

Nichelle moved into his personal space and gazed at him. "Is everything all right?"

Javid smiled, still uneasy about their new dynamic. He hadn't meant to stumble onto this forbidden path, but he'd be damned if he knew how to get out of it now. Nichelle was a warm and shapely body at a time when he needed comfort. Nichelle had only been sixteen when she had Klaudya, which made her only six years older than him. It was well within societal norms for them to hook up. But it was only physical for Javid. Klaudya had his heart. He hadn't meant for one night of pleasure to turn into a permanent thing, but Nichelle Mathis wasn't the type of woman who a man could refuse. And now with Klaudya getting out of jail any day now, he was in one hell of a fix. Javid wanted his wife back, but Nichelle expected him to serve Klaudya with divorce papers.

This mess was his fault.

"Javid?" Balancing the cookie tray with one hand, Nichelle cupped his right cheek in the palm of her left. "Are you all right? You look tired."

At her touch, he jolted back and shook the wild thoughts out of his head. "Um, yeah. I'm fine."

"Maybe you should hit the sack early? Hmm? I can handle the kids for the rest of the evening."

The static from her touch still burned his cheek. The earnestness in her eyes, the sexiness of her smile, and the "fuck-me-now" perfume she wore fogged his brain and restarted the triple-X reel in his head.

CRASH!

Javid and Nichelle jumped.

"What the hell?" Javid swore.

The tray of cookies wobbled, but Nichelle's waitressing

game was no joke as she claimed her balance before a cookie could hit the polished floor.

Javid stepped around Nichelle, breaking her spell, to go and investigate.

The twins raced into the living room the same way they left, shoving and arguing.

"Daddy, did you hear?" Mya asked.

"Yeah, sweetheart. You and your brother stay with your grandmother."

"What was it?" Nichelle lowered her tray for the children to grab as many cookies as they wanted.

Javid stepped over broken glass and crept toward a broken window. Among the shards of glass lay a tennis ball–sized river rock, like the ones lining the dry creek bed in the backyard. He peered out of the unbroken panels in the window and into the night where silver sheets of rain fell at a forty-degree angle. The howling wind made his heart race, his skin pimple with goose bumps, and the hairs on the back of his neck stand at attention. Was he being watched?

Calabasas wasn't the type of place where people made a habit of locking their doors but, tonight, danger thickened the air.

"What's the matter?" Nichelle persisted. "What are you looking at?"

Javid strained his eyes for a second sweep of the backyard and shook his head.

"Nothing." But his gut told him he was wrong. He picked up the rock. At its weight, there was no way it could have possibly sailed through the window without a considerable amount of heft, and it wasn't exactly tornado weather raging outside.

"I thought I saw . . ." Javid's gaze scanned the vast backyard of the estate during the next flash of light, but he wasn't quick enough to cover it all. He didn't even know what he was looking for.

"You thought you saw what?" Nichelle asked, stopping to stand next to him before the bow window to inspect the darkness herself.

Javid forced a laugh out his dry throat. "I'm tired. That's all." Again, he turned away from the window as another lightning flash illuminated the sky.

A lone figure among the silver, slanted sheets of rain and tucked beneath a tall tree caught Nichelle's eye. She gasped.

"What is it?" Javid spun back around.

She shook her head and slapped on a plastic smile before pulling him away from the window. "Nothing. It's . . . getting crazy out there. Maybe we should check the Weather Channel?"

Bang!

The children screamed as the entire house pitched into darkness.

"It's okay," Javid said, racing to the children and wrapping his arms around them. "I'm here." Confused, he added, "The backup generator should have kicked on."

The hairs on the back of Nichelle's neck rose. *She's here.* "Fuck."

"Oooh. Grandma said a bad word," Mya tattled.

Grandma. Nichelle took advantage of the dark and rolled her eyes. She was too damn young to be a goddamn grandmother. Carefully, she inched her way to the coffee table and set down the rest of the cookies. "We should light some candles or find a couple of flashlights."

"Yeah. That's a good idea," Javid stood only for the twins to cling to his legs.

"Daddy, don't go. I'm scared," Mya whined.

Nichelle rolled her eyes again and mumbled, "Such crybabies."

"There's no need to be scared," Javid said. "You're safe. Lights go out during storms all the time, sweetie. It's no big deal. You two stay here with granny and help her light candles while I go and check the fuse box."

Javid pried Mya's arms from around his leg while she cried.

Nichelle swallowed her annoyance before she inched around the room in search of the long matches kept by the fireplace.

Javid quieted Mya's tears as Nichelle bumped into a large vase, causing it to crash to the floor . . . on top of her foot.

"Goddamn it!"

The children gasped.

"Nichelle!"

But the pain was too great for Nichelle to give a shit about her language or her perfected Mary Poppins bullshit. For thirty seconds, her inner hood-rat-slash-convict tumbled out in front of her shocked grandchildren. When the pain receded, she explained, "I think it's broken."

Javid huffed and crossed the room to offer assistance. It surprised her when he swept her into his arms.

"Oh, my," she laughed, wrapping an arm around his neck. "Look how strong you are."

"Please. You weigh close to nothing, and you know it." Javid carried her over to the over-pillowed sofa.

Nichelle smiled while she enjoyed his sinewy muscles and intoxicating male scent. All her hard work was paying off. She'd been wiggling her ass in front of her son-in-law since she'd gotten out of prison and shown up uninvited at the front door. In all honesty, she was stunned at how well her daughter was living. Klaudya had shown signs of becoming a stunner in her earlier years, but there were never guarantees in life. Never in Nichelle's wildest dreams did she envision for one second that her daughter would land herself a white millionaire and be living like a fucking queen in Calabasas.

Nichelle's pride in her daughter only lasted a few minutes. Jealousy reared its head and overrode everything. She could admit it now. As the days and months passed, Nichelle justified her emotion. After all, she had lost twenty years of her life because of Klaudya.

"Mya and Mykell, you two come away from the broken glass," Nichelle snapped.

Javid's parental alarm bells went off at seeing how close the twins were to injuring themselves. "Whoa, whoa. Back it up," he instructed and ushered them out of the room to the dining room to finish with their late-night snack. When he returned to the living room, it was with a broom and a dustpan.

BOOM!

The twins squealed again as the entire property shook. Earthquake?

Klaudya's picture fell off the wall. The edge of the frame clipped the side of Javid's head and smashed his big toe, exposed in his Adilette slides. He jumped as if Freddie Kruger had leaped out of a nightmare. While his heart rammed against his chest, Javid swore his wife's picture now held a look of amusement. His eyes had to be playing tricks on him. Right?

Javid grabbed a flashlight and slipped out of the downstairs backdoor. Immediately, he regretted not stopping an extra two minutes to grab a jacket or at least better shoes. Drenched within seconds, Javid may as well have been naked the way the wind sliced through him. He sloshed through the soggy grass, telling himself it would only take a few minutes to fix whatever was wrong with the backup generator and he'd be back inside his warm house. The only problem was Javid wasn't much of an electrician. He centered his flashlight over the generator's box. Was there a wire out of place or a particular switch he was supposed to push? Suddenly, Javid's man card was on the line. Men were supposed to be able to protect and fix things around the house. Javid Ramsey, a trust fund kid from Bel Air, wasn't exactly raised doing alpha male things. If something broke, you called a repairman. He didn't hunt, and the only thing he knew about cars was how good they looked and how much the best ones cost. So why in the hell was he out there acting like he knew what the fuck he was doing?

"C'mon, baby. Tell Daddy what's wrong with you." Javid

scrambled around the unit, wishing he'd paid more attention to the technician who installed the unit. But he knew why he hadn't. Klaudya was the jack-of-all-trades in the family. In truth, he'd learned there wasn't much she didn't know how to do. The rare times when she didn't, she made sure to find out and master it.

"Goddamn it!" Javid's patience snapped. Nothing stood out as being obviously wrong with the unit. He was at a loss. The freezing temperature made its way into his marrow while his back teeth clacked together. "Fuck it." He closed the unit and stood. Whatever the hell was wrong with the damn thing would just have to wait until he could get a repairman out there. Everyone could just camp out by the fireplace and light candles. They could make a game of it—make it fun.

Snap!

Javid froze and swung his flashlight further into the back-yard. Thunder rolled while he narrowed his gaze to search whether he was alone. "Now you're hearing shit." At the next flash of lightning, Javid quit and sloshed toward the house. As he neared the house, Javid, again, sensed he was being watched.

After opening the back door, Javid made another cursory glance around the yard. His attention focused on the woods. Hell, it could be anything from coyotes to bears out there. His nerves jumbled into a knot.

He dismissed the ominous feeling and stepped into the house. As he closed the door, he scanned the woods again. Something was out there.

Minutes later, he returned to the upstairs family room. Nichelle and the children had already lit every candle in the room.

"Well?" Nichelle asked.

"No luck." He shook his wet hair. "Maybe the power company will get the main power restored soon. I'll get some-one out here tomorrow to take a look at the backup generator. I couldn't see what the hell was wrong."

Nichelle looked at the children. "Well, I guess I'll get you guys off to bed."

Mykell and Mya groaned.

"No, we want to sleep in here."

Nichelle started to argue back when Javid cut her off.

"Let them. It'll be fun to camp out here around the fireplace."

Nichelle clamped her jaw tight while a smile strained her lips. "I guess it's settled. You sleep in here tonight."

The children erupted, "Yea!"

Javid smiled. "C'mon, I'll walk you guys to your bedrooms so you can change into your pajamas and grab your sleeping bags. I gotta change, too, anyway."

After another jubilant shout, the children clustered around their father while he led them out of the family room.

At Mykell's bedroom door, Javid handed over the flashlight with the instructions for his son to escort his sister back to the second floor after they changed clothes and grabbed their sleeping bags. Mya snatched the flashlight from her brother.

"I'll do it," Mya said, indignant. "I'm the oldest."

"Just by two measly minutes," Mykell complained.

"It still counts."

Javid smiled. "All right, you two. No fighting." But feeling his son's pain, Javid added, "Mya, just because you're the oldest doesn't mean you can't allow your brother to be a gentleman and escort you to the family room."

Mykell's bottom lip stretched out further.

"Fine. All right," Mya said, handing over the flashlight. "You can have it."

Mykell beamed.

Javid ruffled his son's loose curls and headed off to the master bedroom, where he peeled out of his wet clothes. He had every inch of the room memorized, and moved around in the dark easily. Since it was the end of a long day, he hit the shower. Most of the day's tension washed down the drain, but not all of it. Tonight, he had Klaudya on the brain. Nothing he did shook her off, especially the memory of the first time he'd laid eyes on her dancing on a golden pole.

The shower door opened, jarring Javid out of his private memory. When he spun around in the marble enclosure, his eyes played tricks on him. "Klaudya."

Nichelle cocked her head and settled her hands on her naked hips. "Try again."

CHAPTER 6

Lieutenants Armstrong and Schneider had connections in a lot of law enforcement and federal agencies. A casual drink with his buddy, Agent Leo Sullivan with the Federal Bureau of Investigation, led to an exchange of information he wasn't supposed to be privy to about a hot case against a drug kingpin, Emilio Vargas. Their case was heating up when an inside man had recently turned federal witness. When Armstrong heard the name, he choked on his drink.

"Arlington Chase? The same Arlington Chase who was a business partner with my murdered vic, Javid Ramsey?"

"The one and only."

"Is this your way of telling me that you're taking over my case?"

"Not yet. But I figured as a courtesy that I'd let you interview."

"Aw. You want to see if I can eliminate the mother-in-law as the murderer first."

"No sense in our showing our hand prematurely. We'll get Vargas on the drugs and money laundering charges. Murder these days is getting harder to prove."

"You don't say."

"So do you want to talk to him or not? In a few days, he's going to disappear until we solidify our case and have the bastard on trial."

"Witness protection?"

"Likely."

"Yeah. Sure. When can I do this?"

"We can go now."

"Deal." Armstrong stood from the bar and tossed down a folded twenty. A few minutes later, they drove to a low-rent hotel outside of Orange County. When they entered the room, the first thing Armstrong noticed was Mr. Chase looked as if he hadn't slept or shaved in a week—the same amount of time his business partner had been dead.

"You're investigating Javid's murder?" Ari asked.

"I am."

"Then you should look at Emilio Vargas."

"Any proof?"

"He's not the kind of man who leaves proof."

"That puts me at a crossroads since the court will be needing it. Why don't you believe the mother-in-law did it?"

"I guess she could've, but it's a little too neat for my blood."

"Neat?"

"Obvious, I should say. But anything is possible. I just know that shit is cutting a little too close to home, if you know what I mean."

"Why don't we just back it up a little? How long have you known Klaudya Ramsey?"

Chase bounced his shoulders. "For as long as Javid had. I was there the night they met . . ."

2007

Javid Ramsey was in love.

He was drunk—but he was in love, too. It didn't take al-

cohol to fall in love with curves like the goddess sliding on the pole in front of him. *Their potential client and Colombian drug kingpin, Emilio Vargas, sat equally mesmerized.*

The woman had moves, not just the well-rehearsed moves of seduction. No. This beauty had a natural rhythm that hypnotized. Long legs, pillowy breasts, and a face etched from a dream.

"I found the future Mrs. Ramsey," Javid said after the dancer, Baby Doll, exited the stage among a shower of dollar bills and thunderous applause.

Arlington Chase, Javid's partner and best friend since grade school, tossed back his head with a loud laugh before dropping a heavy hand against his buddy's back. "Slow your roll, Romeo. You've had too much to drink. One fiancée at a time."

Javid's scotch raced down the wrong pipe and jetted out his nose.

"You okay?" Ari questioned, whacking Javid across the back.

"Yeah. No thanks to you," he joked but meant it.

"Sorry about that. But maybe you forgot you already proposed to one girl this year. It's not supposed to be a habit."

Emilio Vargas exploded with laughter and wiped a residue of cocaine from his nose. "Sound advice. I wish someone told me that when I was your age. I'm on my sixth wife."

"Sixth?" Javid and Ari wore matching shocked expressions.

"What can I say? I'm a fool for love." Vargas saluted before finishing his drink.

"But you're not a fool in business," Ari segued before blowing Vargas's head up with all his accomplishments. It wasn't necessary, Vargas knew more about them than they knew themselves. He was looking for a new firm to help launder the cartel's illegal money and was confident he'd found the *perfect west coast candidates with the Ramsey & Chase financial firm.*

Ari and Javid had about nine months' worth of capital to keep their boutique company afloat and weren't in a position to turn down a deal that would prevent them from closing their doors permanently. Javid didn't want to run back to his wealthy father with his tail tucked between his legs. As far as he was concerned, they could do this for three years and then get out of the game. It was just temporary.

Though he needed to focus on the deal at hand, Javid's mind kept zooming back to the luscious Baby Doll.

"Look at him." Vargas laughed. "Your boy is sprung."

Ari halted his spiel to cast another look at Javid.

Sensing everyone's eyes on him, Javid jerked back to the present. "I'm sorry. What were you saying?"

Vargas laughed harder. "So you like black girls, huh? The man has taste."

Ari's brows careened together, but at the client's laughter, he forced out a few more chuckles of his own.

For the rest of the night, the men talked business and enjoyed a bevy of beautiful dancers—but none of them held a candle to Baby Doll.

After the deal was struck and cemented with a handshake, Javid and Ari waved goodbye to their new client outside Kitty Kat.

"We're fucking good," Ari marveled, turning toward Javid. "We fucking did it!" They slapped palms and exchanged brohugs.

"Yo, man. Do you know what this means?" Ari asked. "We're set!"

"No doubt."

The partners slapped palms again as they headed toward Javid's car. Before he slid the key into the ignition, he looked in his rearview mirror and instantly recognized a pair of golden brown legs marching across the parking lot. After un-lodging his heart from his throat, he twisted around in his seat to track Baby Doll to her car.

Then another man jumped out from behind the car. *"Where's my fucking money, bitch?"* the man growled, clutching Baby Doll by the throat and pinning her to her car. *"And I know it was you and your bitches Sassy and Brandi behind the lick! I ain't stupid!"* He placed a gun to her temple. *"Talk, bitch."*

Javid's eyes widened. *"Yo, what the fuck is this?"*

"What?" Ari twisted in his seat.

"Hey," a woman shouted across the parking lot before she and another woman raced to the defense of their friend. *"Let her go!"*

The armed man sneered, *"Speaking of your bitch-in-crime, here she comes."* He moved the gun from Baby Doll's head and leveled it at them before shouting, *"Where's my money, you ugly-ass yellow bitches?"*

Ari rolled his eyes. *"Man, this is some hood drama going down. We better get out of here. We don't want to witness shit out here."*

Javid opened his glove compartment and withdrew his .45.

"Whoa, man. What are you doing?"

"Playing hero," Javid said, sensing an opportunity for the sexy dancer to be indebted to him.

"Hero? Since when are we heroes?"

"You strapped?"

"In this neighborhood? Is that a rhetorical question?"

"C'mon," Javid instructed, opening his door.

"I don't give a fuck about neither one of you hoes," the angry gunman barked. *"I want my stacks back, and I know you bitches were behind the shit because you pulled the same lick on my nigga Cameron out in Long Beach. Your little tag team act is over. So start talking before I pump the three of you thieving bitches full of lead."*

Fearless, Sassy got in the man's face. "Bullshit. We ain't got shit to do with your punk ass getting jacked. And you need to get that gun out of my face." She mushed him upside his head and dared him to shoot.

When he clicked off the safety, it was clear he was willing to take her up on it.

Javid and Ari crept up to the other side of Baby Doll's car.

Brandi was the first to see the men's approach, and when her gaze shifted to them, it alerted the gunman. However, it was too late for him to spin around before he heard the two handguns rack.

"Let her go," Javid said.

The gunman shifted nervously but barked, "Look, man. This shit ain't got nothing to do with you. These bitches stole from me. I just want my shit back."

"I'm not going to repeat myself," Javid said.

Sassy smiled. "You heard the man. Let her go." She grabbed Baby Doll by the arm and jerked her out of his grip.

At the first burst of oxygen, Baby Doll doubled over coughing.

"All right. All right." The gunman held up his hands, his finger off the trigger. "I let the bitch go. Are you happy?"

Javid rushed around the vehicle and took the man's gun.

The gunman scowled when he saw the two suits who had got the drop on him. "Who the fuck are you two mutha-fuckas?"

"Hey! What's going on out here?" One of the club's brick wall-sized bouncers finally appeared.

"This shit ain't over," the angry gunman told the women, waving his finger as he backed away from the scene. "It ain't over by a long shot."

Baby Doll glared. "Fuck you, Dorian. If you ever put your hands on me again . . ." She searched around and then grabbed Dorian's gun from Javid's hand and took aim.

Dorian ran, but not before the stripper pulled the trigger.

Javid and Ari jumped but were relieved by the fact the girl had missed.

The bouncer's heavy boots chomped up the pavement.

"Trick muthafucka!" Baby Doll fired again, though it was clear now she aimed above his head.

Javid was appalled and turned on at the same time.

The bouncer arrived and snatched the gun from the stripper's hand. "Klaudya, what the fuck are you doing out here shooting? Have you lost your mind? We don't need the muthafuckin' cops out here."

"Where the fuck was you?" Brandi snapped. "We got johns out here lying in wait and jumping on us. Ain't it your job to make sure we make it to our cars and shit safely?"

He blinked and then stared at Javid and Ari.

"Not them," Sassy snapped. "If it weren't for them stepping in, the cops sho' nuff would be out here white-chalking our asses outside this five-dollar pussy establishment."

While the other women argued with the bouncer, Javid's gaze found Klaudya's while he chiseled on a smile. "Hey."

She returned his warm look with suspicion. "Hey yourself." She tucked Dorian's gun into her coat and went to open her car door. Plopping behind the wheel of her sun-bleached blue '98 Ford Taurus, Klaudya jimmied a metal clip so that the two wires jutting from under the dashboard would touch and turn on the lights. They came on for a few seconds and cut off.

Javid leaned into the car. "You're welcome."

"What the hell?" She jiggled the clip and . . . nothing. "Fuck!" She pressed the overhead interior light on, but it didn't come on either. Her heart stumbled over a few beats, the way it always did when car trouble was on the table.

Javid heightened his voice. "Oh, thank you for coming to my defense. I don't know what my friends and I would've done if you'd hadn't helped us."

Klaudya jammed the key into the ignition and, sure enough, it didn't turn over. The engine didn't even try. "No. No. No."

Twisting the key again, she pumped the accelerator for a magical spark. "C'mon, baby. C'mon," she begged. At the car's continued silence, Klaudya dropped her head against the steering wheel repeatedly until her eyes stung with tears. Car repairs would eat into her savings and push back the date of her moving out of her shitty apartment.

"Why can't I catch a fucking break?"

"Do you need any help?" Javid asked, despite being ignored.

She shook her head. "No thanks. Everything is fine."

"Are you sure?" he double-checked. "Doesn't look like everything is fine. I have jumper cables in my car. It shouldn't take more than a few minutes to get you started right up."

Klaudya hesitated while she looked him over. Her heart found its rhythm again, even though this potential serial killer looked more like Jared Leto back in his heyday.

Seeing the contemplation on her face, Jared Leto 2.0 expanded his smile. "I'm harmless." He held up two fingers. "Scout's honor."

Klaudya's shoulders collapsed. She even chuckled. "I never met a Boy Scout before." She opened the door and climbed out of the car. "You sure you don't mind?"

"No. It's no trouble at all." Her knight-in-shining-armor backpedaled. "I'll be right back." He jogged to his black Mercedes.

Ari looked up from his conversation with Brandi. "Are we leaving?"

"Not yet," Javid said. "I'm going to give her a jump."

Klaudya whispered to her car, "Looks like you're about to get some expensive juice, Betsey."

Javid pulled his car next to hers. Klaudya scowled for initially being impressed. After all, Mercedes were a dime a dozen in L.A. Usually assholes who drove them acted like they owned the roads. They were either movers and shakers or hustlers and posers. The Kitty Kat attracted them all.

"All right, let's see what you've got here." Javid popped the hood and sprang out of his car.

Klaudya flashed him a smile and popped her hood, too. She hovered and watched him clamp the cables on the corresponding prongs.

"Start her up," he instructed.

"Huh? Oh!" She sprinted back to her car, her cheeks inflamed. With a quick prayer, she twisted the key—the interior lights came on, but the engine remained silent.

"All right. Turn it back off."

"It never came on," she mumbled.

"Give it a moment," he suggested, folding his arms.

Klaudya reluctantly gave it a rest while he hung out at her window, grinning. "So how long have you been working here?"

"Why?"

He shrugged. "Just making conversation."

"I'm not much of a talker."

"You don't have to be with a body like yours. It does a helluva lot of talking for you."

Despite trying not to, she chuckled. "That's a corny-ass line."

"Yeah, but it made you laugh. Mission accomplished."

"So it did."

"All right. Now give it another try."

"C'mon, Betsey. Start for Momma," Klaudya begged.

The car started.

Klaudya sighed. "Thanks, old girl. Momma is going to get you a nice oil change for that solid." She rubbed the dashboard before she hopped out. "Thank you so much. I appreciate it."

"Ah, it was nothing." He removed the clamps from the battery. *The second he did, her car shut off and went dark.*

Confused, Klaudya asked, "What happened?"

He sighed. "Looks like your battery has seen its last days."

"Huh?"

"Your battery is dead. It won't hold a charge. You'll need a new one."

"Shit!" She dropped her head into the palm of her hand and rubbed her temples.

"Do you, um, have a tow service?" the stranger asked.

Hell. Klaudya didn't even have insurance. "No," she croaked.

An awkward silence lapsed between them before he offered, "We could give you a lift."

Klaudya peered at him through her spread fingers.

"We can even grab a cup of coffee along the way?"

"Uh, that's not necessary." She shook her head. "We'll call an Uber."

He cocked his head. "C'mon. We're already right here."

"Yeah—but I don't know you, and I don't hop into cars with strangers—or customers."

"Sooo . . . what? You're like on first-name basis with everyone at Uber?"

Klaudya opened her mouth to refute, but the man had a valid point.

His smile bloomed, making something flutter in the pit of her stomach. "C'mon, I'm a good guy." He placed a hand over his heart. "Scout's honor."

"You're working the hell out of the Boy Scout angle."

"Is it working?"

"Surprisingly, yes."

"Excellent." He winked. "Oh, by the way, I'm Javid Ramsey."

He offered his hand.

Klaudya whipped out her cell phone and snapped a picture.

"Whoa. What are you doing?"

"David Ramsey?" She grabbed her cell phone.

"No. Javid. J-A-V-I-D."

"Thanks." She typed in his name, moved to the back of his car and took a picture of his license plate."

"What are you doing?"

"Texting your information to our roommates so they'll have your details for the police . . . just in case."

He grinned. "Ah. Smart."

"In this millennium, it's necessary."

He whipped out his cell phone and snapped a picture. The flash blinded her for a second. "And what's your name again?" He grabbed his phone, too.

She frowned.

"Just in case." He smiled. "You know, this millennium and all." He wrangled another smile from her, and it only made her more beautiful.

"Klaudya." She slipped her small hand into his larger one. Instantly, a kinetic spark shot up her arm. She was suddenly drowning in the pools of his blue eyes. "Klaudya Mathis."

"Nice to meet you, Klaudya. Now about that cup of coffee . . . ?"

Her smile expanded as she looked at her girls. "We can do coffee."

"And that was the night Javid fell in love. They were married four months later. Javid's father was pissed that he hadn't married the woman he had picked out for him. But you only live once, right?"

CHAPTER 7

"She did it," Lieutenant Schneider told his partner over coffee the next day. "I don't know why this is so hard for you to admit. Once a murderer, always a murderer."

"C'mon. You don't believe that." Armstrong pushed his coffee away.

"Don't I?" Schneider laughed. "I'm an old enough cat to know people don't fundamentally change. They may play around the edges: get a new haircut, lose some weight, and move from an old neighborhood. But they are the same people they always were."

"All right, Dr. Schneider. Thank you for your dissertation."

"Your problem is guilt."

"Guilt?"

"Yeah. Guilt. You're the one who broke the Ramseys' happily-ever-after . . ."

2014
Calabasas, California . . .
Nestled in their seven-million-dollar dream home, Javid and Klaudya rose early to get in some playtime before the

children woke up. As usual, Javid woke with a brick-hard hard-on and Klaudya was ready to take advantage of it.

"Sex with me is amazing," Klaudya sang softly with a nice, slow grind.

Javid's curled toes dug into the mattress while his hand locked onto her hips and his head lolled among the pillows. After seven years of wedded bliss, his wife still rocked his world to its foundation.

"Ah, baby. You feel so good," he groaned, licking his lips.

Klaudya gloated and watched the range of emotions on his face. "You fuckin' love this pussy, don't you, baby?"

"Aw, fuck, yeah. Baby, you're the best."

"Damn right." She bucked, clapping her ass around the base of his cock in quick succession until her toes curled. "Yeah, baby. That's it. That's my spot," she cried.

As each of their nuts built to a climax, their attempt to remain quiet went out of the window. Before it was over, Klaudya flipped onto her stomach and Javid worked her body like a pro.

A knock sounded at the door, and seven-year-old Mykell's voice floated inside. "Mommy?"

"Shit." Javid took a pillow and plopped it over his wife's head to buffer her cries.

Unfazed, Klaudya threw her ass back into him, challenging him to keep up.

He obliged.

"Daddy?" Mya joined her twin brother on the other side of the door.

"We'll be . . . out in a few minutes, sweetheart." He smacked Klaudya's ass and took pride in his glowing handprint.

"Whose shit is this?" he growled.

The pillow muffled her answer, but it didn't matter. Every inch of her fine body belonged to Javid. He could do whatever he wanted with her.

The kids knocked again.

*"Go downstairs and get Ruthie to fix your breakfast,"
Javid barked, annoyed.*

*Whether the kids followed his instructions or not, he didn't
care. He wanted this next nut, this next blast to heaven.*

*Klaudya's body detonated first, sending an oceanic wave
of honey gushing around his cock. He cried for the almighty
before tilting forward and collapsing against her back, spent.*

*"Damn, baby," he panted. "What the hell am I going to
do with you?"*

*She pushed the pillow off of her head. "You're going to
keep doing what you've been doing."*

*"Oh, yeah?" He rolled onto his back and dragged her
into his arms. "And what's that?"*

"Love me." She kissed him. "And never let me go."

"Go? Oh, no. Never. Until death do us part, remember?"

"Yeah. I remember."

*They snuggled for a few more minutes before the commo-
tion downstairs propelled them out of bed and in for a quick
shower.*

*"You two behave," Klaudya shouted to the children while
she raced to answer the front door. However, it wasn't the plumber,
whom she was expecting. "Lieutenant Armstrong?" She peered
around his six-foot frame, but there wasn't a patrol car. "What
are you doing here?"*

*He smiled and removed his shades. "Hello, li'l K. It's
good seeing you, too."*

*"Li'l K?" She laughed, folding her arms. "I haven't been
called that in a long time. I've grown up."*

*Armstrong's gaze swept over her while his smile ex-
panded. "Yes. You most certainly have. May I come in?"*

*Klaudya's instincts were to say no and slam the door, but
she hesitated.*

"For old times' sake?" he asked.

Klaudya lifted an eyebrow. It wasn't like they were friends. "Fine. Come on in." She stepped back.

"Thanks." Armstrong crossed the threshold with his eyes widening. "Whoa. Nice place." He made a small spin in the middle of the foyer. "A place like this had to set you back a pretty penny."

Klaudya's smile tightened as she closed the door. "One or two."

He lowered his head. "Bad social grace to talk about money. Sorry, I was raised better."

Klaudya's face remained tight. "Don't worry about it." She crossed her arms again. "So what brings you all the way out here to Calabasas?"

"Would you believe I was in the neighborhood?"

"No."

"Ah, well. I was never a good liar," he joked to an una-mused Klaudya.

A glass shattered in the kitchen.

Mya screamed.

"Damn it!" Klaudya raced to see the latest destruction the twins had created. Sure enough, Mya and Mykell were engaged in a full-fledged food fight.

The sixty-five-year-old housekeeper refereed.

"Stop it. Stop it!" Klaudya clapped her hands, trying to gain the children's attention. But they were focused on killing each other with pancakes. Though Mya screamed the loudest, she was winning the fight. "Give it to me." Klaudya wrestled the last pancake from Mya's fist. "I swear I can't turn my back on you two for a minute!"

Armstrong chuckled.

"What's so damn funny?" Klaudya wrestled the sticky breakfast out of the child's closed fists but ended up with the mess all over her clothes.

"Nothing." Armstrong grabbed a roll of paper towels from off the kitchen counter and came to her aid. "It's just . . . I re-

member a time when my wife and I tackled our kids like this every morning. It was a real pain." He laughed. *"I miss those days."*

Against her will, Klaudya's heart softened toward the cop. *"I'm still waiting,"* she reminded him as she wiped Mykell's face clean. *"You weren't just in the neighborhood. All my crimes are well past the statute of limitations."*

"That's not exactly how it works. But I get your point." He chuckled.

"So?"

"Well, it's about your mother."

Ice slid through Klaudya's veins as her face turned to stone. *"My mother? What about her?"*

"Well . . . I don't know if you know, but she's out now. Sort of."

"And?"

Armstrong blinked in the face of her emotionless reaction. *"And . . . she's not doing too well. Your mother is having a hard time finding a good place to live and keeping a job. She's already violated her parole. She spent the last two nights in jail, unable to make bail. But I know a guy who knows a guy."*

"Great. Everything has been taken care of then. Is that's all?"

Lieutenant Armstrong frowned.

Klaudya slid her children's morning juice in front of them. *"Maybe you should cut the bullshit and tell me what it is you're expecting from me, lieutenant."*

"I'm sorry." Disappointment blanketed his face. *"I thought . . ."*

"What? That I give a shit about what happens to her? I don't. In her own way, she abandoned me, too."

His bushy brows jumped again. *"Does that mean you remember what happened?"*

She pulled herself together. *"You should leave."*

"I'm sorry. I made a mistake."

"Damn right, you did."

Javid's heavy footsteps thundered down the stairs.

"Shit," she muttered before her husband rushed into the kitchen.

"Sorry, sweetheart. I had to take a call and . . ." Javid stopped when he spotted Armstrong in the middle of the kitchen. "Hey, um." He glanced at his wife for an explanation while he approached Armstrong with his arm extended.

Jaw tight, Klaudya fussed with the children again.

"Lieutenant Erik Armstrong, this is my husband, Javid Ramsey. Javid, this is Lieutenant Armstrong."

The men shook hands.

"Lieutenant?" Javid attempted to catch his wife's eye again but failed. "Is there a problem, officer?"

Klaudya cut in, "There's no problem. The detective—"

"Lieutenant," Armstrong and Javid corrected her.

"He was leaving," she said.

The men stared at her while tension mounted.

Mya threw a greasy sausage at her brother, but instead of him screaming his head off, he grabbed a fistful of scrambled eggs and launched it upside his sister's head.

Klaudya's blood pressure shot through the roof. "Fuck it. I can't deal with this shit right now." She threw the roll of paper towels and stormed out of the kitchen.

The children fell silent and joined their father and Lieutenant Armstrong in staring after her.

Finally, Javid turned toward the cop.

"Sorry," Armstrong apologized again. "I didn't mean to upset her. I . . . thought she wanted to know about her mother."

Javid blinked and cocked his head. "Her mother? I thought her mother was dead?"

CHAPTER 8

The storm

Klaudya had been in the freezing rain so long she was numb. Despite knowing she needed to leave, her heart overrode her head and had her sloshing her way out of the woods and creeping toward the house. It was her house, goddamn it. She had every right to be there, had every right to see her babies and her husband. He was still her fucking husband, even if her mother had turned him against her. A lump swelled in her throat. For all her street smarts and hustle mentality, she'd failed to stay two steps ahead of her mother. Klaudya was lucky she'd landed in jail and wasn't pushing up daisies in a cemetery somewhere.

Nichelle, the liar.

Nichelle, the manipulator.

Nichelle, the gold-digger.

Klaudya should have slammed the door the moment Lieutenant Erik Armstrong appeared at her door. She listened as her babies shrieked and giggled in the midst of a pillow fight. As usual, Mya was determined to prove she was as crafty and as strong as anybody. She had her mother and grandmother to thank for that. Smiling, Klaudya maneuvered around the second-floor family room's entrance and crept up the second staircase toward the third floor.

The children's boisterous laughter faded, replaced by the sound of running water. Dread slithered up her spine; as its smooth scales glided over her delicate bones, it caused the hairs on the back of her neck to rise. The static in the air was wrong, and the steel knots in her belly threatened to do her in. However, determination forced her to put one foot in front of the other. When she took one step across the platform, her sneakers squished and squeaked so loudly, she had to stop dead in her tracks.

Convinced she'd given herself away, she froze and remained stopped in her tracks for a full minute. When no one came rushing out of the bedrooms to bust her, she exhaled a relieved breath. But before she took another step, she slipped out of her wet sneakers and headed the rest of the way toward the master bedroom barefoot.

Inside the marbled shower, Javid swallowed his disappointment and forced the corners of his lips to curl upward. He should have known she would be looking for a chance to pull a move like this. Nichelle was a smart woman. Undoubtedly, she'd sensed him pulling away from her. She'd been more than clear about what she expected in their new relationship.

He hadn't.

In fact, he'd stumbled into something he might not be able to get out of.

Nichelle took this as a sign of approval and slinked closer while she slid her arms up his chest and locked them behind his head. "I figured we could steal a few minutes alone before joining the kids downstairs." She leaned forward and drew him into a kiss.

Against Javid's will, and better judgment, his cock hardened.

Nichelle chuckled against his lips. "I knew you'd be happy to see me." Her slender fingers wrapped gingerly around his wet cock. As she stroked him, his limited number of brain cells died. "It's been a minute since we've been alone. If I didn't know any better, I'd say you were losing interest." Her lips grazed the column of his neck and across his collarbone. "It's not true, is it?"

Javid moaned and shook his head.

"Good." She sank to her knees. Without missing a stroke, Nichelle kissed the tip of his cock.

Javid shuddered at the sensation of her silky tongue running along his shaft. His knees buckled, and he almost melted down the shower's drain. The rest of her honeyed words were lost in the wind as he gave in to his desire. It didn't last long. When he was flying high, a tidal wave of shame crashed over him.

Klaudya would be released soon. She would never understand, and she would *never* forgive him. Hell, she'd warned him.

Javid peeled open his eyes, and his heart stopped with a gasp.

"What?" Nichelle peered at him. "What's wrong?"

Javid blinked. The shadow at the bathroom door disappeared.

"Nothing." He pulled his soft cock from Nichelle's hands and turned on the water for a final rinse. His mind was fucking playing tricks on him again. It had been happening for a few months now. Everything and everywhere he looked, there she was.

Once again, Nichelle approached him from behind, sliding her arms around his waist, but this time he snapped. "Nichelle, stop." He pulled her arms and broke her hold. "You shouldn't be in here. The kids could come in here any minute."

"So?"

He spun and looked at her incredulously. "So? Don't you think it'll be difficult to explain why their father and their grandmother are naked and taking a shower together?" He shut off the water and opened the glass door.

Nichelle followed, chuckling. "You gotta give them more credit than that. They are adaptable, especially nowadays. Two mothers, two daddies—anything goes. Haven't you heard?"

"Hardly the same thing." He wrapped a towel around his hips and marched out of the bathroom and into the adjoining master bedroom.

Nichelle wasn't far behind him with her own body covered. At the bathroom door, she studied him. "What difference does it make? We got to tell them eventually, right?"

Javid snatched open the top drawer and retrieved a pair of boxers.

"I asked you a question," Nichelle said, the sweetness leaking out of her voice.

"Look. I . . . I don't know what the hell this is. I don't know what the hell I'm doing anymore. Okay? There. I said it."

A long silence hung in the air. "Look. I'm sorry. I didn't mean to hurt you. I . . . I don't want to hurt anyone."

Nichelle pushed away from the doorframe and sauntered toward him. And though he towered a good seven inches above her, fear made his heartbeat pound faster. When she stopped in front of him, he made out her hard features. "Men never *intend* on hurting anyone. It comes naturally to you."

As their gazes clashed, thunder rumbled overhead.

Javid didn't know what to do or say, but was grateful when Nichelle sauntered past him and exited out of the bedroom door.

Nichelle stormed out of the master bedroom as if her hair were on fire. After all her plotting and planning, she couldn't lose Javid now. Not with Klaudya scheduled to be released any day. They needed to be themselves as one united front. When Klaudya saw her former life with the multimillionaire was over, she'd throw in the towel. It all belonged to her now.

Almost belonged to her.

Javid still had to present Klaudya with the divorce papers. And she still needed to get him in front of a priest or a judge. There were too many eggs outside of the basket, and she didn't like it. Lost in her tangled thoughts, Nichelle lost her footing and skidded a few inches across the top landing. Luckily, she regained her balance before landing flat on her ass.

"What the fuck?" She glanced around and tried to make out what was all over the floor. "Water," she concluded, shaking her head. Javid must have tracked it all through the house after he came back from checking the generator. He could get Ruthie to clean it. *I'm not the damn maid in this bitch.*

She marched on to the bedroom where she'd been staying since Lieutenant Armstrong had brought her to this palatial estate. She stopped before her bedroom window, where a sliver of moonlight sliced through the storm clouds and reflected her image back onto the glass. It also revealed a woman standing behind her.

Before Nichelle could spin around, Klaudya snatched her by the back of the head and slammed her face into the edge of the window's pane. Nichelle even heard the sickening crunch before she was pitched into total darkness.

CHAPTER 9

Two days after Javid Ramsey's funeral, Armstrong and Schneider arrived at the Ramseys' estate surprised to see three moving trucks in the driveway. It was awkward ringing the doorbell when the door was wide open, but Armstrong did it anyway.

"Lieutenant Armstrong," Klaudya greeted, sounding like she'd spent the morning sucking on a lemon.

"Ms. Ramsey." He tilted his head. "Moving?"

"Very observant. I bet it's that kind of detective work that makes you a shining star down at the department."

Schneider snickered until Armstrong's sharp look cut him off.

"Mind if we come in and ask you a few questions?"

She sighed. "Sure. Why not?" She turned and led them through a half-empty house to the backyard, where she offered them a seat on the patio furniture. "So what do you want to know? How much you ruined my family's life after you brought my poisonous mother here?"

Armstrong blinked.

"What? You think I don't blame you? Well, I do." Klaudya crossed her arms. "And I blame Javid, too. I warned him . . ."

2014

After Armstrong's surprise visit, Javid rushed upstairs to the master bedroom and found Klaudya at the window, staring across their vast backyard. "Baby? Are you all right?"

She remained silent.

"Klaudya?" He crept behind her. When she still refused to respond, he placed his hands on her shoulders. The moment he touched her, she bunched her shoulders and stepped away.

Javid dropped his arms. "C'mon, baby. Talk to me."

"There's nothing to say."

"There was a cop in the kitchen, telling me your mother rose from the dead and needs your help."

Klaudya sighed. "That big-mouth muthafucka."

Javid sighed. "Baby. Language."

"Give me a fuckin' break. The kids aren't in here." She stormed away from him and the window.

Cautious, Javid watched her. He'd gotten used to her performance as the perfect trophy wife and was caught off guard when her street side cropped up every once in a while. "Okay. How about we tackle one thing at a time?" He watched her remove a joint from the bottom of her jewelry box. "Are you sure that's a good idea? The kids."

"Fuck you, Javid. I need this."

He folded his arms while she lit the joint. Even after a couple of puffs, Klaudya remained coiled as tight as a cobra, ready to strike.

"This fucking weak-ass bougie shit," she said, disgusted. "I should fuck up that kid for even calling this shit weed."

"Are you finished?"

She cut him a nasty look.

"Why did you tell me your mother was dead?"

"Because she is dead . . . to me. I don't want anything to do with her."

"Okay. So you two don't get along. When was the last time you two talked?"

She laughed. *"A long fucking time ago. And I prefer to keep it that way."*

Javid hung his head and scratched the back of his neck. *"Honey. You can't mean that. We can choose a lot of things in this world, but family isn't one of them. Family is the most important thing in this life."*

"Oh, gawd." She rolled her eyes. *"If that was true, why aren't you and your parents talking? Oh, that's right, they weren't too happy about you dumping the blond princess they'd picked out for you to marry my black, stripping ass from the wrong side of the tracks."*

"We're not talking about my family."

"Lucky you."

"Your mother hurt you. That much is clear," Javid concluded, crossing the room toward her again.

Klaudya shook her head. *"Drop it."*

"How can I drop it? Look at you. You're a wreck. A cop shows up at the door, telling us your mother is homeless and needs help, and you're in here puffing like a chimney. All I'm saying is whatever is between the two of you, maybe it's time for you two to squash it and bury the hatchet."

Klaudya blocked out her husband's words.

"You do this every time I ask you about your past. Why? We've been together for nine years. How much longer will it take for you to trust me?"

"Trust?" She laughed.

"Yes. Trust. The thing marriages are built on."

Silence.

"I trust you—with my life." Javid wrapped his arms around Klaudya's hips and pulled her flush against him. *"Look. I don't know what happened, but I do know there's nothing that can't be forgiven. Families are supposed to love each other no matter what. And if my father ever answers the phone when I call, I'd tell him, too."*

Klaudya lowered her head and expelled another stream of ganja.

"C'mon, baby." Javid lifted her chin, and she blew smoke in his face. He turned away, coughing.

"Sorry."

He waved the smoke away and gave her a stern look. "Stop being stubborn . . . and selfish."

"Selfish?"

"Yeah, are you forgetting about Mya and Mykell? They have a new grandmother. They'd love to get to know her."

"Hardly." She laughed. "My mother is . . . trouble. With a capital T. Wherever she is, she's better off there. We're better off."

Javid opened his mouth, but Klaudya quickly placed a silencing finger against his lips.

"I get how important family is to you," she said. "I do. It's one of the things I love about you, but believe me, you don't want my mother around our kids."

"Why?"

Klaudya sighed, knowing there was no way out of this conversation. "I don't like talking about my past because I went through some horrible things. I'm talking about the kind of shit kids never get over."

He frowned.

"Did that motor-mouth cop tell you my mother spent twenty years in prison?"

The lines in Javid's face deepened. "No."

"I didn't think so. He dumped that shit on my lap to tell you." She took two more puffs.

"What did she go to prison for?"

"Murder."

"What?"

"Two counts."

"You're shitting me." He looked distressed.

"Nope."

"Holy shit." Javid raked his hands through his hair. "Fuck! Why didn't you tell me?"

"Because I never planned on seeing her again. Not now, not ever."

He shook his head. "I wish you would've told me."

Klaudya's gaze narrowed. "Why? What did you do?"

"I told the lieutenant we would help her."

"What?"

"Well, I didn't know she was a murderer! That's usually something you would tell a person."

"Wait. So, you're going to put this all on me?"

"It's not my fault," he thundered. "I thought you two were fighting over some trivial mother-and-daughter bullshit. How was I to know your mother was a fucking killer?"

"What? You thought they climbed out from under rock? They have families, too. The ones they manage not to kill," she amended.

"What are we going to do? Already told the kids about her. Lieutenant Armstrong is on his way to get and bring her here."

"What? Well, go call him and tell him she can't come."

Javid stared "I can't."

"Why not?"

"He didn't leave a number." He rushed toward the phone by the bed. "I'll call the local precinct and get in touch with him there."

"You better. Because if that asshole brings Nichelle here, we'll never get rid of her."

Klaudya crossed her arms and smirked at Armstrong. "But of course, we couldn't get in touch with you in time, and you did bring her here. "Lucky us."

Lieutenant Armstrong squirmed in his chair. "I was simply . . ."

"What?" she challenged.

"I was simply trying to help."

"Yeah, well. I'm sure you remember the day you brought her here . . ."

Nichelle spun around the vestibule trying to take in the whole place. "Holy shit, Klaudya. What muthafuckin' bank did you rob to land a crib like this?"

Still holding the door, Klaudya stood in shock as her brain processed who'd entered her home.

Nichelle stopped spinning and set down her bags. "Well? Are you going to stand there or are you going to give your momma a hug?"

Klaudya inched toward her mother like a zombie while shooting invisible daggers at Lieutenant Armstrong, who entered the house last.

Nichelle snatched her daughter into her arms and damn near squeezed the life out of her. "Oh. My big baby. Let me get a good look at you." She thrust her back at arm's length and studied her. "I always knew you'd be a stunner. Look at you." Her gaze raked every inch of her daughter, but instead of pride, jealousy roared through her veins. Suddenly, Nichelle's carefully selected Salvation Army outfit was rough and itchy against her skin and the two inches of the new growth beneath her six-month-old perm itched. "Beautiful." She released her daughter and hid her raggedy fingernails behind her back.

Klaudya stared at Nichelle, either at a loss for words or teeming with regret.

Nichelle decided it was the latter and took it like a knife to the back. "So this explains why I haven't heard from you," she said tightly. "Ashamed of your jailbird mother, I take it?"

"No, I, um . . ." Klaudya looked to the lieutenant for help and received none. "I didn't know you were out. That's all."

"How could you? It's not like you kept in touch while I was locked down, right?" Nichelle held onto her smile even

though it was tight as hell. Heavy footsteps pounded on the staircase, wrestling Nichelle's attention away from her daughter. Immediately her stiff smile softened. "Now you must be the man of the house." She stepped past her daughter and met him when he stopped on the bottom step. He wasn't her preferred flavor of chocolate, but he was hot for a white boy. Tall, lean, with soft, curly black hair and inquisitive blue eyes. But best of all, he was young. At least Klaudya hadn't sold her soul to suck on a pair of eighty-year-old balls to live in such luxury.

"And you must be Nichelle Mathis," he said, stretching out a hand. "I'm Javid Ramsey. Your son-in-law."

Nichelle gave his hand a cursory glance. "Now that's no way to greet family." She threw her arms around his neck and caught him off guard. Good. When she released him, she was all smiles. "Now that's how you greet family."

Javid relaxed. "I see where Klaudya gets her beauty."

Nichelle smiled, but patted at her new growth and became self-conscious all over again.

The husband and wife exchanged an odd look, and Nichelle guessed her time was limited.

"Sooo," she stalled. "I can't wait to hear how you two met. Maybe over a cup of coffee or tea?"

"Of course," he answered instead of Klaudya. "Espresso?"

"Fancy."

He chuckled and led the way to the kitchen.

Klaudya watched her mother trail Javid to the kitchen and hung by the front door to singe Armstrong with an evil glare. "I'll never forgive you for this."

Armstrong coughed after Klaudya recounted the story. "I see you're remaining true to your word."

"Can you blame me?" she asked, folding her arms. "Look around. I have to start all over again."

Schneider cleared his throat. "If you didn't want your mother here, why not tell her to leave?"

"You think I didn't try? After she fed Javid a self-defense story against my father, he warmed to her. And I knew that was even more trouble. So I caught myself taking her out to a nice lunch and laying down the law . . ."

2014

Nichelle, shining like a new penny to blend with the other bougie trophy wives of Calabasas, handed her menu back to the waiter and directed her attention to Klaudya. "What does your husband do for a living?"

"Why?"

"Well, whatever it is, he must be damn good at it."

"He is," Klaudya said before thanking their server.

Alone, Nichelle continued her interrogation. "So? What does he do?"

"He's part owner of Ramsey & Chase Financial. They do financial planning and shit."

"So . . . he manages other people's money?" she clarified. "I'm impressed."

Klaudya sipped her lemon water.

"And how did you two meet?"

"Moomm."

"What? I can't know how you two happened to cross paths?" Nichelle asked innocently.

Klaudya nibbled on her bottom lip, but her mother waited her out. "We met at the Kitty Kat. I was a dancer."

"Kitty Kat?" Nichelle perked. "You were a stripper!"

Klaudya rolled her eyes.

"What? There's nothing wrong with it. No need to be embarrassed."

"I didn't say I was embarrassed."

"See? We do have something in common. I met your fa-

ther when I was dancing at Nikki's back in the day. Of course, back in the day, they never pulled the kind of clientele that could land a girl in the lap of luxury. You did good." Nichelle lifted her glass for a toast.

Klaudya left her hanging.

"Ninety days, Mom," Klaudya said, the moment the waiter arrived with their lunch. "That's more than enough time for you to get back on your feet and find your own place."

"You're still angry." Nichelle stabbed a chunk of ham in her Cobb salad. "I wish we could work out our issues. When you were a kid, you used to send me a lot of disturbing drawings. I worried about you."

"I just bet you did."

"No, I did." Nichelle lowered her voice. "Did you ever see someone? You know for a psych evaluation?"

Klaudya's knee bounced a mile a minute under the table. The idea was to bring her mother to a public place to avoid a full-on fight. Now she wasn't sure it was going to work. She wanted to launch across the table and wrap her hands around her mother's neck. "Look," she snapped. "I didn't want to give you the ninety days. Javid insisted after that brilliant performance at the house." She clapped. "Bravo. Academy-Award-winning stuff. But let me be clear. I. Want. You. Gone."

"So angry." Nichelle sighed. "You act like you don't re-member what it was like living with your father. His anger is-sues. The abuse."

"I remember the abuse went both ways," Klaudya coun-tered.

"Oh, you suddenly got your memory back about what happened?"

Klaudya thrust up her chin. "I didn't say that."

"No, of course not. You want the luxury of sitting there judging. Damn the truth, right?"

Klaudya resented being hemmed into one of Nichelle's new webs.

"We should go to counseling."

Klaudya glared.

"You know, work out our issues."

"The only issue I have is with you popping up in my life and refusing to leave."

"You're being unfair."

"Am I?"

"Yes. Now, why wouldn't I want to have a relationship with my only daughter and my . . . grandchildren?"

Klaudya snickered. "You can barely say the word."

"It's an adjustment. Do I look like I could be a grand-mother to you? I look as good as most of these young twenty-somethings running around here." As she said the words, a gaggle of long-limbed teenagers sauntered by their table.

Klaudya had a migraine. In fact, she had had one every day since her mother moved in. "I don't know why you can't get it through your head that I'm not interested in developing a deeper relationship with you. Our situation is what it is." She snatched open her Hermès bag and rummaged around.

"What are those?" Nichelle asked, watching Klaudya tossed back two pills. "You keep popping those like candy."

"I have a headache," she said pointedly.

Nichelle ignored the bait. "What happened to my sweet little girl? We used to be so close."

"And you can't think of anything that might have changed that?"

"You've allowed people to poison your mind against me. I'm not the bad guy here. And I don't buy the amnesia act. I did what I did to protect you. And this is how you repay me?"

"You're delusional."

"You keep telling yourself that. Clearly, it helps you to sleep well at night."

"What is that supposed to mean?"

"It means that I don't deserve your anger or your hatred. If anything, I deserve your gratitude."

Klaudya tossed her head back with a loud, "Ha! Are you high?"

"Keep digging that ditch, sweetheart. You may not remember that night, but I do, and I say that you can take your ninety days and shove it. I'm not going anywhere. Momma is here to stay."

Klaudya popped two more pills and washed them down with alcohol.

CHAPTER 10

Armstrong and Schneider returned to Arlington Chase for a second interview. At least this time, Ramsey's larcenous partner had finally allowed himself the luxury of a shower and a shave. However, he still behaved like a long-tailed cat in a room full of rocking chairs.

"You believe Emilio Vargas killed your business partner," Armstrong said, cutting to the chase. "Why? What's the motive? You guys have been working for the cartel for a long while. What did Ramsey do to piss off Vargas?"

Arlington lowered his head.

"Or what did *you* do?" Schneider corrected.

Guilt washed over Mr. Chase's entire body as he confessed to the floor. "I got greedy . . ."

2014

Ari watched his partner take a couple of laps around the large office. His partner grew harder to read with each passing day. "Well? What do you think?"

Javid shrugged. "What am I supposed to think?"

Ari rolled his eyes. "Don't leave me hanging. Do you like it or not?"

"My liking it is not the issue. We can't afford it."

The real estate agent shot Ari a look and, in turn, he gave him a reassuring smile. "Of course we can. Don't be such a wet blanket." Ari pounded a hand on his shoulder. "C'mon. Live a little. You know as well as I do you have to spend money to make money. Right?"

Javid ignored Ari's excitement and shook his head. "It's not going to happen."

"C'mon. It's time to expand. Show the world we're one of the big dogs."

"It's too big and too flashy. We don't need the extra scrutiny."

"Says the man living in a seven-million-dollar house in the middle of Calabasas."

"That's different."

"Oh?" He lifted an eyebrow. "How?"

"Klaudya and I built our house with the money I inherited from my grandfather."

"Must be nice," Ari spat sourly.

The agent spoke up, "I'd hate to rush you guys, but a property like this isn't going to be on the market for long. So I'm going to need a decision soon."

Javid bounced his shoulders. "Oh, that's easy. The answer is no."

"The answer is maybe," Ari countered before giving Javid his best puppy-dog sad eyes.

Javid pulled Ari farther away from the real estate agent. "Where is this shit coming from? Are you going through some midlife crisis I should know about?"

"No, I just . . . I mean when the hell am I allowed to enjoy the fruit of our labor if I'm always watching every dollar in fear of triggering some federal investigation? Why do we care? Our shit is tight. Nobody is going to find shit."

"Shh. Shut the fuck up," Javid hissed, shooting another look at the agent. "What's with the diarrhea of the mouth?"

"Will you chill out? All I'm saying is, it's time to expand the business and attract some bigger and legit clientele. To do that we have to have "the look." The boutique shit is old school."

"The look, huh? Is that why you bought a new Porsche and Aston Martin in the last month? You going for a new look?"

"C'mon, not that shit again. I told you, I got a deal I couldn't refuse." He sniffed.

Javid eyed him up and down and zeroed in on Ari's dilated eyes. He stepped closer and hissed, "Are you fuckin' high right now?"

"What? No."

Javid hung his head. "I'm out." He headed toward the door.

"What?" Ari turned, stunned his boy left him hanging. "But what about the space?"

"It's still a no," Javid shouted and walked out.

CHAPTER 11

Emma Richards had returned home after a long, exhausting day of shopping with an armload of luxury designer bags draped from both arms when Lieutenants Armstrong and Schneider pulled into her winding driveway. After flashing their badges and requesting a few minutes of her time, they entered another Calabasas estate.

"Oh yeah. K and I go *waaay* back. I believe she and Brandi used to dance at the Kitty Kat together. She found her Prince Charming about a year before I found mine and we became neighbors. It's just a shame all the drama she's been going through this past year. It's all anyone talks about out here. I wouldn't blame her if she did move and start all over some-where—preferably where no one knows her name."

"You consider yourself close to Mrs. Ramsey?"

"I'd like to think so. We have a close-knit group of girl-friends who got together every month for a girl's day out. Of course, it's been a while since she has joined us, but she's wel-come back at any time."

Schneider pulled out his steno pad from his jacket. "What did you girls do on a typical girl's day out?"

"Normal stuff: Blow a hole in our husbands' credit cards, or spend a day at the spa, or even just sip cocktails by the pool. We'd talk about life, love, or our badass children. The last time Klaudya joined us, Tabitha hosted, and the conversation was interesting."

"How so?"

"We talked about soul mates . . ."

2014

Klaudya would have never survived Calabasas had she not found four cool-ass chicks to clique with when she'd moved into the neighborhood. Together, they held graveyards of secrets stuffed into their princess closets. Every third Friday of the month the women would have a girl's day out. Today, Tabitha Montgomery played host out by her pool.

Klaudya was happy to leave Ruthie with the kids while her mother pretended to look for a job and an apartment.

Tabitha handed out drinks. "Question of the day: Would you leave your man if he cheated?"

"Depends." Brandi raked her red hair out of her eyes.

Tabitha frowned. "On what?"

"On the details of my prenup."

The women laughed.

Bethany slid on a pair of sunglasses. "I'd be gone in a heartbeat. Life is too short to be dealing with unfaithful ass-holes."

"That explains the four divorces," Brandi joked.

"I'm serious," Bethany pouted. "Marriages aren't like what they used to be. No one takes them seriously anymore. If anything, they're an excuse to throw big-ass, ridiculously expensive parties. Nobody means their vows anymore. For better or for worse. Until death do us part. They're just words. If you're not going to take the vows seriously, why say them?"

The women agreed.

"Some people mean it," Bethany said. "Do you ever watch the ID channel?"

"Oh, girl. That shit is addicting," Emma said. "My father was a cop, and my brother-in-law works at the county morgue. If you ever need help getting rid of a body or making it look like an accident, I'm your girl." She winked.

Laughter ensued while they sipped on their cocktails.

Encouraged, Bethany added, "If you ask me, the problem is women are too damn easy. They have no moral code or compass. Most see men's wedding bands as nothing more than jewelry instead of the stop sign they were meant to be. They pursue men like prey and never make any of them work hard for anything."

Emma shook her head. "It cuts both ways."

"That makes it worse," Tabitha said. "Men nowadays have a wife, a girlfriend, a side chick, baby mommas, and a couple of Instagram thots on standby."

"Wow." Klaudya drained her mimosa. "You have been burned."

"Oh. Like I'm the only one?" Her gaze searched around the small group.

The women's gazes scattered.

Klaudya confessed, "I wouldn't leave."

Eyebrows shot up.

"Really?" Tabitha asked.

Klaudya shrugged. "I don't know. Maybe it's because I was raised in an unstable environment. It makes you unstable. You know what I mean? You never feel like you belong anywhere. I don't want that for my kids."

"So you'd stay for the children?" Tabitha crossed her arms.

The girlfriends groaned.

"What?"

Tabitha shook her head. "Honey, that is one of the worst things you could do."

"Agreed," Brandi added her two cents. "Now I know something about that. My parents stuck it out for my brothers and me. I can't tell you how many nights I'd lie awake, listening to my parents fight like cats and dogs and praying they'd put us out of our misery and get divorced already."

Emma co-signed. "Yeah. Living in a house where everyone walked on eggshells was not fun."

Klaudya clarified. "No. It wouldn't be just for the kids." A smile tugged at her lips.

"Oh?" Tabitha leaned forward.

Klaudya blushed along with the sweet buzz her pain pills and cocktail gave her. "Javid is my soul mate."

"Ooooh?" Giddy, Bethany and Emma leaned forward with their brows high.

"Soul mates?" Tabitha crossed her arms. "I didn't know they still made those."

"It sounds silly," Klaudya confided. "But it's true. I love my husband with every fiber of my being. I can't imagine my life without him."

"Spoken like a true future divorcée," Brandi joked.

Klaudya's smile vanished. "Forget it."

"No, no." Bethany waved off Tabitha and Brandi's pessimism.

"Yeah," Emma said. "Don't listen to them. They're bitter and jaded. It's wonderful you still believe in a soul mate in today's climate."

"Yeah, but what kind of soul mate cheats on you?" Tabitha asked. "That's the question. Would you leave your man if he cheated on you—even if he's your soul mate?"

Klaudya sighed. "My answer is the same. I don't mean I would take it on the chin if he did. I'm sure I'd be angry and even make his life a holy-hell for a while. But leave? I doubt it."

Tabitha looked annoyed. "All right. What if he left you? Then what?"

"Oh, then I would kill him."

Bethany and Emma gasped.

Tabitha and Brandi grinned.

Cool as a cucumber, Klaudya added, "Until death do we part? I meant that shit."

CHAPTER 12

Ruthie Ann Coates sat nervously across from Lieutenants Armstrong and Schneider and spilled her guts immediately.

"Mr. Ramsey was a good man. He was fair and decent. Hands down, he was one of the best employers I ever had."

"And you were employed for how long?"

"I came to live with them right after the Ramseys finished building their house. Before that, I worked for his father—Javid Senior in Beverly Hills." Her expression soured. "Trust me. Those two were like night and day."

Armstrong cut in. "So you've known Javid his whole life?"

"Oh, no. I came on board with the Ramseys when Javid was entering high school. Still, that's a good long while." She smiled. "He was such a bright kid—always seeking his father's approval. But it didn't work out in the end. I always knew that whatever Javid pursued he would be successful." Her expression changed again. "I hope Nichelle burns in hell. Not only did she kill a great man, but she also destroyed a wonderful family."

Armstrong cocked his head. "You don't care for Mrs. Mathis?"

"Humph. No. I never did. I saw she was trouble the first damn day I met her. The moment she moved into the house, she acted as if she owned the damn place. God forgive me, but I don't blame Klaudya one bit for trying to take her out last year. I mean, what kind of mother goes after her own daughter's husband like a bitch in heat?"

2014
After a two-hour morning workout in the home gym, Javid followed the scent of cooking bacon into the kitchen. Seeing his wife working her magic at the stove, he moved behind her, giving her ass a good squeeze.

She froze. "Oh?"

"I take it we're no longer vegan?" He kissed her neck.

Nichelle spun around with a sly smile. "Definitely not vegan."

Javid leaped back, his face flaming with embarrassment. "Oh, my god. I'm sorry. I thought you were Klaudya." He kept backpedaling.

"I gather that much." She laughed, pointing a fork at him. "You should see your face." When he looked sick, she added, "Don't worry. I won't tell about your mistake."

"All clean!" Mykell and Mya shouted, racing into the kitchen to show their grandmother their hands.

"Good. I guess that means you two will get chocolate chips in your pancakes."

"Yea!" The twins bounced around and scrambled into their chairs at the breakfast table.

"What about you, Javid? Have any special request for breakfast?"

"I'll just have some eggs and toast."

"That's it? No bacon? It's apple smoked," she teased.

Javid hedged while a smile crept around the corners of his lips. "Maybe a couple of strips."

She winked. "You got it."

Javid rustled Mykell's hair and delivered a quick peck on Mya's cheek.

"Ew, Daddy. You stink," Mya wailed, pinching her nose.

Javid grinned. "And that's my cue to go jump in the shower."

"Oh. I don't know," Nichelle said. "There's something about the natural sweat of a man. I read somewhere it has something to do with pheromones."

"Yeah?" He grinned, eyes sparkling.

"Oh, yeah." She bit her lower lip and met his gaze straight on.

Javid, not for the first time, roamed his gaze over his mother-in-law's svelte figure. His cock bulged against his briefs. "Well, I'll be back in a few."

"Take your time." She winked and turned back to her sizzling bacon.

Javid gave her round bottom another look before departing for the staircase. Upstairs in the master bedroom, he found his wife still in bed—again. He pushed off jumping into the shower to check on her. "Honey? How are you feeling?" He pressed the back of his hand against her forehead to see if she had a temperature.

Klaudya groaned and rolled away from him.

"Honey, the kids. Aren't you supposed to meet with the caterers this morning? C'mon, shake a leg." Javid playfully smacked her ass but awakened a demon.

"What the fuck?" She came up and socked Javid in the jaw.

"The fuck?" He leaped from the edge of the bed, his fists reflexively balled at his sides.

"Why can't you leave me alone?" Klaudya screeched. "Is it going to kill you to let me get some sleep? I'm fucking tired. You got me running around putting together this fucking party that I don't want to do. The children are fighting all the time. The third party planner quit on me yesterday, and every *damn time I turn around, there's my mother, watching and scheming behind my back."*

Javid relaxed. "Baby, stop. Not this again. You're starting to sound crazy."

He took in the sight of her hair standing straight on the top of her head and added, "Not to mention, you also look kind of crazy, too."

"Oh, this is funny to you, is it?" Her eyes went wild. "Fuck you. Throw your own goddamn party." She snatched a pillow and launched it.

Javid dodged the pillow. "I don't know what's gotten into you lately. But maybe you need to put in a call to Dr. Helmsley to increase or lower your meds. Something."

"Not funny!"

"I'm not trying to be funny. Look at you. If anything, your mother is picking up the slack. She's downstairs cooking the children breakfast. Didn't she take the kids to the Pacific Park yesterday while you lay up in bed?"

"I was tired!"

"All day?"

"Yes, all day. You have no idea how much work I do around here. You never did."

"Right. You have it so hard with a housekeeper and a mother-in-law doing all the work."

"What?"

"Okay. Okay." He held up his hands. "Truce. I don't have time to stand here and argue. I gotta shower and get to the job that pays the bills around here." He swiveled and stormed toward the bathroom.

"And what the fuck is that supposed to mean?" She snatched the bedding back and finally jumped out of bed to storm behind him into the bathroom, their arguing voices echoing off the bathroom walls and carrying all the way out-

side their bedroom door, where Nichelle stood listening and smiling.

Ruthie shivered in her seat. "Horrible, horrible woman."

Armstrong and Schneider shared looks.

"You had a front seat view of what happened the night Mrs. Ramsey and her mother clashed, didn't you?" Schneider asked, flipping through his notebook. "You testified in the assault case."

Ruthie tensed before admitting, "I've tried to forget about that night. It was the beginning of the end . . .

2014

Klaudya was still dressing for the Vargas's party. "Everything is going to be fine, sweetheart," Javid assured Klaudya as he moved behind her while she stood before the full-length mirror. I'm the one that's supposed to be nervous, remember?" He kissed the crook of her neck. "Ari thinks Vargas is going to expand our operation."

Klaudya's smile tightened. "Is that supposed to be good news? I thought you were getting out?"

"I will. We will. But not right now."

"Uh-huh."

"What?"

"The more you do, the more we're exposed. You're already washing more money than every Whirlpool in America wash clothes. When is enough enough?"

Javid's lips twitched. "If I didn't know any better, I'd say you don't have much faith in your man."

"I have faith in you. It's Vargas I don't trust. And you're crazy if you do."

Javid laughed as he spun her around in his arms. "Trust is a dicey thing in this line of work. I run shit like a well-oiled machine. It's as simple as that."

Klaudya shrugged. "I guess."

"You guess?" He cocked his head. "Don't tell me you suddenly have a problem living like a queen?" He held her flush against his body. "Valentino gowns, Cartier jewels—a closet that looks like a boutique store." He laughed, looking around. "I'll never understand why women need so many clothes."

Klaudya refused to be amused. "The few times I've met Vargas, he . . ." She shook her head. "He creeps me out."

"Vargas is an intense guy."

"You think?" She chuckled, sliding her arms around his neck. "He has to be like Man of the Year for most of the morgues and cemeteries from here to Colombia."

"Hey, hey. I don't concern myself with that part of the business. I'm a money man."

"I get that, but . . . why a big flashy party?"

"Who knows? But it would've been rude to turn down the invitation."

"It's just . . . odd." She shook her head. "Does everybody else at the party know what he does?"

"What kind of question is that?"

"One I'd like an answer to. I ask too many questions, and you don't ask enough."

He chuckled.

"Well, at least it'll be a night away from my mother."

Javid kissed his wife but still rolled his eyes. "I thought you two were starting to get along."

"I swear you never listen to a muthafuckin' word I say."

"Don't start. Of course, I do. It's just that—"

"What? Because we haven't killed each other, it must mean we get along?"

He shrugged. "Well, yeah. It's been my experience that's how you can tell whether any two women are getting along."

"Not funny."

"Not trying to be." Javid glanced at his watch. "How late

is fashionably late again?" He grasped hold of her dress's zipper as his eyes met hers in the mirror. "Up or down?"

"We're already running late," she teased, eyes sparkling.

"So this is the one night you don't want to be fashionably late?"

She smiled while his hands roamed her body-hugging Valentino gown and glided over the curves of her hips. "You have no right to be so fuckin' sexy. You know that?"

The back of her gown rose.

"You clean up well, too, Mr. Armani suit."

"You think so?" His fingers brushed beneath one breast while his other hand found the waistband of her Cosabella panties and tugged.

"You're naughty," she said.

"Yeah, but you don't mind, right?" His breath warmed the crook of her neck.

Instantly moist, Klaudya entertained the idea of a quickie. A giggle bubbled up her throat. "What are you doing back there, Mr. Armani?"

"What do you think?" Javid squeezed and spread her ass cheeks. "So fuckin' fat."

"Yeah?" She gave it a jiggle. "So what are you going to do about it?"

Javid unzipped his pants. "What the fuck do you think I'm going to do? Huh?" He locked an arm around her waist and dragged her over to the closet's golden chaise, where he quickly bent her over its arm. With her ass up, he took his time caressing and squeezing.

Klaudya grinned as she glanced back over her shoulder. "Now that it's in your face, whatcha gonna do with it?"

Javid knelt as he grinned back. "The only thing you can do with a big, beautiful chocolate cake. I'm going to eat it."

Whatever trash talk she was about to say died on her lips

the second his silky tongue slid in between her cheeks. From there on, she was in heaven.

Nichelle wasn't going to miss this party for anything in the world. How could she? A house filled with rich mutha-fuckas? Shit. Klaudya wasn't the only one with skills on how to get on. At forty-four, she still had a body that men did double-takes to check out. Like Cinderella, all she needed was a gown. Klaudya would never miss the few pieces of jewelry Nichelle had lifted from her vast collection to pawn off to pay for a Gucci gown. Hell, she was going to return the damn thing tomorrow anyway and pocket the cash.

As for the kids, fuck baking cookies and playing with dolls all night. Let Ruthie take care of that shit since she liked it so much.

No fancy limousine, but a rented Mercedes did the job. Nichelle arrived at the Vargas's fancy party with a fake invitation. She had copied Javid and Klaudya's. However, she was surprised to be stopped by a wall of tough-looking security men with visible weapons on their hips.

Curious looks from the glittering party guests floated her way and Nichelle's face grew hot. She hadn't gone through all this trouble to be humiliated even before she was in the door.

"It's all right, gentlemen," a rich baritone told the brick wall of security. "Ms. Mathis is a distinguished guest."

As if by a commandment from Moses, the wall of muscles parted and revealed a handsome and distinguished Latino. Money and power radiated off the man in waves. Instantly, Nichelle's knees weakened and her tits tightened against her Gucci gown. "My hero."

"My lady." He took her hand and brought it to his lips. "I see where your daughter inherited her beauty. Exquisite."

"You're too kind."

"Drink?" He turned toward a passing waiter's tray as if

he had eyes on the back of his head and swooped two chilled champagne glasses.

"Thank you." She accepted the offered glass and took a tentative sip as she eyed him.

"So how long have you been out of prison? Four months?" Nichelle choked.

He grinned. "Murder, wasn't it? Two counts?"

"Excuse me?"

"Don't worry. I like a woman with spunk."

Nichelle stood shell-shocked, debating whether to curse this muthafucka out or slap the shit out of him. But his power still radiated and prevented her. "You have me at a disadvantage, Mr. . . ."

"Vargas. Emilio Vargas."

Nichelle's heart stopped. Surely, she'd heard him wrong. He couldn't be the Emilio Vargas who ran one of the biggest drug cartels in Mexico. Could he? She took another look at the man's luxurious home while more pieces of the puzzle finally snapped together. A financial advisor, my ass.

Vargas spotted Javid with a glowing Klaudya on his arm. "Ah, if it's not the man of the hour."

Something clicked inside of Nichelle. She'd acknowledged Javid was a good-looking man, but there was something about seeing him in a suit that pushed all her right buttons.

"You have a beautiful daughter," Vargas complimented again.

"Huh? What?"

Vargas frowned. "Your daughter. She is a beauty."

"Oh, yes. Thank you." Her attention drifted back to Javid as he swiped champagne flutes from a passing waiter and handed one over to Klaudya.

However, Klaudya had already spotted her mother in the crowd. Her fiery gaze smote Nichelle where she stood.

Vargas didn't miss a thing. "I take it you and your daughter aren't exactly on good terms. Pity."

Nichelle dismissed his observation with a nervous laugh. "It's nothing time won't fix."

Vargas lifted a single brow but said nothing.

Javid and Klaudya made small talk with the other guests as they crept a beeline toward Vargas and Nichelle.

"Señor Vargas." Javid extended his hand. "I didn't know you knew my mother-in-law."

"Actually, we just met," he said. "Fascinating woman, I must say. You're a fortunate man to have two beauties under one roof."

"It's temporary," Klaudya said icily, but her smile was as warm as the sun.

"I see."

At the front door, Javid's business partner, Arlington Chase, entered the party with a leggy blonde.

"If you ladies could excuse us, I'd like to have a private word with Mr. Ramsey here."

"As long as you promise to bring him back in one piece," Klaudya challenged, still smiling.

"I'll see what I can do." He winked and, to Javid, he said, "Shall we?"

"Of course." Javid kissed his wife's hand and departed with Vargas.

Nichelle stepped closer to her daughter while they watched the men go. "You want to tell me how your husband happens to know the man who runs one of the most dangerous Colombian drug cartels?"

Ari's smile melted when he spotted Vargas. His troop of muscled and armed henchmen parted the crowd. However, he rebounded and slapped on a smile by the time Javid and Vargas stopped in front of him and his date.

"Evening, gentlemen," Ari greeted. "Señor Vargas." He stretched out a hand, which Vargas ignored.

"My office," Vargas said and kept moving.

"*Of course,*" *Ari responded and abandoned his date.*

At Vargas's home office, two men posted outside of the door and two men inside. A few seconds later, Henry Goodson and his two sons, who worked the docks for Vargas, were also escorted inside. They greeted everyone with bright smiles and firm handshakes. Javid had to look close to notice their nervousness.

Javid and Ari didn't dare sit before their host.

"*Can I get anyone a drink?*" *Vargas offered, making a sudden detour toward the bar.*

Everyone politely refused the offer. It was best to be clear-headed when talking to the kingpin.

"*I'm not going to take up much of your time,*" *Vargas said.* "*I want everyone to get back and enjoy the party.*"

"*We're thrilled you invited us.*" *Javid tried to relax but found it impossible.* "*I've been following your son's reelection campaign. It looks like he has this one in the bag.*"

"*My son's reelection campaign does eat a lot of my time. You have no idea how much bribes have gone up in four years.*"

The men laughed.

"*Yeah, whatever happened to loyalty? Eh? It's hard to believe there was once a time when men were men of their words. Today?*" *He sighed.* "*Not so much. Everyone is obsessed with fucking over everyone else. Everywhere I go, more and more people sneak their hands into my pockets.*" *Vargas's gaze hardened as it leveled on his financial advisors.* "*But you two know about that, right?*"

The cheap laughs evaporated and the business partners exchanged alarmed glances.

"*I mean, I pay you guys a lot to wash my money, but I'm getting reports saying shit ain't adding up.*"

Ari shook his head and blurted, "*If so, it's not on our end.*"

"*Yeah, all our numbers are legit,*" *Javid vouched.* "*I run the numbers twice every week myself.*"

Vargas hung his head.

"It has to be on the other end. What? You're dealing with hundreds of shady dealers, distributors, and packaging plants?" Ari laughed. "That's where you're going to find your discrepancy, not here. Not with us."

Javid's heart hammered.

Emilio opened his top desk drawer, pulled out a Glock .45, and set it in the center of his desk. The conversation shut down and the tension thickened.

"Whoa. Whoa. Whoa." Ari lifted his hands in surrender. "There is no need for this. There must be some misunderstanding somewhere. We're more than willing to help clear it up. Ain't that right, guys?"

The men agreed—everyone except for Javid. His life streamed in front of his eyes. Was this it? Had he rolled the dice one too many times? Why didn't he get out of the game after his initial five-year plan? How did Ari talk him into laundering for another five years? Or was there an option? Did anyone ever retire from the cartel?

"A misunderstanding?" Vargas repeated, amused. "How so?"

Ari drew a blank. "I-I don't know. I guess we need to review everyone's books. I know our firm is meticulous. I'm confident whatever error you've found is not on our part."

Vargas glared at Ari so long, Javid thought the kingpin was reading his partner's DNA.

"What about you, Henry?"

Henry Goodson owned a shipping and trucking company out of Los Angeles. Javid and Ari didn't know all of the intricacies of how Vargas got his product through the ports, but they knew Henry and his sons had worked for Vargas far longer than they had.

"Me?" Henry asked, blinking like he'd finished reviewing his own life. "I have no idea. You know I run a tight ship. All my men are top-notch and loyal."

"Loyal?" Vargas repeated. "Loyalty is the one thing I value above all else. I mean, without loyalty in this business—you're nothing." As fast as a serpent's strike, Vargas picked up the gun and fired a single shot into the center of Henry's head.

"Oh, shit!" Ari sprung out his chair and backpedaled. "Oh, shit!"

Javid remained rooted in his seat next to the dead man. Despite the calm exterior, inside he was on the brink of a heart attack.

"I'll ask you one time." Vargas leveled his gaze on the Goodson boys. "How did you do it?"

Blake Goodson shook his head,

Logan Goodson spilled his guts. "It was Blake's idea. I didn't even want to do it. He came to me."

"The fuck?" Blake smacked his brother on the back of his head. "Shut the fuck up."

"It's true. Pop had no idea," Logan cried. "We're sorry."

Vargas looked at Ari. "You see how loyalty works?"

Ari looked to Javid who, beneath his expensive suit, was covered in sweat.

Logan pleaded, "Look, Señor Vargas. We can make it right. It was a huge mistake and we'll never do it again."

"Are you going to make me ask twice?" Vargas said.

"The scales," Logan said. "The gas scales were adjusted to read full when they were light. But we will make it up to you. We will work for free. Whatever it takes."

"How much?"

"Twelve million over the past five years," Logan confessed, unaware of Vargas's heavies creeping up behind him. "Please, we can—"

Two more succinct shots were fired, silencing Logan as he and Blake dropped like lead balloons.

Ari's eyes looked ready to pop out of his head as they shifted from Vargas to Javid, and then to the dead bodies lying on the floor.

"Fucking thieves." Vargas stuffed his weapon back into his drawer. *"I can't fucking stand them. No matter how good you are to people, they just leech off of you until they drain every ounce of blood from you. You know what I mean?"*

"Yeah, but you don't have that problem with us," Ari croaked. *"We believe in loyalty. One hundred percent. Isn't that right, Javid?"*

Javid nodded. *"Absolutely."*

Vargas grinned. *"See? That's why I like you two. That's why I wanted to talk to you. I'm expanding our operation, and I'm going to need you guys to wash more money—faster. After this mayoral race, my boy has his eye on the presidency, and power doesn't come cheap."*

"Expand?" Javid stared at the dead bodies as Vargas's men rolled them into a rug.

Vargas stopped next to the bar. *"Is that going to be a problem?"*

"It'll be a challenge," Javid admitted, running numbers through his head.

"But not a problem," Ari amended, cheesing despite the sweat glossing his forehead.

"Ah, good." Vargas smiled. *"Whiskey?"*

Ari nodded.

Javid asked, *"Can you make it a double?"* when he wanted the whole damn bottle.

After tossing back the alcohol, Vargas pounded them on the back. *"Let's get you back to the party. We can discuss reviewing the numbers another time."*

Javid exhaled, relieving his burning lungs.

Vargas continued, *"You guys just keep doing what you're doing."*

"Yes, sir," Javid and Ari echoed before falling in line behind the kingpin.

However, Javid's heart hit the floor when he spotted Klaudya, barefoot and on a centerpiece table, dancing like she was back on the pole. The crowd around her cheered her on.

"What in the hell?"

Vargas chuckled. "I see some things never change. Eh, Ramsey?"

CHAPTER 13

The storm

"Is Grandma going to camp with us?" Mykell accepted his s'mores from the fireplace.

Javid sighed. "I'm not sure, li'l man. But we're having fun, right?"

"Yeah," Mya co-signed. "We don't need her around every time we do something."

"Mya," Javid chastised.

"What?" Her large hazel eyes blinked. "We don't."

"No," he agreed. "But . . . be nice."

Determination glinted in her eyes. "I *am* being nice. Just because I don't see why she has to *always* be around, don't mean I'm not a nice person."

Javid traipsed lightly. "No, I'm not saying you aren't a nice person."

"You're suggesting it," she countered.

Javid had a future lawyer on his hands. His daughter didn't know how to walk away from an argument. "I'm not saying *you* are bad. It's just what you're saying isn't nice."

Her frown deepened. "What's the difference?"

At this point, he didn't know.

Mykell rode to the rescue with a mouthful of melted marshmallow. "Nice people can say not nice things just like mean people do sometimes. Anyway, I *like* having Grandma around. She's nice."

Javid smiled. "Thanks, son. I'm sure she likes hanging around you, too."

Mya made a face. "Nichelle isn't nice. She's pretending to be nice."

"*Mya,*" Javid thundered.

"What? It's true. She doesn't even like us calling her 'Grandma.' She's too busy trying to take Mom's place. I don't even think she wants her to come back home."

"That's not true," Javid countered, floored by the words flowing out of his daughter's mouth.

Mya's gaze narrowed. "Do *you* want Momma to come home?"

"What? What kind of question is that?"

Mya's thin shoulders bounced. "I don't know. A regular one. Do you?"

"Of course, I want your mother to come home. I want her to get better and get back to being a good mother to you and Mykell." He covered her hands. "You believe me, don't you?"

Mya eased her hands out from under his and refused to answer his question.

The maneuver was a dagger to the heart. "Mya, baby . . ."

"I'm going to invite Grandma to come camp here with us," Mykell announced, springing from his sleeping bag. "Maybe she's not here because we didn't invite her?"

"No, don't," Mya barked.

"Dad, where's the flashlight?" Mykell asked.

Still troubled by the conversation with his daughter, Javid didn't hear Mykell until he shouted his name a third time. "Huh?"

"The flashlight."

"Oh." He searched around and found the flashlight next to one of the pokers on the hearth. "Here you go, son. You want us to go with you?"

"I'm not going," Mya insisted, crossing her arms. "I don't want her here." At the look on her father's face, she added, "And I'm *not* being mean, I'm being honest."

"I'm starting to believe there's such a thing as being too honest." Javid stood. "C'mon, li'l man. Let's go."

Mya folded her arms with a huff and watched them head out of the family room.

"You can come with us if you want to," Javid said, sensing she didn't want to be left alone. But on top of being argumentative, Mya was stubborn. "Suit yourself."

"Don't worry about her," Mykell told his father. "She's mad because she thinks you like Grandma more than you like Momma."

"What?"

Mykell hitched his shoulders as he climbed the staircase. "Yeah, she said she saw you kissing Grandma like you used to do Momma, but I know she's making it up because she wants Grandma to move out."

Javid glued his lips shut while they lumbered up the stairs. He'd tangled himself in a web. It was only going to get worse when Klaudya was released.

"Whoa." Mykell skidded across the floor and fell on his ass.

Javid glanced around. "Sorry, son. I must have tracked more water in the house than I thought. Are you all right?"

Giggling, Mykell lumbered back onto his feet and reclaimed the flashlight. "Yeah. I'm all right." He rushed to his grandma's closed bedroom door and pounded on it like the police. "Nichelle," he called. "Are you up?"

At Nichelle's silence, Javid sighed. "Hey, let me try." Gently, Javid moved his son away from the door and knocked. "Nichelle?

Can you hear me? The kids would love it for you to join us in the family room. We're doing a whole camping thing and—"

"We're making s'mores," Mykell yelled.

"Yeah, it's going to be fun."

Something rustled behind the door.

Javid placed his ear against the door. "Nichelle?"

No answer.

"Maybe she's already asleep," Mykell suggested.

Javid twisted the doorknob. It wasn't locked. He looked at his son and opened the door. "Nichelle?" He crept inside, his gaze going to the open window. A fierce wind billowed the curtains while sheets of rain poured inside onto something lying on the floor. "Son, give me the flashlight."

Mykell handed it over.

Javid swept the beam of light across the floor. "Nichelle!"

"Grandma!"

They raced to the motionless body.

Javid rolled Nichelle over. A thin stream of moonlight highlighted her face and the ghoulish gash across her forehead. "Nichelle! Nichelle!"

Mykell inched away. "Is she dead?"

Javid's heart plummeted. *Was she?* He checked for a pulse. There wasn't one.

"Call 9-1-1!" Mykell snatched the abandoned flashlight and raced to Nichelle's nightstand for the portable phone.

"Bring it here," Javid ordered.

When Mykell returned to Javid's side, he frowned. "I can't hear anything."

Javid snatched the phone. No dial tone. "What the fuck?"

Mykell gasped. "Oooh. Daddy, you said a bad word."

"Not now, son." He raked his hand through his hair, urging his brain cells to work. "My cell phone. Take the flashlight and go into my room and grab my cell phone off the charger."

"Okay."

"Hurry!"

Mykell took off like a flash.

Javid attempted to find a pulse, but with his own racing heart, he had a hard time distinguishing if anything moved beneath the pads of his fingers. "Here you go, Dad."

"Thanks, son." Javid took the cell phone, but after punching in the emergency number, he got nothing but dead air. "No. No. No." He looked at the top of the screen. "Cellular service is out."

"Does that mean you can't call for help?" Mykell asked.

"Shit."

"Daaad."

"Mykell, please. I need a second to think."

Mykell buttoned his lips but couldn't hide the hurt of his father yelling at him.

"I'm sorry, son. I didn't mean to snap. But we're going to have to get your grandma to the hospital, okay?"

Mykell wiped the tears from his face and nodded.

"Good. Now, go and tell Mya I need you two to get dressed and put on your coats and meet me in the car." Javid carefully slid his arms underneath Nichelle's body and lifted with a groan.

"You all right, Dad?"

"Yeah, go do what I told you."

"Yes, sir." Mykell raced out again.

"All right. Nichelle, don't you die on me." He struggled toward the door. "We're going to get you some help." He feared the worst while he lifted her dead weight. More than ever, Javid hated the time he'd missed in the gym, especially when he failed to protect Nichelle's head as he bounded onto the staircase.

Thump!

"Fuck. Sorry." He hobbled to the second floor. "Guys, hurry!" He rushed to the second staircase and burst out of the front door into the torrential rain with arms ready to dump Nichelle onto the asphalt. It didn't help he'd forgotten to grab his car keys.

"Shit. Shit. Shit." He tried the back door to the Mercedes and was relieved when it opened. "Okay. Here you go." He slid Nichelle onto the backseat. "All right. Hang in there." He slammed the door and turned back toward the house for the car keys and the kids.

"Mya! Mykell! We gotta get going. Now!" He grabbed the car keys from the hook in the kitchen and stopped long enough to jam his feet into a pair of Nikes. But the kids were still nowhere in sight.

"C'mon, guys! We don't have all night." He jingled the keys.

Still no answer.

"You got to be kidding me." Javid took the stairs two at a time. "What is taking you guys so long?"

On the second landing, Mykell appeared at the family room's entrance.

Javid spread out his hand. "Well, c'mon, buddy. What's the hold up?" He looked over Mykell's head. "Where's your sister?"

Mykell's eyes watered. "I don't know. She's not here."

"What? What do you mean she's not here?" Javid thundered past his son to take a look for himself. Sure enough, the room was empty. "Well, where is she?"

Tears splashed Mykell's face. "I don't know. I looked everywhere. I can't find her. She's gone."

CHAPTER 14

2015

A beautiful blond, blue-eyed Barbie answered the front door, took one look at Lieutenant Armstrong, and launched into a sex kitten act. "Well, hello."

Armstrong smiled. "Good evening. Are you Tabitha Montgomery?"

"Depends on who is asking."

He flashed his badge. "I'm Lieutenant Erik Armstrong, and this is my partner, Lieutenant Joe Schneider. Do you have a few minutes? We'd like to ask you a few questions about your neighbors—the Ramseys."

"Oh?" Tabitha pulled the door open wider. "That poor family. They have been through so much."

"Can we come in?"

"Why, sure." She stepped back from the door to allow them entry. After closing it, Tabitha led the way, exaggerating the sway of her hips, to an over-decorated salon. "Can I get you gentlemen anything to drink? Water? Tea? Me?"

Schneider brows jumped.

"We're good," Armstrong cut in before his partner said the wrong thing.

"Are you sure?" she asked.

Schneider opened his mouth.

"We're sure," Armstrong answered again.

"All right. So, what can I help you with?" Tabitha asked, settling into the plush sofa across from them.

"How well do you know the Ramseys?" Schneider asked.

"Well enough, I guess. How much can you *really* know anyone these days? They built their house about two years after we built ours. Our kids are about the same age. They went to each other's birthdays and play-dates. You know, the normal bougie shit." She smiled and opened a crystal decanter and removed a joint.

Armstrong lifted a brow.

"Don't worry. It's for medicinal purposes." She winked before she lit up.

The partners shifted glances but said nothing as Mrs. Montgomery puffed on her thin joint.

"Back to the Ramseys," Armstrong said. "Klaudya and Javid. Ever notice any problems between them?"

"Notice? It was kind of hard to miss. Especially after that party last year." Tabitha threw her head back with a laugh. "People are *still* talking about that one. I didn't know Miss Thang used to be a stripper until that night. But, honey, she showed us. She still had the moves."

"What else do you remember?"

"Well, I spotted Klaudya a few minutes after I arrived . . ."

2014

"So, what's with all the firepower around here?" Tabitha asked, pushing her way toward Klaudya.

"I was trying to get to the bottom of that," Nichelle said, eyeballing her daughter.

Tabitha finally noticed Nichelle. "Oh, hello. I'm Tabitha

Montgomery. I don't believe that we've met." She offered her hand.

"No, we haven't. Nichelle Mathis." Nichelle accepted Tabitha's bejeweled hand. "I'm Klaudya's mother."

Klaudya groaned.

Shocked, Tabitha turned toward her. "Didn't you tell me your mother was dead?"

Nichelle choked on her champagne. "Dead?"

"A girl can dream," Klaudya deadpanned, glancing around for a tray of alcohol.

Nichelle laughed bitterly. "My daughter and I are working trying to heal our troubled relationship. So far, it's a long, hard, bumpy road."

"Aw, that's nice." Tabitha sighed. "I wish me and my mother had patched things up before she died. But we were both so damn stubborn. When I look back on all the fights we used to have, they all seem so petty. You two are doing a good thing."

Nichelle's smile bloomed. "There. You hear your friend, Klaudya? We're doing a good thing."

Klaudya rolled her eyes and searched for a nearby waiter.

"I'll get you a drink," Nichelle said. "Maybe it'll cool you off, and you can enjoy the party."

"Thanks." Klaudya rolled her eyes at her mother's back. Once Nichelle was out of earshot, Tabitha asked, "So what's the real deal between you two?"

"She was released from prison, and the cops dropped her off at my door," Klaudya admitted.

"You're kidding me. Prison? For what?"

Klaudya sighed. "It's a long story."

"I love long stories," Tabitha admitted, inching closer.

Klaudya shook her head.

"I went to jail once," Tabitha confided.

Klaudya eyed her suspiciously. "For what?"

"I did some shit. You and Brandi aren't the only ones

with a past. You guys always think I'm such a goodie-two-shoes—but I have a couple of skeletons in my closet, too, you know."

"Yeah? Like what?"

Tabitha's voice lowered to a whisper. "I dealt drugs for some extra cash while I was in college."

Klaudya assessed Tabitha like it was the first time she had ever laid eyes on her. "You're shitting me."

"My not looking the type was exactly why I was so good at it." She winked.

"Here we go," Nichelle said, returning with a bar drink. "Whiskey sour. Your favorite, right?"

Klaudya grunted. "No. it's your favorite." She accepted the drink anyway.

Since she didn't get an answer to her question, Tabitha went to the source. "So, Nichelle. You were in prison?"

Nichelle's fake smile melted before she stabbed her daughter with a hard gaze. "Wow. You guys had an Oprah moment in ten minutes?"

"Excuse me." Klaudya drifted away from the conversation to make small talk with the other guests. All the while, she kept an eye out for Javid's return. But the more she sipped on her whiskey sour, the more tension ebbed from her body. In no time, she felt good. Damn good.

She laughed at every joke, told a few corny ones, and danced with anyone who was willing. Soon she was lost in the music and hopped onto a table. Before she knew it, her red-faced husband charged through the crowd.

"What are you doing? Get down from there!"

The crowd booed and jeered him.

Worse, Klaudya resisted his attempts to drag her off the table. That angered him even more.

"Get down! Get down!" He swiped at her legs until he knocked her knees out from under her and toppled her toward him.

Everyone gasped, but Javid's ex-college All-Star football

player reflexes kicked in in time to catch his intoxicated wife before she hit the floor. He also pulled a muscle in his back. Where moments earlier, Klaudya was shrieking for him to leave her alone, she was now laughing hysterically and blowing kisses to the crowd.

"What the hell is wrong with you?" Javid tossed her over his shoulder and marched toward the front door.

Tabitha shook her head. "Frankly, I thought she livened up the party. She gave everyone there something to talk about. I loved it." She puffed out a ring of smoke.

Armstrong stood from the sofa. "I see. Thank you for your time."

"Anytime." She raked her silver gaze over him and smiled. "Are you sure there isn't something else I can do for you, officer?"

Armstrong's brows furrowed at the way she licked her lips.

"The kids aren't due home for a few hours," she added, making her intention clear.

"I'm good," he said, struggling to hold on to his stony expression. "Schneider, let's go."

Tabitha stood. She twirled her hair around her finger as her gaze raked him a second time. "Pity. Well, you know where to find me if you have any more questions."

"We'll be in touch. And we can see our way out."

CHAPTER 15

2014

Javid tossed Klaudya into the limousine and climbed in. "What the fuck? What in the hell has gotten into you?"

"Oh, calm down." Klaudya giggled, worming her way into his lap as the vehicle pulled off.

Javid shoved her back to the other seat.

"Hey!"

"Hey yourself," he roared back. "This isn't funny. You made a complete ass out of yourself in front of everyone, including Señor Vargas."

"Oh, fuck Señor Vargas. Did I ever tell you he used to have the hots for me when I danced at the Kitty Kat?"

"Oh, fuck Señor Vargas? So fuck me, too? Is that it? That man has the power to make muthafuckas disappear, and you just made a fucking scene at his place like that shit ain't going to blow back on me? What the fuck? Are you high?"

"Lighten up!" She laughed. "If anything, I livened up the party. Everyone was having a good time."

"I don't know about everybody else, but you were." He tugged his tie loose. "I don't know what's gotten into you

lately, but you need to snap out of it. The drinking, the smoking, the pills—it's like I don't fucking know you anymore."

Klaudya sighed but didn't give up trying to seduce her husband. She turned up the heat by spreading her legs and caressing her inner thighs. "You sure you don't want to play right now?"

Javid frowned. "Are you fucking serious?"

"Yeah. It's been a long time since we've done it in the back of a limousine." She peeled out of her panties and tossed them at him. She glanced toward the driver's rearview mirror. When their eyes connected, Javid hammered his fist down and powered up the partition.

"It's not happening," he growled.

Klaudya's playful mood deflated. "Party pooper."

"No. The party ended when Vargas threatened to kill me."

"What?"

"Oh, do I now have your attention? While you were shaking your ass among the hors d'oeuvres, my life was flashing before my eyes."

Klaudya attempted to concentrate. "What did he say?"

"Nothing much. He only accused Ari and me of stealing from him—and in the next second blew holes into Harry Goodson and his two sons while we watched with our fucking dicks in our hands. The shit was right out of a fucking Godfather movie. I gotta get out of this shit. I ain't about this life no more. Bullets are fucking hazardous to a muthafucka's health."

"But why? Do you think he's on to us?"

"How the fuck would I know?"

They rode the rest of the way home in silence. And when they climbed out of the limo, Javid crammed his wife's panties into his jacket pocket.

In their bedroom, Javid paced back and forth while Klaudya undressed. It didn't take long before the pacing got on Klaudya's nerves. "I don't think there's anything to worry about. If he suspected you, you would be dead."

Javid laughed in her face. "When it comes to Emilio Vargas, there is always something to worry about. When you're sober, you know that shit." He pulled a deep breath. "I have to go to the office and look over the numbers. Vargas is fishing for a reason. He didn't need us in that room to witness that shit. It was a warning."

Klaudya pressed her body flush against her husband and looped one arm around his neck. "You're working yourself up for nothing. Let me relax you." She tugged on the belt of his trousers.

"Baby, this is not the time."

"It's always the right time." She sank to her knees.

"I'm serious, Klaudya. Not—"

The zipper zoomed down, and Klaudya grabbed his cock.

Angry, he leaped back. "I said not now!" He crammed himself back into his pants and zipped up. "I got shit I gotta take care of." He marched toward the door.

"Where are you going?"

"I told you. To the office. I got to check those numbers. I'll be back."

"I'm on my fucking knees, and you're walking out on me?"

"Get some sleep. We'll talk about your behavior tomorrow."

"Well, hell, I should go back to the party instead of wasting my night off from the kids."

"No! You stay the fuck right here. You're fucking blitzed out of your mind and have done enough damage."

"I'm not a child." She jumped to her feet.

"Great. How about you stop acting like one?" He opened the door.

"Fuck you!"

"Good night, Klaudya."

He slammed the door so loud it rang Klaudya's ears. By the time she heard the rattle, followed by a click, it was too late. "You have got to be fucking kidding me!"

She raced to the door.

Locked.

"Javid! Come back here!" She heard his heavy footsteps, marching away. "Javid!" She hammered the door. "I'm not playing with you! Let me out of here!"

Javid descended the second flight of stairs and spotted a wide-eyed Ruthie, holding a tray of cookies and what appeared to be cups of hot chocolate.

"Is everything all right, Mr. Ramsey?"

Javid kept marching. "Klaudya is under the weather. She is not to be disturbed until I return."

"Sir?"

He stopped at the door. "Problem?"

Ruthie blinked while Klaudya's screams rang from the upstairs. "Um, no, sir."

"Good. It's for her own good. She's fucking crazy as shit lately."

"Yes, sir."

"Where are the children?"

"They are still in my living quarters," she said. "We're still in the middle of a Disney marathon."

"Good. I'm headed to the office. I'll be back later."

"Yes, sir."

He jerked open the front door, hesitated like he wanted to add something else but stormed out of the house instead.

CHAPTER 16

2015

"Evil," Ruthie spat. "I told you before Ms. Mathis is an evil woman. Now I hear she spinning more lies trying to blame Javid's death on Klaudya."

"So, I guess I have an answer to my next question on how you feel about Klaudya."

"Oh, I love her. And that's because she loved Javid. She was good for him. Sure, they had their ups and downs. Every couple does. But those two loved each other. I remember them being over the moon when they found out they were having twins." She smiled. "I used to be in love like that."

"Oh? Is there a Mr. Coates?"

"There used to be. Well, I mean . . . we're no longer together. We divorced a few years before I went to work for Javid's family. In fact, it was the reason why I had to work." Her voice softened. "One day we were in love, and the next day he loved another woman twenty years younger than me. Our vows meant nothing to him."

Armstrong wrangled the conversation back to the subject

at hand. "Do you think Javid Ramsey fell out of love with his wife?"

"No." Ruthie's head sprang back up. "The real trouble started the day *you* brought Nichelle to live there."

Armstrong squirmed in his seat.

Ruthie continued, "She suffered with those massive migraines. She popped pills left and right and washed them down with alcohol. Those two women should have never been back under the same roof."

Schneider said, "It certainly sounds like it."

"You know last year, I read after Klaudya's arrest with that crazy concoction in her bloodstream and I believe her mother was behind it."

"How so?"

"It made no sense: lithium and whatnot. Those were the same medications Mykell takes."

"The kid?"

Ruthie nodded. "He's bipolar. He was put on those mood stabilizers two years ago. It makes no sense for Klaudya to be popping them for headaches. Now, I'm no detective, but I can put two and two together."

"Meaning?" Schneider asked.

"Meaning Nichelle camouflaged and switched the pills. I can't prove it. But she did it. It's the only thing that makes sense. Those mood swings, especially the violent outbursts, sleeping half the damn day, and snapping at the children. Klaudya never did any of it until mother dearest moved in and made her a ticking time bomb. Only she hadn't expected it to go off on her when it did. Serves her right. Humph."

2014

"Javid! Come back here!" She could hear his heavy foot-steps, walking away. "Javid!" Her fists were like hammers against the door. "Man, I'm not playing with you! Let me out of here!" She kicked the door. But there wasn't a lock invented

Klaudya couldn't pick. When she'd calmed down, she picked the bedroom door lock and went looking for her husband.

He was long gone.

Pissed, she contemplated returning to the party, but she didn't want to be at the muthafucka anyway. She texted Javid to bring his ass back home.

He ignored the texted demand, the excessive calls, and voice messages. In a flash, she was back on ten and was pacing in their bedroom like a cornered tiger with a P238 in her hand.

Who in the fuck did he think he was? Who the fuck did he think he was dealing with? Did this muthafucka not know she could still pull any nigga she wanted? His ass wasn't fucking special. Her mental tirade became a souped-up carousel, spinning in her head. She went into the master bathroom, searching for more pain pills. All the bottles were empty.

I just had this one refilled. Didn't I? She paused but couldn't remember. The days were hazy. It could have been last week—then again, it could've been last month. "Fuck." She needed something for her head. Frantic, she searched through her medicine cabinets and her purses. In the end, she had to settle for some over-the-counter aspirin. By that point, her head was set to explode. She took a handful of aspirin instead of the recommended two pills.

Twenty minutes later, while she was still pacing the bedroom floor, she dropped, passed out on the floor, her gun inches away from her body.

Dawn was a couple of hours off when Javid returned home. Instead of heading straight to bed, he sought solace in his home office, where a fully stocked bar awaited him. He started a fire in the hearth before taking a whole whiskey bottle over to his favorite leather chair to watch the flames crackle.

Twenty minutes later, he was a quarter of the way

through the bottle. At least his thoughts had slowed down. He wasn't sure it was a good thing. Images of Henry Goodson and his sons murdered in the middle of a big party blew his mind.

Sure, the drug game was rough. Javid had paid attention to the news. He'd seen the wrath and destruction of the drug wars waged around the world. They were glorified in gangster movies, TV shows, books, and music. But to see the shit play out right in front of him was another thing entirely.

Emilio Vargas was Dr. Jekyll and Mr. Hyde. Tonight Javid had seen the evil lurking behind his black gaze—and it scared him. How the fuck was he going to get out of this bullshit? Could he get out? Javid took another swig from the bottle.

"You're up late." Nichelle's husky voice floated into the room.

Javid lolled his head toward the door and then smiled. Standing at the threshold in a red lace negligee, Nichelle flashed her sauciest smile. A man would have had to be among the walking dead not to have a physical reaction to the woman, especially to those pillowy breasts spilling out of the top of her negligee and those deep curves leading to her round hips. Then there were the long legs peeking out of the deep split on the right side. In an instant, he was hard as steel.

"A man should never drink whiskey alone. Care if I join you?" She entered the room without waiting for a reply.

Speechless, Javid watched the roll of her hips as she sashayed to the bar for a glass. When she crossed back before him to take the chair next to him, he was in trouble. Hell, he had a whole night's worth of trouble. What was a little more?

Nichelle sat and took her time crossing her legs to allow the split in her negligee to expose her legs all the way to her inner thigh—where Javid's gaze glued itself.

"You and Klaudya left the party early tonight."

At the mention of his wife, Javid sighed.

"Oh, don't be too hard on her. It could've been worse.

Back in my day, I had a wild streak, too. I can honestly say that she gets it from her momma."

"Humph."

"Maybe in a way I'm the one who owes you an apology."

"No apology needed. I knew what I was getting when I married your daughter."

"Did you?"

He smiled. "Yeah. Klaudya's striptease tonight is the least of my worries. I have way more important things on my mind right now."

"Oh? You two have already kissed and made up?" She grabbed the bottle of whiskey and poured a double.

"I didn't say that." He took the bottle and continued drinking straight from its mouth.

Nichelle chuckled and shook her head. "I'm having a hard time figuring you two out."

"What do you mean?"

Nichelle bunched her shoulders. "On the surface, you two look like the perfect couple with beautiful children. But . . . what do you two have in common? You're a straitlaced pencil pusher. You're intelligent and successful. And Klaudya . . . ?"

"Yeah?"

"She dances well."

He chuckled. "She sure does. And?"

"Nothing. Forget it. It's not my place to say."

"No, go ahead. You have me intrigued now." With each chug of whiskey, Nichelle looked more like her daughter, and his dick went from steel to titanium.

"All right. The best I can tell Klaudya is a trophy wife. She has a beautiful face, a terrific body, especially for someone who's delivered twins, but what else does she bring to the table? I haven't seen too much ambition. It surprises and disappoints me. If I had the time and resources she does, I'd be in the hall of fame for having acquired the most academic degrees—or I would have started my own business. Something."

Javid laughed.

"What's so funny?"

"Honestly?" he asked. "This conversation is hilarious. Klaudya is a disappointment, but you're the one with the criminal record. Don't tell me you don't see the irony."

"It was self-defense," Nichelle snapped. "If I could have afforded a halfway decent lawyer, I wouldn't have served a day in jail. But the system isn't designed for people like me. Once we're in the system, we're there to stay. Prisons only get paid per body in a cot. Fuck justice. Give them their paper, Uncle Sam."

"Sorry. I know your record is a sore subject."

Nichelle clamped her mouth shut. She did sound defensive. During the next few sips of whiskey, the only sound between them was the crackling fire in the fireplace until she announced, "I am proud of my daughter. By hook or crook, she broke our family's history of systematic poverty. That's not nothing."

Javid was done talking about his wife.

"If my daughter isn't what's keeping you up tonight, what is?"

Javid sighed. "The same thing that always keeps me up. Business."

"Ah." She sipped again. "The business of financial planning, right?"

His smile sloped. "Yeah. Financial planning."

She chuckled. "Man. The world has changed since I got locked up. Back in the day, they called it plain old money laundering."

Javid's smile melted.

Nichelle laughed. "Don't worry. Your secret is safe with me."

"Klaudya told you?"

Her chuckle turned into a full-on laugh. "Hell, no. She thinks my ass is dumb. Maybe you do, too? I can't imagine a drug kingpin like Emilio Vargas needing anything close to fi-

nancial planning, given the life expectancy in his line of work."

Javid shook his head. "*You're mistaken.*"

"*Yeah, okay.*" She grinned. "*Like I said, your secret is safe with me. I'm no snitch. Klaudya can vouch for me that much.*"

It was time to end the conversation. The whiskey had saturated Javid's bloodstream. Maybe it was best for him to sleep in the office. Even if Javid made it out of the chair, getting him upstairs to his bedroom would take a miracle.

"*Are you in any trouble?*"

"*Trouble?*" he slurred.

"*You did disappear with Vargas for a long time, and now you're marinating your liver.*"

"*Nah, no trouble. If anything, my partner and I will be expanding the business.*" He held up his bottle.

"*I see.*"

"*I don't know about any illegal business my client may or may not be involved in. What I do for him is above board.*"

"*Riiiight.*" She winked. "*Of course it is.*"

"*I'm serious,*" he persisted.

Refusing to call him out on the lie, Nichelle grabbed the bottle and poured herself another double. "*Then I guess we're celebrating. Congratulations.*" One spaghetti strap tumbled off her shoulder.

Javid tracked it as if it happened in slow motion.

The room's temperature skyrocketed. It was hot enough to set the whole state of California ablaze.

Javid tugged on his collar even though it was already open.

"*Cheers.*" Nichelle held up her glass.

Javid struggled to lift his gaze from her creamy breasts. He was unaware of his tongue gliding across his bottom lip, but he was conscious of his dick fleeing the seams of his briefs.

"Are you going to leave me hanging?" Her red-lipped smile spread wide. *Like her daughter, Nichelle had the perfect set of fuckable lips. When she raised a brow, he lifted the bottle for a toast.*

Nichelle smiled around the rim of her glass and Javid couldn't get the idea of fucking her mouth out of his head.

Klaudya woke up sick.

Even before her brain processed anything, her stomach clenched and ejected everything she'd eaten in the last twenty-four hours. She stumbled and crawled back to the bathroom, leaving a trail of vomit in her wake. She begged God for her life and hugged the cold porcelain toilet. This had to be death. In a few hours, her babies would discover her body in a puddle of her own sick. She was sure of it.

How long she cried and vomited into the toilet, she didn't know. By the time it was all over, she lay exhausted and dehydrated.

Miraculously, she stood from the floor and scooped running water from the sink into her mouth. Once satisfied, she shut off the water and wiped her mouth dry with the back of her hand. When she lifted her bloodshot eyes to her reflection in the mirror, she flinched. A hot mess stared back at her.

Disgusted, Klaudya stripped and jumped into the shower. Submerged under a stream of hot water, snippets of the night's disaster replayed in her head. It seemed more like an out-of-body experience. None of it made sense.

Where was Javid?

Exiting the shower, Klaudya wrapped herself in a towel and returned to the bedroom. She stopped cold at the sight of her gun lying on the floor. What the hell did I do this time?

She searched her scattered memory for an answer but kept ramming into a brick wall. For the second time, she asked, "Where is Javid?"

Klaudya raced to the closet and grabbed another robe. She slipped the gun into her pocket and went to check on her babies.

Their rooms were empty. After the first shot of panic, she remembered, "Ruthie."

Relief washed over her like a tsunami, buckling her knees. "Thank God."

But where was Javid?

Klaudya descended the two flights of stairs, hoping to find him working in his office. Her head pounded the entire way. How much did she have to drink? How many pills did she take? She couldn't remember. Maybe I do have a problem.

A sound caught her ear.

A familiar sound: Javid's sex groans.

She froze while her belly looped into every imaginable sailor's knot, and Jell-O replaced the bones in her legs.

"Ah, shit. That feels good," Javid moaned. A steady pig-like slurping sound followed his praise.

Klaudya unglued her gelatin legs and followed the sound to Javid's office. At the open door of Javid's home office, she went into shock at seeing Javid's head tossed back in ecstasy over his favorite chair, and riding his white pony was her mother.

Without thinking, Klaudya palmed the P238 and fired. The first bullet missed her mother's head by inches, but it got Nichelle's fucking attention.

"Klaudya!"

"You fucking bitch!" She fired again.

Nichelle screamed and leaped off Javid's dick. The next shot clipped her ear as she scrambled across the floor.

Javid, reflexes slow, sprang out of his chair in time to catch a bullet in his arm. "Fuck!" He dropped to the floor.

"You sick muthafucka," Klaudya wailed, tears streaming. "My mother?!"

"Wait, baby. Hold on." He held his hands up. "Let me—let me explain!"

The French doors were snatched open, stealing Klaudya's attention.

Nichelle bolted out, her long legs erasing yards like a natural Olympian.

Klaudya fired and took out two of the door's glass panels. "Where are you going, bitch?" She took off after her mother.

Javid jumped back to his feet and caught Klaudya by the waist. "Let her go!"

Furious, Klaudya clocked him upside his head with the butt of the gun.

Javid released her and stumbled back a foot.

That was all she needed to resume her chase after Nichelle.

Frantic, Nichelle didn't know where she was going or how the hell she was going to get away from her crazy daughter. But she managed to make a half circle around the house to the circular driveway in front.

The car. She needed to get to the rented Mercedes and get the fuck out of there.

Nichelle glanced over her shoulder and saw Klaudya gaining ground. Doubling her efforts, Nichelle made it to the Mercedes. The mercy of all mercies, the car door was unlocked. She hopped inside and locked the door.

Klaudya tried the door.

Grateful to have left the key-fob clipped to the visor, Nichelle jabbed the push-button car starter, and the car's engine purred as it turned over.

Klaudya reared back and smashed the driver's-side window with the butt of her gun.

Nichelle screamed as broken glass cascaded over her, but it didn't stop her from shifting into drive and flooring the gas.

The car took off like a rocket.

Klaudya scrambled to her car in the driveway, after losing time to retrieve her electronic fob from the kitchen. With the same push-button technology, the car turned over.

Ruthie and the twins were at the front door, witnessing the tail end of the madness.

Javid jumped from out of nowhere in front of the car. "Let her go, Klaudya. You're not thinking right."

"Fuck you!" She stomped on the accelerator.

Javid dove out of the way in record time and was left to choke on a puff of smoke from the tailpipe.

The next time he saw either of them, it was with the police after they'd crashed on the Ventura freeway, where the police had handcuffed Klaudya and carried her off to jail.

CHAPTER 17

The storm

"M*ya!*" *Javid roared, tearing through the house. "Mya, where are you? This isn't funny. We've got to go."*

Mykell shadowed his father from room to room. "Where do you think she's at?"

Javid had no idea, but he was out of patience with his headstrong daughter. "Mya, I mean it. I don't have time for this bullshit. Let's go!"

Silence.

After scrounging through Mya's pink princess bedroom, Javid ran out of ideas where to search. It was a big house. "Shit." He scooped out his cell phone to see if he had service.

He didn't.

Mykell voiced a fear creeping around the back of Javid's head. "What if somebody took her? She could be in trouble right now."

"Mykell, stop it," Javid barked. "I don't need you acting like a big baby right now. Can you please suck it up? I need to find your sister." He stormed away from his son before his

shimmer of tears had him apologizing again. He wasn't in the mood to cater to his son's fragile emotions. It didn't take anything to get those tears going.

Javid tugged his son toward the door. "C'mon, we're going to Ruthie's."

"What about Mya?" Mykell whined. "We have to find her."

"I will, son. I will. I promise."

Mykell dragged his feet.

Javid grabbed the boy's raincoat and helped shove him into it.

Mykell cried.

"C'mon, son. I'm going to need you to man up. Stop crying."

At the bass in his father's voice, Mykell cried harder and ran through a list of reasons why they couldn't leave the house. "She could be hurt," was one he kept repeating.

"Mya is fine, son. I promise."

Mykell made a face. His father had broken too many promises in the past year. He didn't believe him now.

Frustrated, Javid lifted the boy and raced out of the back of the house toward Ruthie's private quarters. It was raining harder than it had been an hour ago. A few times he slipped on the soggy earth, but he trudged on. He prayed Mya was hiding in the house and Nichelle wasn't dying in his car.

When Javid arrived at the private cottage, the lights were out there, too. Inside he could make out flickering candlewicks. Sighing, he hammered on the door.

Ruthie took her sweet time disengaging the locks while Mykell cried. When the housekeeper opened the door, she shined a flashlight in their faces. "I figured you'd show up here."

"You did?"

"Of course." She opened the door further and revealed his soaking-wet daughter standing by Ruthie's side.

"Mya!" Javid lowered Mykell to the porch.

The boy spun around and threw his arms around his twin. "Mya!"

"What are you doing here?" Javid thundered. "Do you know how worried me and your brother were?"

Mya pushed away from her brother and folded her arms. "I don't want to camp with Grandma!"

Ruthie shook her head. "I would've called you the second she arrived at my door, but service is out."

"Yeah, I know. We have the same problem back at the house." He relaxed. "Hey, I need you to do me a favor. Can you watch the kids? I have to run to the hospital."

"Hospital? Is there a problem?"

"Grandma fell and hurt her head," Mykell blabbed.

"Oh, my. Of course, I'll watch the children," Ruthie said.

"Thanks, Ruthie." He delivered a peck on her cheek. "I can't tell you how much I appreciate you."

"I have a pretty fair idea." She grinned. "But you be careful out there on the road. I can't remember the last time we've had weather like this."

"I will." Javid knelt to the kids' level. "Now you two be good and listen to Ruthie. I should be back in a few hours." He gathered them into a hug and kissed their foreheads.

The children kissed him back.

After Javid raced off the porch, he turned and gave a final wave.

"And that was the last time I saw him alive." Ruthie lowered her head.

Lieutenant Schneider pushed a Kleenex box toward her.

"Thank you." Ruthie swiped a few sheets to wipe her eyes.

Armstrong and Schneider exchanged looks and thanked Ruthie for her time.

CHAPTER 18

A tired, red-eyed Lieutenant Armstrong entered the interrogation room with his partner. Guilt weighed heavily on him for Nichelle being back in this situation. If only he'd never pressured the Ramseys to take her in, Nichelle Mathis wouldn't be looking at another life sentence without the possibility of parole.

Nervous, Nichelle, in her orange prison garb, hopped to her feet when the men entered. "Well? Did you find Sassy?"

He shook his head. "Yeah, we found her. She wasn't much help, though. She said she hadn't seen your daughter since the day of Klaudya's release from prison."

"That bitch. She's lying."

"You have any proof?" he asked.

The way Nichelle plopped into her seat told all he needed to know. "Look, you got to help me. I didn't do this."

Schneider, unmoved by Nichelle's performance, whipped out a folder. "And what about this?"

Nichelle eyed it like he'd dropped a snake in the middle of the table. "What is it?"

"You don't know?" he asked.

"Should I?"

Armstrong sighed as if he'd spotted a crack in her innocence. "It's an insurance policy."

Nichelle stiffened.

"Ring a few bells now?"

Nichelle sucked her teeth and shook her head. "Okay, I know it looks bad. But it's not what you think."

"Looks bad?" Schneider said. "It's what the prosecution likes to call *motive*."

Nichelle scrambled to explain. "We were getting married. We both took insurance out on each other."

"Yeah, we have the policies you both took out on the same day . . . but you went back—and doubled his from two million to five million—a week before he died."

Nichelle squirmed in her chair and insisted, "I'm being set up."

"You've said that already," Schneider droned on, bored. "But . . . where's the proof? From everything I see . . . you moved into your daughter's place, she experienced some breakdown that landed her behind bars for assault, a considerable downgrade from attempted murder."

"Tell me about it," Nichelle grumbled. "Those high-powered lawyers can work miracles."

Schneider went on, "You stole her husband, took out an extraordinary amount of life insurance, and he ends up dead. But your murder charge is your daughter's fault. Do I have that right?"

"You're underestimating my daughter. She's not as innocent as she appears."

"And yet, before *you* showed up on her doorstep, Klaudya Ramsey was a model citizen. No priors. Performed a ton of community service. Her neighbors loved her."

Nichelle stopped arguing with Schneider and returned her attention to Armstrong. "You believe me, don't you?"

Armstrong hedged.

Tears swelled and rolled like boulders over her face. "I swear to you. I didn't do this."

Both men stared back, their faces unreadable.

"I don't fucking believe this." She rolled her eyes toward the ceiling and blinked back tears.

"This dysfunctional mother–daughter relationship might be clouding your judgment. Do you know of anyone else who might've wanted Javid Ramsey dead?"

She shook her head, sniffing.

"No one? No enemies? What about at his job? He closed his business firm rather quickly, didn't he?"

Nichelle froze. "What do you mean?"

Armstrong tested her. "Ari Chase had been Javid's business partner for more than a decade. Then, one day, they shut down the firm without any prior notice, Chase sold his house, packed up the wife and kids and disappeared."

Nichelle sat mute.

"Know anything about it?" Schneider asked.

Nichelle shook her head.

Armstrong leaned over the table and braided his fingers together. "Ever heard of Emilio Vargas?"

"No." At their exchanged looks, it occurred to her she'd answered too quickly. "At least, I don't think so," she amended.

"So . . . you didn't meet him . . . say, at a party?"

Nichelle's expression hardened. "Why are you asking me questions you already know the answers to?"

"Why else? To see if you'll tell the truth. And you're not."

She shook her head. "Klaudya is going to get away with it again. Isn't she?"

"Again?" Schneider asked. "What do you mean?"

Nichelle speared him with an angry look. "What in the hell do you think? I took the blame the last time. I'm *not* going to do it again. Is it too much to ask you two to do your fuckin' jobs and investigate?"

The men shared confused looks.

"I mean, she was a child the last time. I wasn't about to see my kid get locked up . . ."

1995

Nichelle quietly opened the front door of her house, but the moment she closed the door behind her there, a light clicked on. She spun around and saw her angry husband, Shadiq, in his favorite chair with a bottle of Jim Beam in his hand. "Where the fuck have you been?" he barked.

"One of the girls was late, so I had to perform another set to cover for her," she lied.

"Such a pretty mouth that spits so much bullshit." Shadiq stared as he chugged from the bottle, and then swiped his mouth with the back of his hand. "What's more fucked up is you believing my ass is dumb as hell."

Nichelle sighed. "Shadiq, I'm tired. I'm not in the mood for this." She marched over to him and pulled out tonight's knot of cash and handed it to him.

Shadiq slapped the wad of cash out of her hand to let it rain throughout the living room.

"What the fuck, Shadiq?"

He roared to his feet. "I went to Fat Tacos, and I watched you spend a muthafuckin' hour on some dusty Negro's lap while his head was rolled the fuck back. I know I've seen that muthafucka in there for the last three weeks."

"Shadiq—"

"I knew your ass been collecting side niggas at that club and bringing your stretched-out pussy back home to me like I'm supposed to be grateful or some shit." He leaned his face within an inch of hers. "Tell me I'm fuckin' wrong. I fuckin' dare you."

"You're wrong."

"Bitch!" Shadiq crashed his fist across her jaw.

Nichelle tumbled back. "He's a loyal customer," she screamed.

"Bullshit!" He stormed forward.

She backpedaled but shouted back, "How the fuck are we

gonna pay the muthafuckin' bills around here? Those loyal muthafuckas I keep happy in the champagne room, that's how!"

"What are you trying to say? Are you saying I ain't pulling my weight around here?"

"No. I . . ."

"I'm a muthafuckin' man." He pounded his chest. "I provide for mine. I don't want their jack-off money. In fact, your ass ain't going back."

Nichelle stopped walking. "How are we going to pay bills? You ain't held a legit job in years, and nobody trusts you to move any weight because you're too busy getting high off your supply. You ain't made a grip in six muthafuckin' months! We got kids! How are they gonna eat if I ain't shaking my ass on some dusty nigga's lap?"

Shadiq's hand was like a lightning strike, knocking her to the floor. "Oh, you're a mouthy bitch tonight." He shook his head. "It never fails. Every time bitches get a few dollars in their pockets, they grow fuckin' balls."

Nichelle touched her lips and saw the blood. "Fuck you."

"Fuck me? Nah, fuck you." He launched forward.

Nichelle screamed and scrambled away on her hands and knees. Across the hall, she saw little Kaedon's baseball bat leaning in the doorway. She was inches from it when Shadiq grabbed her by the back of the head and snatched her. Nichelle pounded his grip until he released her.

Shadiq pounced, fist swinging.

Nichelle hung in there as best as she could, but each punch produced bright stars behind her eyes.

"What did I tell you about your slick-ass mouth?" he roared. "Huh? You think you all that because you can get those niggas' dicks hard. Let's see how much they want to nut after I fix your face for you."

Nichelle's head snapped back with another blow to the head.

"Daddy, stop!" Kaedon ordered, launching onto his father's back.

Shadiq flung his son off.

The boy's head made a solid hit against the corner of the coffee table before he fell limp beside it.

"Kaedon!" Nichelle doubled her efforts to escape her husband's swinging fist.

In his rage, Shadiq hadn't noticed what had happened. But the next voice caught his attention. "Stop, Daddy."

The punching stopped when Shadiq saw his little girl aim the gun at him. He grinned. "Looks like shit just got real."

"Daddy, you're hurting Mommy."

"And you're playing with guns after I've done told you they weren't toys."

Klaudya's entire four-foot body shook.

Nichelle inched from under her husband to make it over to Kaedon.

Shadiq asked, "Now, what are you going to do with the gun, little girl. Hmm?"

"I want you to stop hurting Momma."

Seeing Nichelle creep away, he quickly grabbed her again while speaking directly to his daughter. "Klaudya, this here ain't none of your damn business. This is grown folks' business. You understand? Now you hand me the gun, and you and your brother go back into your rooms and shut the door."

Klaudya shook her head.

"Do you hear me, little girl? Go do what I told you," he snapped.

Klaudya clicked off the safety and racked the first bullet just like he'd taught her at the gun range. Tears flowed from her eyes and blurred her vision.

"Klaudya," he warned, finally releasing Nichelle to inch toward his daughter. "Give me the gun."

Sirens wailed in the distance.

Nichelle clutched Kaedon's limp body. "No. No. No."

"Klaudya," her father barked, making her jump. "Don't make me tell you again."

"I can't find a pulse," her mother wailed.

"HAND ME THE DAMN GUN."

Heart racing, Klaudya inched backward, but her father was closing the space faster than she was getting away.

"You little bitch!

Klaudya could barely keep her hands level.

Shadiq lurched—and Klaudya pulled the trigger . . .

Armstrong's brows crashed over his eyes while disbelief blanketed his face. "Klaudya *killed* your husband? And you took the heat?"

"She was a child . . . and she was trying to protect me. I wasn't about to let the system lock her up and brand her as some troubled kid. Plus, after Shadiq and my long and troubled history of domestic violence, I was confident the jury would buy a self-defense argument. I was wrong. There is no justice in the justice system. It's just us locked in it. Had I given up Klaudya, the state would have tossed her into one of those junior jails they love so much. She had already lost her brother and father. I wanted her to have a real chance. I never believed she'd grow up hating me. In the beginning, she'd write me every day. When she became a teenager, the letters stopped.

"One of the reasons I insisted on staying with her in Calabasas after I was not wanted there was . . . well. Damn it. She owed me. I served *her* time while she was out living the good life. Why couldn't she help me until I got on my feet—however long it took?"

"On your feet or on your back?" Schneider asked, disgusted. "How does stealing her husband come into play? You were jealous. Jealous enough to steal the good life you claim you wanted her to have." He looked at his partner. "Are you still buying all this?"

"Fine, I wanted Klaudya's life," Nichelle snapped. "But I didn't kill Javid. I swear."

"Oh, you swear? Well, I guess that settles it." Schneider chuckled.

Armstrong glared at Nichelle. "What did happen to Javid that night of the storm? Why is there no record of him ever taking you to a hospital? Why were you found with him and his blood all over you?"

"All I can tell you is that I woke up with my head pounding in the backseat of a car . . ."

The pounding rain on the car's roof was tantamount to torture. Plus, she was freezing. Her wet clothes plastered to her body. What was she doing out there? How did she get there?

She peered through the heavy sheets of rain toward the dark estate. Nichelle swore there was a light moving around in the house.

"What the hell is going on?" She opened the back car door and climbed out into the pouring rain. When she took a step, the world spun beneath her feet. C'mon, girl. Pull yourself together. It was easier said than done.

Nichelle stumbled to the front door like a drunkard with a broken toe. After opening the door, she held onto the doorknob for a few extra seconds and waited for the dizziness to pass.

"Javid?" She huffed like she'd completed a marathon. "Javid, are you in here?"

No answer.

"Mya? Mykell?"

Silence.

Where the hell was everybody? Nichelle closed the door and was entombed in the house's darkness. Wasn't there a light?

"Hello?" She crossed the foyer to the first staircase.

"C'mon, guys. This isn't funny." She tested her sore foot on the first stair and almost blacked back out from the pain.

A floor creaked somewhere. Someone was in the house. She swore, "These damn kids." When she tested the second stair, the pain was worse. "Javid, c'mon. I need some help with these stairs."

Silence.

"Javid?"

Her annoyance turned into suspicion and a heightened sense of awareness. None of this was right. If no one was here, how had she gotten into the car? What was the last thing she remembered?

Nichelle stopped on the third stair and held onto the banister while she scoured her memory. She was attacked in her room. Klaudya's name sat on the tip of her tongue, but she held it back because it didn't make sense. Klaudya was in jail. She wasn't due to be released for at least another month. It couldn't have been her. Could it? However, her throbbing head said otherwise. Someone had knocked the shit out of her.

Javid? They did argue before she'd stormed off to her bedroom. It hadn't been serious enough for him to attack her—had it?

Rooted on the staircase and bathed in paranoia, Nichelle didn't know what to do. Nothing made sense, not waking up in an empty car or entering a quiet house. The house was never quiet with the twins.

A floorboard creaked again. The echo in the house made it impossible to detect which direction it had come from. The house was huge. It could have come from anywhere.

Holding the banister, Nichelle descended back down the three steps. Whatever the hell was going on, she needed protection. She went to the kitchen and grabbed a large knife from the butcher's block. She had seen way too many scary movies to walk into a trap.

Now armed with a weapon, Nichelle still didn't feel safe. How long should she cower in the kitchen?

A door opened and slammed closed.

"What the fuck?" Nichelle's fear now shifted to anger. She didn't like fucking games, and someone was playing one with her. Nichelle hobbled back to the foyer, wincing with each step. Something scraped, like a stone. Even that didn't make sense, but at least this time she was sure it was coming from Javid's office.

Despite her heart leaping into her throat, Nichelle held on to her anger. Anger fueled her while every hair on her body stood. Her grip on the knife tightened as she rounded the corner to the home office.

Nothing.

Nichelle's eyes widened to adjust to the dark. Of course, she'd been in the room before, but she wasn't as familiar with the layout as she was with the rest of the house. It took longer to make out the different shapes and shadows. The air was different. It was thick and stuffy. It also carried an odor, much like her own: wet hair and mildewing clothes.

Someone is in here.

"Javid?" She lifted the knife and stepped inside of the room. Holding her breath, she listened to every nuanced sound. Her hand, slick with sweat, had her adjusting her grip on the knife. "I know someone is in here," she declared. "Mya? Mykell? If it's you, come out now so that no one gets hurt."

Silence.

She neared the fireplace. "This isn't funny," she snapped before tripping over something on the floor. The knife flew out of her hand as she fell. Her head missed the corner of the hearth by an inch. Wincing, Nichelle rolled over, but there was something around her ankle. "What the fuck?"

It was some sort of bag handle. A duffel bag? As she moved to untangle her foot, stacks of something fell around her. She picked up one and instantly knew what it was. Cash. There were other bags. Were they all stuffed with money?

Excitement crashed through her, but only for a second. Why was there so much money lying around on the floor? There were also bricks on the floor. Despite her aching head, Nichelle put two and two together. The money was in the fireplace.

A floorboard creaked, but before she could turn around, she received her second whack to the back of the head . . .

At the end of her story, Nichelle shrugged. "And that's it. When I woke up, Javid was lying dead on the floor, I had a gun in my hand, and the bag of money was gone."

Armstrong lowered his head while Schneider shook his.

"I know what I saw!"

Armstrong said, "But you didn't see who killed Javid. You put yourself at the scene of the crime. You admit to having the murder weapon. Days before the murder you take out additional life insurance on him—even though he was still married to your daughter."

"I didn't increase the policy."

"The insurance agent, a Mrs. Bethany Grimes, says otherwise."

"This is bullshit," Nichelle huffed. "I'm being set up, and nobody believes me or will do a damn thing about it."

Schneider sighed as he closed his notebook. "Well, I heard all I needed to hear. What about you?"

Armstrong sighed. "Yeah. Me too."

Nichelle panicked when they stood. "No. Wait. What does that mean?"

Armstrong shook his head. "It means that there is nothing else we can do for you. I'm sorry. Good luck with your trial."

The men signaled for the guard and left the broken woman sobbing. Back out in their car, Schneider asked, "So what do you think? You still believe your girl is innocent?"

"I never said she was innocent," Armstrong growled, fishing around in his pocket for his last cigarette. "I said there was more than what meets the eye on this case. That's a big difference."

"Or, more likely, you like making things more complicated than they are."

"Mathis killed her husband; now she killed her daughter's husband. The woman is a cold-blooded murderer."

"You act like it's hard for you to admit."

"Don't psychoanalyze me, Dr. Phil." Armstrong started the car.

"Fair enough. But we still don't know how Señor Vargas fits into all of this."

"Maybe he doesn't—for once. All I know is that I'm through with running around on this case. Klaudya could've killed him, or Vargas could've done it. The one thing that doesn't make sense is for Klaudya to have killed him and not her."

Schneider nodded. "I knew that you'd come around to my way of seeing things."

Armstrong's cell phone buzzed. "Hang on." He scooped it out from his pocket and read the screen. "It's Agent Sullivan."

Schneider frowned while he watched his partner answer the call.

"Hello."

"Erik, it's Leo. Man, I got some bad news. Arlington Chase is dead."

"Shit."

"Yeah, tell me about it. Chase and a couple of our agents were gunned down in broad daylight after gassing up at a Seven-Eleven."

"You're shitting me."

"I wish I was. It's a major blow to our case. But I thought I owed you a heads-up."

"Vargas?"

"It would be my guess."

"All right, man. Thanks." Armstrong disconnected the call and relayed the news to his partner.

"So do you think Vargas is also behind the Ramsey case?"

Armstrong pinched the bridge of his nose. "I have no idea. It's going to be up to a jury to decide. C'mon, I'll buy you a drink."

"How about you buy me two?" Schneider said. "I'm going to need them."

EPILOGUE

Klaudya and the children loved their new life. Living in one of the Balearic Islands off the coast of Spain, their small family enjoyed three hundred days of the year in the sun. It helped the children heal from the loss of their father much faster and to avoid the wild press of Nichelle's second murder trial—which ended with her getting another life sentence without the possibility of parole.

Klaudya loved the people of Sant Joan. They accepted everyone—no judgment. It was a small island, which made it easy to make new friends between the daily siestas. However, it was difficult to keep secrets. But Klaudya was a master.

Their new home was a Mediterranean paradise on top of a mountain, which gave them a lovely panoramic view of the turquoise sea as well as the countryside. The two-story home was made of natural stone with a matching privacy wall and tower.

This morning Ruthie cooked and served the eleven-year-old twins their breakfast while Klaudya's mind drifted as she stared out at the scenic view from the kitchen window. At some point, her mind roamed over her crazy life and what had happened the night of the storm . . .

Javid slogged through the backyard from Ruthie's place, and then stormed into the house through the back doors. After shaking off the excess water, he twisted the lock behind him.

Thump!

Javid froze for a few seconds. Someone was in the house. Finally, he uprooted his feet and crept forward, all the while searching through the dark for anything he could use as a weapon.

Thump!

He froze again while every hair on his body reacted as if he'd stuck a fork into an electrical socket. When his brain came back online, he grabbed a vase for a weapon.

After an eternity, Javid made it to the doorway of his office. It was pitch black—until lightning flashed.

"Klaudya?"

She lifted her head, and the room went dark again.

Though he knew it wouldn't come on, he flipped the light switch.

"Klaudya, I know it's you. What the fuck are you doing here?" He stormed into the office, determined to get to the bottom of this.

Klaudya clicked on a flashlight. "What the hell do you mean? This is still my house, too, or did my mother suck all of your brain cells out through your dick?"

"Ah, there's that mouth again."

"Don't do it." She unclicked the safety and racked the first bullet. "I'm not here for the language police."

Javid raised his hands, chest high. "Whoa. What's this? What are you doing?"

She chuckled. "Take one guess." She swept the beam of

the light toward the fireplace, where bags of money and a body lay on the floor.

"Nichelle!" He took a step forward.

"Ah. Ah. Ah," Klaudya warned, raising the gun. "Don't you even fucking think about comforting her ass in front of me. Are you stuck on stupid?"

"Is she dead?"

"Does it matter?" Klaudya cocked her head.

"No, it's just . . ." His gaze returned to the bags. "You came for the money?"

"Yeah. I figured I'd need it if I am going to start a new life in Ibiza."

"Ibiza?"

"I hear it's a great place to raise the kids."

"The kids? You're not taking the kids from me."

"Oh, don't worry. You're coming, too." She fired; a flash of light filled the dark room.

Javid jerked as the bullet blasted through his shoulder. "You shot me." He dropped to his knees.

"Yeah, but unfortunately, you'll survive it."

Sassy stepped out of the shadows and jabbed a needle into his neck. "Nighty night, sweet prince."

Javid pitched forward and collapsed inches from Nichelle's unconscious body.

Sassy knelt and checked his pulse. "Damn, this shit is good. Are you sure he's not dead?"

"He shouldn't be. But it should fool the right people until his body is delivered to Bethany's brother-in-law at the morgue."

Sassy smiled as she turned her beam of light toward the bag. "I gotta hand it to you, this is the best lick we've pulled."

"Yeah, well. It's not over yet." Klaudya planted her gun in her mother's hand and grabbed the bag of money. "When the time comes, you make sure you play your part until the coast is clear, or we'll have Vargas sniffing around wanting his shit back."

"Please. For this kind of cheese, I'm going to give the performance of a lifetime."

Bethany was right. Between her cop father and her brother-in-law at the morgue, she knew how to help someone get away with the perfect crime.

"Mom!"

"Huh?" Klaudya spun away from the window, sloshing her hot coffee over her hand. "Ah, damn."

Mya shook her head. "Oooh. You said a bad word."

"Sorry."

"Can we have twenty dollars?"

"Twenty dollars? For what?" She headed toward her purse.

"For the pizza party. Remember? You signed the school permission slip."

Klaudya sighed. "Still, twenty dollars for a couple of slices of pizza? That's highway robbery."

Mya and Mykell looked at each other and rolled their eyes.

"Here." Klaudya handed over the money with a delayed smile and then kissed each of them on the forehead. "Have a good day at school."

Mykell winked. "Thanks, Mom."

"Yeah. Yeah." Still smiling, Klaudya fixed another breakfast plate while Ruthie washed the dishes.

"Are you sure that's enough?" Ruthie asked and then piled a few more strips of bacon onto the plate.

Klaudya turned up her nose but having a vegan household had never taken root. Humming, she exited out of the side kitchen door and walked over the blocks of stone leading to the tower. Like a natural waitress, she balanced the breakfast tray on the one hand and retrieved the key to the lock from her robe.

She entered and closed the door with the heel of her foot. Inside, she climbed a set of narrow stairs. At the top was another door, which required a second key. "Good morning."

A chained Javid lay in bed and groaned. He'd been running a fever for the past week while the island had a rare week of rain. The tower was cold and drafty. The one window had been sealed and soundproofed, and Klaudya had the only key, to prevent the children from wandering inside and discovering their father alive.

"Still not feeling well?"

"Please," Javid croaked, licking his lips. "I need to see a doctor." His scraggly wet hair plastered to his head. His skin matched the shade of paste.

She chuckled. "And people in hell want iced water. Guess who will get what they want first?" She went to place the tray on the table by the bed, but it was broken. "What happened to the table?"

Javid writhed. "Doctor," he begged.

"No doctors." She set the tray on the floor. "They don't treat dead people, and you've been dead for three years. Surely you haven't forgotten."

"Please."

Setting her hands on her hips, she assessed the amount of sweat blanketing his body. "I have to admit, you don't look too good."

A nasty cough racked his chest. After a minute, Klaudya edged closer. When she pressed her hand against his forehead, Javid sprung. He raised a broken table leg to strike, but Klaudya's Taser was faster.

"Aaaagh!" His eyes rolled to the back of his head before he crashed back onto the bed.

"Asshole." Also from her pocket, she pulled out a remote. The chains reeled, stretching each of his four limbs to four separate posts on the bed until it was impossible for him to move.

After the immediate danger was over, Klaudya laughed. "Nice try, baby."

Panting, Javid glared. "Get me out of this shit!"

"No. No. No." She leaned over him and brushed his wet hair from his face. "You're not leaving. *Ever.* We said vows. We're in this shit together *for better or for worse* and *'til death do us part.*" She kissed him. "And I meant that shit."

TEARS OF BLOOD

A'zayler

PROLOGUE

May 2010

"**P**ut the money in the bag!" Kayden's black 9mm handgun was pointed at the terrified cashier. "I don't have all night."

The bald spot in the center of his head was on full display as he held his head down and pounded the buttons on the register. With one hand still in the air and the other tapping away on the raggedy, plastic-covered machine, it took a little longer than Kayden would have liked for the cash drawer to pop out. When it finally did, Kayden tossed the dark green Crown Royal liquor bag over the counter, hitting the man's unsteady hands.

"Fill that shit up." Kayden held his gun steady as he looked over his shoulder.

With Davion, a local corner boy, standing guard outside of the door, Kayden was free to handle his business on the inside. A Pepsi and a bag of Hot and Spicy Skins was all it had taken to convince Davion to keep his eyes peeled. Judging by how empty that register looked, Kayden was glad.

There was no way in the world that he was going to give away any of the money, especially to a nigga who hadn't done anything. Kayden was greedy, which was the main reason why he normally did dirt on his own. But tonight was different.

He needed to be in and out with no distractions. It was twenty minutes after seven, and he needed to be in his seat and ready for graduation practice within the next twenty minutes, or he wouldn't be walking the stage. Twelve years of hard work would be shoved down the drain all because he couldn't shake his hunger for dead presidents.

The cashier tossed the bag across the counter. "That's all I have. Take it and leave. Please go!"

Kayden frowned at the man, feeling a tad disrespected, but chose to go ahead and ignore his fearful gesture. Had it been any other night, Kayden probably wouldn't have let him off so easy, but since it was past time for him to go, he would let it slide.

With the bag now tucked securely in the pocket of his baggy jeans, Kayden took off, running out of the gas station. He tossed the snacks to Davion without breaking his stride and continued down the sidewalk, headed up the hill toward his high school.

Though it was spring and it was the furthest thing away from being cold in Texas, he could feel the wind on his face. The warm air brushed against his skin as he darted as fast as he could through the short bushes and tall trees separating his school from the gas station he'd just robbed.

Kayden could hear the traffic and evening noise in the distance as he made his way farther from the scene of his crime. It wasn't until he was on the back stairs of his high school that he stopped. He was winded and needed to catch his breath before entering the auditorium. The last thing he needed was to come stumbling in and have their senior class director to put him on the spot. Which she would probably do anyway, simply because she didn't necessarily care for him.

He looked down at his clothes, fixed his oversized shirt, straightened the gold jewelry on his wrist and around his neck, and took one last deep breath before pulling the door handle. As soon as he walked in, all eyes were on him. One familiar pair stood out among the rest: Aiden Lattimore, the senior class valedictorian, captain of the football team, president of the math club, academic scholarship recipient, and last but most important, his identical twin brother.

He was at the front of the auditorium behind the oak podium with his index cards in hand. The moment he saw Kayden, he raised his hands and eyebrows in question. Kayden being the vibrant young tyrant that he was, he smiled and held the peace sign up while heading to his seat.

"Where do you think you're going, young man? You are late." Mrs. Peterson marched toward Kayden with a vengeance. Her one-inch heels clicked against the tiled floor the entire way.

Kayden sucked his teeth and turned around in a huff. He'd already known she was coming, so he didn't even bother trying to fight it.

"I have told you all week that you needed to be on time for rehearsal." She started in on him the moment he was facing her.

"I'm sorry, Mrs. Peterson. It was my fault." Aiden met them in the middle of the floor. "I asked my brother to run back home and check for one of the note cards for my speech. I must have lost it somewhere." He looked as pitiful as he could as he stood lying to Mrs. Peterson. "I knew I would probably have to rehearse the most since I'm the biggest part of the ceremony, while Kayden not so much." Aiden shrugged. "Please don't be mad at him."

Mrs. Peterson stood with her arms folded across her chest looking from Aiden to Kayden with a very deep frown still on her face. Kayden could tell she was trying to decide whether she wanted to believe his brother or not, but he honestly didn't give a damn if she did or if she didn't. That was her business.

"Kayden, you are one lucky little deviant. Find your seat."

Her eyes tracked from his feet back up to his face before she walked back up the aisle.

Aiden waited until she was out of earshot before leaning over and whispering to Kayden. "Nigga, where the hell were you?"

Kayden's long fingers patted the denim material of his jeans. "Getting us some graduation money." His smile was broad as he watched Aiden's eyes get large before shrinking back to their normal size.

"Man, your ass won't be satisfied until you get caught. I've told you to stop doing that shit."

Both of them laughed after Kayden shrugged his shoulders nonchalantly.

"Gentlemen, if you don't mind." Mrs. Peterson's voice came from the front of the room.

Aiden rolled his eyes to the ceiling before turning around and walking back to the front, while Kayden went to his seat. The rows were small as he maneuvered through his classmates. Between talking and stopping to dap his friends up, it took him a little longer to get to his chair than need be.

His butt hit the seat simultaneously with him making eye contact with Mrs. Peterson. Kayden could tell by how red her light-colored face was that she was angry. He didn't care about her attitude any more than he'd cared about the gas station cashier's fear for his life.

When everything was finally back to its regularly scheduled program and Aiden had resumed his speech, Kayden relaxed in his seat and stretched his legs out in front of him. He watched his twin brother with admiration. Aiden was everything that he wasn't. Everything good that Aiden was, Kayden was the exact opposite.

Aiden made good grades; he didn't. Aiden had college offers; he didn't. The list went on. And though on most days he wished he could change it, Kayden had come to terms with the choices he'd made for his life, and he was okay with them. Though most people would probably be envious of someone surpassing them and winning in everything that they did, Kayden was nothing of the sort.

He loved Aiden and probably wanted him to succeed more than anybody else in their life. Although Kayden was probably one of the city's most troubled youth, and would more than likely end up in jail, Aiden didn't judge him. He loved Kayden just as much as Kayden loved him. It didn't matter how different they were, the love they had for each other was the same.

Aiden had been taking care of Kayden for as far back as Kayden could remember. From diapers to high school graduation, they'd been together. Even with Aiden taking the higher road to everything and Kayden taking the lower, illegal one, they were inseparable. The only thing that proved to be successful at separating the two was Kayden's actions, and just like every other time it happened, it was a total inconvenience.

"Excuse me, we're looking for a Kayden Lattimore." The boisterous voice at the back of the auditorium grabbed everyone's attention.

As soon as Kayden and Aiden laid their eyes on the police officer who had just busted through the auditorium door, both of their heads dropped. Although neither of them said anything about who was who, it was obvious. Almost everybody in the room had looked at Kayden.

Being who he was, Kayden stood up and accepted his defeat like a man. He looked over toward where Aiden was standing and shook his head from side to side in a dejected manner before walking toward the officer at the back of the room.

They grabbed and handcuffed him immediately, but not without informing him of the charges and his rights first. As he walked out to the squad car preparing to be loaded into the backseat, the only thought that crossed his mind was how much he wished he could have at least given Aiden the bag of money.

CHAPTER 1

Ten years later
June 2017

"Damn, man, my boy Gotti got these li'l thots out here showing out." Jackie, one of Kayden's little workers laughed. "They Snapchatting their pussy for real." He pulled his phone out and tapped on the screen a few times. "What's her Snapchat name? I'm about to follow her and see if I can get some pussy pictures, too."

All of the men in the room chuckled at his immaturity, Kayden especially. He remembered like it was yesterday when he was the youngest hustler of the crew. Now he was the person in charge. Niggas were breaking their necks to answer to him, and that's the way he liked it.

"Y'all li'l niggas stop fucking off and come count up this money. I got some places I need to hit."

"Got you, boss."

"On it."

They all answered in various ways as they got back to

work. It had been a long day and Kayden was ready to hit the rack. He'd been up bright and early that morning supplying the streets with the drug they loved to hate, while picking up and dropping off money. It was the beginning of the month, and it was time for his team to eat.

"There's fifty stacks in each one." Jackie set two large duffel bags on the table in front of Kayden.

"Here's thirty more." Another bag was placed in front of him.

Kayden nodded his head and stood. He dapped Jackie up before grabbing the bags.

"Y'all make sure y'all lock up tonight. Any of my work come up missing, so will you."

The men in the house expressed their understanding as he walked out of the house. Kayden looked up and down the street before going to his truck and placing the money inside. After slamming the tailgate closed, he hopped in and drove off. He'd told Aiden he would be there within the hour and that had been thirty minutes ago. Aiden was his twin brother and the city's next mayor.

Kayden and Aiden had been born only minutes apart, and had been joined at the hip ever since. The only things separating the two were what they chose to do with their free time. While Aiden chose to spend his time going to school and involving himself in the activities of the community; Kayden would rather run the streets and commit crimes that Aiden had to eventually aid in getting him out of.

It had been like that all their lives. Long before Aiden ever became a lawyer, he had been talking Kayden's way out of trouble, but their love went both ways. There was a lot of shit that Aiden wanted to do that he never had the money for, starting back in high school with Kayden buying Aiden the new Jordans that came out.

The list went on from clothes to cars, college tuition, and Aiden's most recent endeavor, campaign fees, all things that

Kayden took care of for him with no problem. Since he was in the lower income part of town, it had taken him a little over twenty minutes to get to Aiden's campaign headquarters, but he'd finally pulled in and parked. He called him as soon as his truck was in place.

"Aye, I'm outside."

The noise in the background was a clear sign that Aiden was still working. "Headed out there now."

Kayden ended the call and tossed his phone in the cup holder and got out. Before moving, he grabbed both sides of his baggy Balmain jeans and pulled them up so that they were back onto his waist. Satisfied with the slight sag of his pants, Kayden began walking around to the back of the truck. He'd just stopped at the rear bumper when he spotted Aiden walking toward him.

The tailored black suit and red-and-gray dress shirt Aiden was wearing looked expensive as hell as he moved toward the truck. Whatever the perfectly fitting pants and jacket hadn't given away, the suede fabric on his tie and handkerchief most definitely did. That suit had to have been pricey, and Kayden could tell that without having ever worn a suit in his life.

"Look at your black ass out here looking like money." Kayden held his hand out and Aiden slapped it while using his other hand to touch his tie.

"You know I'm allergic to that fake stuff."

Kayden laughed and opened the tailgate. "Shit, me too. You know I rocks nothing but the best." He looked down at the jeans he'd spent almost two thousand dollars on. "I'd just rather have on shit I can move in. You can have all them tight-ass, expensive-ass, colorful-ass suits."

Aiden nudged Kayden's shoulder as they shared a laugh. "The difference between me and you, though, is my suit looks like it cost a few thousand and your jeans don't."

"See, your shit fits your style, like mine fits mine." He shrugged. "We live two different lives, my nigga, and the way we carry ourselves shows that." Kayden grabbed the bag that had thirty thousand dollars in it and handed it to Aiden. "I'm a street nigga, while you…" He waved his hand toward the building Aiden had just come out of. "Are about to be the fucking mayor."

Aiden looked over his shoulder and nodded while placing the bag of money on his arm. "We are who we are." He dapped Kayden up again. "Appreciate this."

"As many times as you've had to defend me in court, nigga, you know I got you."

"A'ight, then. I'm wrapping things up in here now so I can head home and get some sleep. Where you about to go?"

They walked back toward the front of Kayden's truck. "Home, nigga. I'm tired as hell."

"If you'd stay your ass out them streets and get you some rest, you'd be all right."

Kayden opened the door to his truck and got in. "I got more time than I've got money, so I'ma spend all of that shit racking up these coins."

Aiden shook his head at his brother before dapping him up once more and walking back into his office. Kayden made sure he was good before pulling out of the lot and heading to his next destination. He'd ridden around for two more hours before heading to his second to last stop of the night.

The bass from Kevin Gates's "Satellites" vibrated through the back speakers of Kayden's midnight blue Denali as he crept slowly up the street. It was a little after midnight, so the block was black, illuminated only by the glow from the streetlights, when Kayden pulled into the small parking space in front of the building. He was greeted with love as soon as he hopped out.

"Kayden, what's going on, man?" One of his corner boys held his hand out to dap him up. Kayden obliged. "Where you at with it tonight? I know it's somewhere." He showed every single tooth in his mouth as he smiled.

"Nah, young nigga, I've been hitting the clock all day. It's time for me to take it on in." Kayden's eyes wandered off to the three women who had just come out of the building. As soon as they saw him, they were all smiles. One of them even had the nerve to jack her skirt up some more, as if that meant anything to him.

"Hey, Kayden," they spoke in unison.

"What's going on, ladies?"

The one with the short skirt that she'd tried to make shorter walked to him and touched his arm.

"You should take me for a ride in your truck. It's really nice."

Kayden's nose turned up. "For what?"

"I don't know. Maybe I can help you unwind a little before you go home." She shrugged and rubbed her hand over his chest.

"Help me unwind?"

She nodded.

"I think I'll pass, but thank you, though."

The girl looked a tad dejected but she smiled anyway before walking back to her friends, who were also eyeing him lustfully.

"Well, I'm in need of some unwinding." His corner boy smiled at the girl and received an eye roll in return.

Kayden, being the goofy nigga that he was, starting laughing.

"I don't know why these hoes love your ass."

"They don't love me. They're just looking for a come-up." Kayden dapped him up again. "Be glad they ain't checking for you. I'll slide through tomorrow. I just pulled up on you since I was out here."

"Bet. I'll have that package for you, too."

Kayden nodded and dapped back to his car. Once he was back in, he saw various shadows lurking in the darkness, moving so slowly that they were damn near crawling up the sidewalk. Kayden shook his head in disbelief as he observed what the drugs that he distributed on a daily basis had done to their consumers. Some of their bodies were so small and frail that they could have easily passed for skeletons, creeping back and forth terrorizing the hood.

Their tattered clothing was the only thing that made them differ from the plastic cream-colored skeletons that he recalled from his tenth grade physical science class. Their eyes were bulging and taking over their faces so dominantly that when looking at them, that was all he could see.

The more he watched the people, the more disgusted Kayden got. True enough, he was one of the main suppliers, which was why he was even on that side of town that late at night anyway. It didn't mean he enjoyed what he was doing or the effect it was having on the people that he served.

It didn't matter how disgusted he got, this was his life. The one he had stuck his hand in the middle of the universe and chosen for himself. A young, rich nigga with more felonies than he could count on one hand, and the local trap star that everyone in the hood looked up to.

From robbing and fighting to his frequent stays in the juvenile detention center, Kayden had been frowned upon and easily became the black sheep of the family early in life; the second son to parents who had died doing all that they could to save him from himself, and the younger twin to the intelligent, business savvy, dominating criminal defense lawyer, Aiden Lattimore, Kayden carried a lot of weight on his shoulders.

After his parents' untimely demise, Aiden had taken over the responsibility of looking out for Kayden, which was more of a burden than anything. No matter how Aiden tried to act as if he never got tired of bailing Kayden out of trouble, Kayden knew that Aiden had to be at his wits' end with him. It had been years, and he was still getting into trouble.

Though their lives weren't as carefree as they were back when they were kids, they still had fun together, even if the majority of it was spent bailing Kayden out of trouble. Kayden loved his brother and would do anything he could to help him succeed in life. Most people in Kayden's position would probably be envious of Aiden and all that he'd accomplished while winning over the people in the process, but he wasn't.

Kayden loved the life that he lived. It had been working for him for years, and he didn't foresee it changing anytime soon. He had a heavy hand in the streets that had a reach much longer than Aiden's, and he used it every chance he got not only to secure the life he led but the one his twin brother led as well.

Many people in the community looked at Aiden like the smart, hardworking citizen that he was, never bothering to educate themselves on what he'd had to go through in order to get there. Though that was cool with Aiden, it irritated Kayden to no end. It was like they loved his brother's image, but didn't love him.

Just like Kayden, Aiden was a product of the hood, raised in a low-income neighborhood with parents who could barely make ends meet from one check to the next. But instead of embracing that part of him, they clung to the cases he won, the plans he had for the city upon becoming the next mayor, and lastly, the handsome features that he possessed.

Tall, dark, and handsome was cliché as hell in Kayden's opinion, but it described him and his brother to a tee. They were both six foot five around 230 pounds with skin the color of milk chocolate and the facial structure that one would only see in magazines.

Their lifestyles fit their personalities, and even though everybody on the outside tried their best to maximize their differences in efforts to tear them apart, it only drew them closer.

The bond that Kayden and Aiden shared was inexplicable and deeper than any words could ever explain. Which was probably the main reason why he'd circled the same block three times in a row with his pistol in his lap.

Kayden leaned forward and squinted his eyes, doing his best to make out the facial features of the man who had just begun hopping down the stairs. It was so dark that he could barely see anything, but even if he couldn't make out the face, he could tell that walk from anywhere. It was Joe, a local club owner who had been jealous of Aiden for years and had taken it upon himself to begin slandering him publicly.

He had gone to high school with the twins and had called himself having some sort of underlying beef with Aiden. It was really starting to get on Kayden's nerves. Aiden might not have cared to address it, but Kayden was a different type of nigga.

With a quick movement of his hands across his gun, Kayden put a bullet in the chamber and slid out of his truck discreetly. He moved in a hurry toward his target, being sure to catch him on the side of the building and out of plain sight of anybody who happened to pass by.

An expert at doing hood shit, Kayden had the barrel of the same 9mm gun he'd had since he was a kid pressed against the middle of the Joe's throat before he'd even seen him coming. Like every other man he'd run up on unexpectedly, Joe's hand went up in surrender immediately. His eyes were large and held a hint of shock, but more fear than anything.

"Hey, Kayd—" Kayden pressed his gun further into Joe's neck.

"Don't say my fucking name."

Joe's eyes bucked, but he was unable to say anything due to the fact that he could barely catch his own breath.

"It ain't no need in explaining myself, because I'm sure you already know why I'm here." Kayden gripped the front of Joe's shirt a little tighter, adding more pressure to his neck.

"I've heard one too many things yo' bitch ass has spoken about my brother." He pulled the gun from Joe's throat and slapped him hard across the top of his head with it.

Joe grabbed the top of his head as he fell to the ground, nursing his wound. It was dark, but Kayden could see the blood trickling from the top of Joe's head into his eyes.

"Nigga, get your ass up." Kayden snatched him from the ground. "I ain't got time to baby your punk ass." With his gun now pressed to the side of Joe's head, he went back to what he was there to say. "My brother has too much other shit going on to address you, but guess what, pussy." Kayden leaned closer to Joe so that their noses were almost touching. "I ain't that nigga. I will blow your muthafuckin' head off . . . you feel me?"

Joe nodded his head rapidly. "Ye . . . yeah . . . yeah, Kay. I meant, yeah, I understand."

"Remember the next time you open your mouth to speak my brother's name that he's got me, and I ain't got shit to lose. You feel me? I will find your ass and dead you on sight. You got it?"

Joe's head was moving up and down quickly as blood and tears began to smear all over his face.

Kayden frowned. "I know your grown ass ain't crying?"

Joe sniffed and looked straight doing his best to avoid eye contact.

"Damn, Joe. I thought with all the shit you talk that you would be the last nigga to bitch up like this," Kayden taunted. "That was my fault, though. I should have known a nigga named Joe would be a hoe." Kayden's laughter sounded throughout the dark pathway. "Joe the hoe." He laughed again. "From now on that's your new name." The broad smile on Kayden's face drew more tears out of Joe's eyes, only fueling Kayden's laughter even more.

"Man, let me go. You ain't nothing but pussy, Joe the hoe."

With that, he stepped back and allowed Joe to fall to the ground again.

Kayden looked him up and down before sticking his gun back into the back of his jeans and taking a few steps backward.

"Remember what I said. I won't tell you again. Aiden's name better not cross your muthafuckin' mind."

He gave Joe one more look before turning to head back to his truck. It was still parked in the middle of the street where he'd left it, untouched as he'd known it would be. The streets knew who he was and how he got down. A nigga would be committing suicide laying a hand on anything that belonged to him without permission. So they made sure to never do it. It would be nothing for Kayden to make an example out of them. Kayden played a lot of games, but his temper could go from zero to one hundred within seconds. Anyone who knew him personally knew this, so they made sure to tread lightly. If they didn't, he would need Aiden for more reasons than one.

Once he was back in his driver's seat and comfortable, Kayden stuffed his gun into his armrest and sped off toward his house. The drive home was at least twenty minutes, so even though Aiden had told him he was headed home to get some sleep, he pulled out his cell phone and called Aiden anyway. He answered on the second ring as he always did when Kayden called. It never failed. Anytime Kayden called, Aiden answered.

"Everything a'ight?" Aiden answered groggily.

Kayden chuckled because anytime he called in the wee hours of the morning, Aiden assumed it was because he was in some sort of trouble and needed him to come rescue him.

"Hell, yeah, everything a'ight, nigga. Wake yo' ass up."

An exact replica of Kayden's laughter came through the phone. Not only did he and Aiden share the same face, but their voices were identical. The only way that anyone could ever tell them apart would be through fingerprints, personalities, and their clothing. Other than that, they were the same.

Aiden cleared his throat. "You know I have to check with your ass. You always in some shit."

They shared a brief laugh before Aiden took over the conversation again. "Where you coming from this time of night anyway?"

"You don't want to know."

"I always want to know. What's good?" Aiden's tone was sincere.

"A'ight, so I was at the trap shooting dice about an hour ago and one of my li'l block boys was telling me that he ran into a nigga named Joe. As soon as he told me the name I knew who it was, but anyway, he said the nigga was on some ole bitch shit talking down on you and stuff, so you know I couldn't let that slide."

Aiden released a deep sigh. "Man, Kay, I told you not to worry about that dude, man. I'm not thinking about him. He's a fucking peasant."

Kayden had already known that Aiden was going to say something like that, which was why he had decided to run up on that nigga and then tell him about it after the fact.

"Yeah, I know you did, but fuck all that. You know me. I couldn't sit on that shit."

"What did you do?" Aiden sounded like a stressed-out parent.

His reaction was expected and quite comical to Kayden, so before he could tell him what he'd done, he had to laugh first. He was laughing so hard that Aiden had begun to laugh as well.

"Kay, you think this shit be funny. Your wild ass be having me stressed the fuck out. I'm tired of being your fucking daddy."

That only boosted Kayden's laughter. "Shit, I feel like your damn daddy, too, as much money as I spend on your ass."

Neither of their laughter could be suppressed then, but it

was always like that. That was the kind of relationship they had. Brothers and best friends. It was a rare occasion for them to be around each other without laughing and joking practically the entire time. They talked about serious stuff and conducted business together as well, but that was rare. For the most part, they were just two young brothers that shared a sibling bond like no other.

"Man, Kay, I ain't got time for this shit, nigga. I was knocked out. Tell me what the hell you did to that man."

"I ain't really do shit. I just ruffed his hoe ass up with my pistol. That was it. He'll shut the fuck up from now on. I put money on that. I've let him slide long enough just off the strength of you, but that shit is dead now. He gon' learn today, gotdamn." Kayden mocked the famous comedian, making Aiden laugh again.

"You got to learn to let stuff go, bruh."

Kayden took the exit off the freeway to his house and sped up to catch the light. "No, I don't. As long as I got you to get me out of shit, I can do what I want."

"Spoiled ass . . . but you right. I got you forever, my nigga."

"Likewise, bruh. But aye, I'm at the house now and it looks like I'm about to have to go in here and show my ass some more. Jessica got cars all over my damn driveway, which means she got hella bitches up in my spot that I'm finna have to throw out."

Aiden snickered. "Well, if they fine, send 'em over here. I got a king-size bed I'd love to share."

"Well, scoot over and grab these bitches a pillow, because I'm about to run up in here and clean house."

"Man, leave them damn girls alone."

Kayden got out of his truck and headed up the driveway. "Hell, nah. Go unlock your front door, because I got some hoes on the way."

They shared another brief laugh before ending their call.

Kayden stuck his phone in his pocket and snatched his gun out of his waistband. He already knew what he was about to do was childish, but he was a childish-ass nigga, so he did it anyway. Hopefully things didn't get too out of hand, but knowing him it probably would.

CHAPTER 2

Kayden took the stairs two at a time until he reached the front door of his house. It had been a long day and all he wanted to do was take a shower and lie down. He'd been out on the block all night serving. The last thing he felt like doing was being bothered with Jessica and her loud-ass friends.

The sleep that he had planned to get was much needed, and the only thing that had been on his mind for the past few hours. So, having a house full of people blew his mood instantly. His girlfriend and the mother of his unborn daughter, Jessica was a nursing student and always felt the need to have her friends study at their house.

Kayden was very supportive of her dreams, so on most nights he tried to ignore it. Tonight wasn't one of those nights. Kayden made sure that there were no bullets in the chamber before twisting the doorknob and kicking the front door open. With his gun pointed and a frown on his face, he surveyed the room as the women screamed and began scattering.

"The fuck y'all asses doing up in my shit?" He tried to suppress his laughter as he watched Bronx, Amy, Jessica, and Amelia fall all over one another trying to get away from him.

Amelia and Amy were huddled in the corner beside the recliner and end table, while Bronx flipped over the arm of the sofa and was sprawled out in the middle of the floor. Jessica was also on the floor from having jumped so hard upon his entry.

"Kayden! Why you got to be so stupid!" Jessica yelled as she stood from the floor. "You play too damn much. It's too late for this shit."

Kayden could hardly breathe, he was laughing so hard. He'd lowered his gun and was holding his stomach as tears fell from his eyes.

Jessica's hands landed all over his back and head as she slapped at him for being so ignorant. "You make me so fucking sick, man, I swear."

"Jess, that nigga needs some damn help," Jessica's cousin Bronx told her as she took her seat back on the sofa. "Stupid ass." She rolled her eyes hard.

Kayden stood back to his full height and pointed his gun at Jessica and Bronx. "Call me stupid one more time, either one of you, and I'll shoot that damn weave out y'all's head." His smile was still in place as he joked with the petrified women.

"You ain't gon' do shit. Put that gun down, crazy-ass boy." Jessica walked to him and wrapped her arms around his waist.

"Aye, y'all get up. I ain't gon' do nothing to y'all scary asses," he told Amy and Amelia, who were still crouched down beside the table.

They were Jessica's classmates and had only met him in passing, so he wasn't surprised that they didn't find any humor in what he'd just done. Bronx, on the other hand, had known him just as long as he'd known Jessica. She knew that Kayden was a jokester and liked to do dumb stuff. Her laughter right then was evidence of that.

"Y'all get up. That nigga just playing. Forgive him for being a grown-ass kid." Bronx looked at Amy and Amelia. "He still hasn't grown all the way up yet."

The girls moved slowly from the floor and began gathering their things. Kayden could tell they were still a little leery, so he put his gun back in the waistband of his pants and held his hands up in surrender.

"My fault, y'all. I was just fucking with y'all," Kayden said.

All eyes were on Amy and Amelia as they stuffed their things into their bags, preparing to leave. Jessica immediately began begging them to stay so they could finish studying for their finals. Bronx sat watching them with a smile on her face. It was clear she still thought the whole ordeal was funny.

"Damn, B, why everybody can't be like you?" Kayden walked toward Bronx and plopped down on the sofa next to her. "They need to learn how to take a joke."

"No, you need to learn that pulling a gun on someone isn't a joking matter," Amy spat.

Kayden and Bronx looked at each other before he sat up on the sofa. He may have been a jokester, but he didn't tolerate disrespect in any form. He didn't give a fuck if he had just pulled a gun on the hoe, she was in his house and had better watch her mouth talking to him crazy.

"Bitch, you better get your shit and hurry your ass up out my spot with that noise." Kayden spat, clearly angry.

Bronx grabbed his arm and gave it a light squeeze. "Just chill, Kay. They just don't know you."

Kayden was still irritated as hell, but he heeded to Bronx's attempt to calm him down. She was right, they didn't know him, or Amy would have known better than to ever in her life talk so rudely to him.

"She's right, Kayden, damn! That shit was out of line." Jessica caught him off guard with her comment.

The fuck?

He turned toward her with a frown on his face. She of all people should have known how he was and should be on his side no matter what. It didn't matter if she agreed with him or not. She should have kept that shit to herself and vocalized her thoughts later and not in front of company.

"At least someone has some sense," Amy mumbled under her breath, but still loud enough to be heard . . . by Kayden.

Bronx's hand on his stopped Kayden from pulling his gun back out. He looked at Bronx, ready to go off on her as well for stopping him, but when he looked at her, he couldn't even do it. She was shaking her head from side to side subtly with a look of genuine concern in her eyes.

"You'll mess around and get a charge fooling with these stuck-up bitches," Bronx said. "Just let it go."

"You see this shit?" he asked, referring to Jessica huddled with her friends, agreeing with the things they were saying.

"Yeah, but you know how Jessica is," Bronx said, then lowered her voice. "She's probably just scared they'll call the police on you or something." Bronx was practically whispering. "You know she loves you, even if she likes to put on a front for other people."

Kayden was breathing hard as he sat staring at Bronx, wanting to believe what she was saying, though it looked very different in that moment.

"B, she know how I am. She knows damn well I wasn't gon' do shit."

"She does, but those are still her friends."

"Fuck them! I'm her nigga."

Amy, who had apparently been listening to their entire conversation, looked over her shoulder as she headed for the door. "She needs to find herself a new one."

Kayden hopped up. Bronx was right behind him, grabbing onto his arm at the same time that Jessica stepped in front of Amy, using her body as a shield to push them out of the door. She may not have been checking them for the slick shit they were saying, but she knew just as Bronx did that Kayden was a certified fool.

"B, take him in the back!" Jessica yelled as she hurried to close the door behind her and the other girls.

"Kay, stop!" Bronx made her way in front of Kayden and pushed him backward.

Her body was pressed flat against his chest as she used everything she had to push him away from the door. Kayden was mad, but he wasn't so mad that he didn't see what was going on. It was hilarious to see how fast Bronx and Jessica moved once they saw how he'd hopped up. They knew he was crazy and would spazz out without thinking twice about it.

"I know your silly ass ain't laughing."

Kayden looked down at Bronx's body sprawled against his. She was so tiny compared to him. "Just what in the fuck did you think you were about to stop?" He raised his eyebrows at her. "Little tiny self."

"Leave me alone, man. I was just trying to keep your ass from having to call Aiden to come get you out of the county jail tonight." Bronx laughed but didn't move.

Her breasts moved against his stomach as she giggled. Kayden tried not to let his mind wander off in that direction, but he couldn't help it. She was right up on him, and even if he could make his mind ignore it, his body was probably a lost cause.

"I was on the phone with him when I pulled up. He told me to send y'all over there."

Bronx giggled. "I bet he did. Y'all two are too much for real."

"You the one too much. I'm calm now." He looked down at her. "You can get off my dick."

Bronx jumped backward off of him and shook her head, obviously ashamed for getting caught. "I didn't even realize I was still on you."

"Yes, you did. You just wanted to feel on me," he joked with her. "It's cool. I won't tell Jess you want her D."

"Oh, my God!" Bronx's small hands went to cover her face. "You get on my nerves, man."

The two of them stood laughing together.

"I'm just fucking with you, man. Chill out. It ain't no thing. You know you my li'l baby. We good."

Bronx smiled at him before turning and going back to the living room while he headed for his bedroom. He wasn't even all the way down the hallway yet before he heard the door opening. Kayden turned right back around. When Jessica came in he noticed that the girl, Amy, was gone, but Amelia was still with her.

When Amelia looked up and caught eyes with him, she gave a flat smile and held her hands up in mock surrender. "I didn't say anything."

"You good. I was only fucking around," Kayden said. "That was your friend on that fly shit."

Amelia nodded. "She's always like that. She just has a smart mouth."

"Well, I don't fuck with smart mouths. They make my trigger finger itch."

"Got you." Amelia sat back down on the loveseat next to an array of loose papers and a few textbooks.

Kayden nodded his head at her quickly before looking over at Jessica. "Aye, Jess, let me holla at you real quick."

Jessica looked up from where she'd just sat and allowed her smile to fade. Her eyebrows rose in question as she looked to him for some sort of warning or explanation for his curt request. When he walked back out of the living room not bothering to give her anything, she stood and followed him down the hall.

As soon as their bedroom door closed behind Jessica, Kayden was in her face. "What the fuck was that? You in there teaming up against me?"

"Really, Kayden? You want to blow up on me because you play too much? You can't be serious right now."

"Why wouldn't I be? I'm your man, Jessica. You should never go against me in front of people."

Jessica rolled her eyes. "I wasn't against you. I was just trying to spare you from an unnecessary run-in with the police. Amy would have called the boys on you had you touched her. I didn't want that." She looked at him to make sure he was listening to her. "I like you being here with me. So, if I have to save you from yourself, then that's what I'm going to do." Her voice softened at the end.

Kayden stood near the dresser, staring across the room at her. Jessica was a hard person to stay mad at. He wasn't sure whether it was because he loved her so much, or simply because of how sexy she was. Jessica was a thick redbone with a crazy-ass body. Her succulent thighs and wide hips literally hypnotized him every time she walked by. Her bow legs and soft, plump breasts were also two of his favorite assets, but neither of them had anything on her beautiful face.

The slanted hazel eyes and short blond haircut that she wore were a match made in thug heaven, and Kayden enjoyed every piece of her on a daily. Much like any other confident woman, Jessica knew she was bad. Because of this, more times than not she got away with things that Kayden wouldn't dare tolerate if she was someone else, especially when it came to defiance. Jessica was a strong-minded woman, so it was rare for her to comply with his demands. It angered him every time, but he never left. Not that he could, or even wanted to, now that she was eight months pregnant with their daughter.

"Baby," she whispered sexily as she walked toward him and wrapped her arms around his waist. "Don't be mad at me. I just need a few more minutes to study and I'll make them leave . . . okay?"

Kayden moved his head out of her reach so that she couldn't put her lips on him. He then looked away. If he looked at her too long, then he might fall into the deep pools of hazel temptation that made up her irises, something he most definitely didn't want to do right then. He wanted to stay mad a little longer. If he made eye contact with her, it would be over with for him then. Jessica had Kayden wrapped tightly around her finger, and because she knew this, she used it to her advantage.

He had been trying as hard as he could to keep a straight face and remain angry, but he was failing miserably. The more she touched him, the more his anger dissipated. Before long, all he found himself wanting to do was throw her company out, make love to her, and fall asleep. He could already tell that wasn't about to happen. At least not anytime soon.

Judging from the way that she was pleading for the presence of her friends, he was fighting a losing battle. She wasn't going to give up until he gave in. And as sad as it was, it wouldn't be long. He was already melting beneath her fingertips and she hadn't even been touching him that long.

"Man, how long they gon' be here?" He looked down at her and she smiled.

"Not long, baby. Thank you." Jessica pecked his lips quickly before scurrying from the room, with Kayden watching her the entire way.

As soon as he heard her and her little group whispering about their work and whatever page they were on in their book, he figured the coast was clear enough to take a shower. Kayden kicked his shoes off in a hurry before heading across the hallway to the bathroom.

He and Jessica had one in their bedroom, but he hated the water pressure in that one. He only used their bathroom when Jessica wanted to do couple stuff like take baths together and silly shit like that. Their guest bathroom across the hall from their bedroom was his favorite, and the only one he took showers in. The water pressure was so strong it felt like he was getting a massage. Right about now, that's exactly what he needed.

Once Kayden was undressed and completely nude, he tested the water before getting into the shower and washing his body.

It didn't take long, so he was back out of the shower and wrapping the towel around his waist in no time. He checked himself in the mirror to make sure nothing was showing before he exited the bathroom.

As soon as he opened the door and walked out, he slammed into Bronx. Her small frame had been so light on the floor he hadn't even heard her coming down the hallway until they were pressed against each other.

"Oh, damn. My fault, B." One of his arms went around her waist to steady her on her feet.

Bronx held on tightly to his forearm to keep herself from falling, probably out of instinct more than anything.

"Dang, Kay, you almost took my head off."

Kayden chuckled and rubbed the hair that was sticking up on the side of her head back down, all the while still holding her close to his body.

"I'm sorry, B. I promise I ain't see you."

When Kayden finally released her, the thin towel that had been wrapped loosely around his waist snagged onto her belt and fell down a little. Bronx's eyes followed it, catching a glimpse of the top of Kayden's dick along the way.

Neither he nor she spoke on it; they simply stood there and allowed it to happen. Obviously embarrassed by what was happening, Bronx's eyes widened in shock before she hurried to look away. Kayden, on the other hand, wasn't the least bit shy, nor did he care that his girl's cousin had just seen his joint. That didn't mean shit. He was sure she'd seen plenty of naked men in her lifetime. He wasn't hung up on stuff like that, but it was evident that she was.

The smirk on his face was the total opposite of the petrified look on Bronx's pretty brown one, and it was hilarious to him. She was standing there looking like a damn virgin, and he knew for a fact that wasn't the case. All she did was talk about niggas and sex, so she could kill the innocent act.

Kayden chalked her shyness up to it being *his* dick and not some random nigga's. One that didn't belong to her cousin. To ease some of the tension, Kayden wrapped the towel back around him and tucked it securely to ensure that there wasn't another slipup before he could get into his bedroom.

"You good?" he asked her quietly. The last thing he wanted to do was make Bronx even more uncomfortable by having Jessica come back there wilding out.

She finally looked at him, and he smirked when she nodded her head. "Yeah. I'm straight. It ain't nothing." Bronx looked over her shoulder quickly. "It looked nice, though." She winked.

Kayden was shocked by her rapid change of attitude, so he decided to be a little more aggressive and flip her whole world upside down.

"It looks nice, but it feels better. Let me know when you're trying to feel it." With a sloppy kiss placed to the side of her head, he turned and walked away, smiling the whole way. He heard her gasp just as he closed his and Jessica's bedroom door behind him.

Though Kayden loved Jessica and everything she had to give, he'd always been secretly attracted to Bronx. Although neither of them had never spoken on it, or acted on it for that matter, he liked to think that she felt the same way. There had been too many times in the past where they'd caught each other's eye and held it one second too long, or accidentally touched the other and moved a tad bit too slow when it was time to break the connection.

In his mind, there wasn't anything wrong with it, either, because it was unspoken. It wasn't like they were sneaking around town fucking every chance they got. It was innocent. She was a gorgeous young woman who kept herself together at all times, while he, too, was attractive and commanded the attention of most females. Being attracted to each other meant nothing as long as they never acted on it. It didn't matter how many times Bronx found herself in the same vicinity as his male parts.

Kayden chuckled to himself as he dropped the towel and slid beneath his covers. Bronx was probably on the other side of the door about to have a mental breakdown while he didn't give two fucks. Snuggled warmly in his bed, Kayden closed his eyes and got some much needed rest. Now who he would dream about, Jessica or Bronx, was left to be seen.

CHAPTER 3

"How's it going, Mr. Lattimore? You ready for tonight? I can't believe it's voting day already!" Silvia, Aiden's assistant, made small talk as he passed her desk.

Aiden gave her his signature smile while nodding excitedly. "I've been waiting months for this. Can't wait to see what happens."

"I'm sure we both already know the outcome."

"I appreciate your confidence." He winked at her before continuing on to his office.

Aiden had exactly four hours before he was due at his campaign headquarters. Tonight was the night that he'd find out whether all of his hard work had paid off or been in vain. He and his team had been going nonstop for the past few months trying to ensure his position as Dallas County's newest mayor.

From visiting schools and churches to standing alongside of the streets shaking hands and taking pictures, Aiden had done it all in hopes of taking the next step in his life's journey. There were a lot of people depending on him, and Aiden had no interest in disappointing any of them, the main one being Kayden.

Kayden had not only poured countless dollars into his campaign and organized city functions, but he believed in him. He believed Aiden would become more than they'd ever thought possible. He and Kayden had been overlooked on so many different occasions because they'd come from the projects and hadn't had as much as everybody else growing up, but that time was over.

From the time Aiden had been in the sixth grade to now, he'd been doing anything and everything he could to make sure the public saw that he and his twin were more than just products of the hood. Though his hard work had given people a reason to respect him, Kayden continued to give people a reason to think of him the way that they did.

However, that was the one thing that Aiden didn't allow to fly with him. He didn't care if Kayden picked up the entire city of Dallas and threw it in the river, he would gladly stand next to him in the courtroom defending his honor. No questions or judgment mattered to him when it came to his brother.

Kayden never really gave people the opportunity to get to know the real him, but he really was one of the best people Aiden had ever known, and it wasn't just because he was Aiden's twin brother. He really was a loyal and genuine person who would do anything a person needed him to do. How he chose to do it was always the problem, but that's what he had Aiden for.

There had never been a time when Aiden had needed Kayden and he wasn't there, starting with their freshman year in high school. Against his parents and Aiden's wishes, Kayden hit the block every day after school until the sun rose for them to go to school the next day, making runs for the older dope boys.

Because of this, he fell behind a lot in school. He managed

to do the bare minimum in order to meet his requirements. Whatever he needed to get to the next grade, that's what he did, nothing more. Aiden watched from afar, sometimes doing his work for him, and talking to teachers on his behalf to make sure they gave him an adequate chance.

The summer heading into their freshman year quickly became one of the best. Kayden had been able to assist their parents with household bills and had even bought all of his and Aiden's school clothes. That summer changed him, and he hadn't been the same since. That and the day their parents died in a car crash on their way home from the grocery store had been life-changing moments for him, and Aiden had been by his side every step of the way.

A loud knock at his door startled him out of his thoughts.

"Mr. Lattimore," Silvia said, pushing the already cracked door open a tad more. "You have a delivery." Her smile was bright as she leaned only her head in the door.

"Send it in."

Silvia disappeared back out of the door. Moments later, three women walked in dressed alike in short, black dresses. Their red lipstick stood out against their beautiful brown skin as they all stood smiling at him. Aiden smiled back, not having the slightest idea of what was going on, but appreciating the view. They all stood smiling at him for another few seconds before the shortest of the three stepped away and looked at him.

"Aiden, a personal friend of ours asked us to stop by and give you an early congratulatory present."

He was really confused then, but not for long, because the gorgeous choir of women began to sing "The World's Greatest" by R. Kelly. All confusion was cleared up in that moment, because there was only one person in the whole world who knew that was his favorite song. Aiden's eyes watered briefly as his best friend's face and laughter popped into his head.

He wiped the water on the brink of falling from his eyelids away quickly and gave the ladies his undivided attention. He enjoyed the whole singing performance and even walked around the front of his desk to hug the women when they'd finished.

"Thank you all so much." He placed kisses on their foreheads. "I appreciate that so much. Y'all have no idea how beautiful that was." Aiden expressed his deepest feelings to the group of black queens who had been sent just in time.

His nerves had been shot all morning, and their voices had put him completely at ease.

"You are more than welcome. We've been instructed to sing it again at your headquarters tonight after you win," the same one who introduced them told him as his large arm rested on her shoulders.

"I'm looking forward to it." He smiled at them all before kissing each of their cheeks again.

After they bid him goodbye, they left, and he returned to his desk and fished in his top drawer for his cell phone. He hadn't even had time to retrieve it before his office door was opening again.

"The world's muthafuckin' greatest!" Kayden yelled with his arms outstretched. "You ready, my nigga?"

Aiden was around his desk and headed to his brother within seconds. As soon as they were close enough, they embraced in a brotherly hug. Kayden was just as excited as Aiden was and it showed. They held onto each other for a few minutes before Kayden whispered in his ear.

"You've got this, man. You hear me?" He palmed the back of his brother's head. "You made it, bruh. You proved these people wrong. Anybody that has ever slept on you are about to wake the fuck up tonight." He hugged him tighter before slapping his back hard. "I'm proud of you, man. You fucking made it, my boy."

Aiden nodded his head as his brother spoke his admiration and praise in a whisper that only the two of them could hear.

Kayden was proud of him; now he could go win. To have his brother's praise meant the world to him, because he was all he had. They were the only family that the two of them had, and the only ones who knew personally what they'd been through to get where they were in that moment.

"I love you, twin," Aiden told him as they embraced.

"I love you, too. Now go put all my fucking money to good use."

Their deep laughter broke their embrace and allowed them time to fix their clothes and faces. Kayden, too, had shed a few tears and proceeded to wipe the moisture from his face. Once they'd gotten themselves together, Kayden looked over his shoulder.

"Let me go out here and get this damn girl."

"Who?" Aiden wiped his wet hand on the dark blue dress pants he was wearing.

"Jessica. I told her to give me a minute with you before she came wobbling in here with balloons and flowers and shit."

Aiden chuckled as he watched Kayden dap out of the room and return with a very pregnant Jessica and a very stunning Bronx. They were both holding balloons and flowers in their hands with smiles on their faces.

"Aidennnnn!" Jessica screamed as she wobbled to him.

"Congratulations, twin!" Bronx was right behind her rushing to him with their gifts.

Aiden opened his arms and welcomed both women. They each held onto him, giggling and expressing how proud of him they were.

"All y'all up here acting like I've already won."

Kayden was seated in one of the chairs in the front of his brother's desk with his legs spread wide. "Shit, you have. That old bitch ain't no match for you. I don't see how she's held on this long. I would have thought she would have been had sense enough to drop out and take her loss like the man she looks like."

The room erupted in laughter as Kayden made light of the nerve-wracking situation.

"I'm serious. I saw a picture of her on the news last night and I could have sworn I saw a mustache across that hoe's lips."

"Man, Jess, get this clown." Bronx leaned back against Aiden's desk with her arms folded.

"Y'all know he ain't got no sense." Jessica walked to him slowly and sat on his lap.

"Now, Jessica, you being real mean right now." Kayden looked up at her. "You know Aiden wants me to come to his li'l thing tonight. Why you trying to break my legs before I even get there?"

Jessica and Bronx both squealed with laughter. "Man, this fool said you're being real mean right now." Bronx held her stomach as she laughed. "I cannot deal with him today."

Kayden chuckled along with them. "I'm for real. She know she too damn big to just plop down on my legs like that. She could have at least warned me, made that loud beeping noise as she backed up or something."

All of the friends shared constant laughs as they chilled with Aiden.

"So what time your li'l party start?" Kayden asked Aiden.

"They announce the winner around eight o'clock, so I've asked everybody to be there by eight. That way we can hang out and relax our nerves before it really gets going. The news channel should be there immediately after the polls close. I need to have everybody in place long before then."

"Bet." Kayden stretched his long legs out in front of him. "I'll slide through around eight-forty."

"Nigga, why? Didn't you hear me say they announce around eight tonight?"

"Yeah, which is why I'ma come after that. I already know you gon' win, so I ain't tripping on that. I just know y'all gon' be taking all them pictures and shit afterward, and I don't want my face to get caught in none of them and fuck up what you got going on."

Bronx looked at Kayden with a confused expression. "Kay, y'all have the same face."

"Mine is a little more thugged out than this nigga's is. The city knows me. I ain't about to embarrass my boy like that."

Aiden sat back in his chair, shaking his head at his brother. "Hell, nah. You be there at eight just like everybody else. I need you with me."

Kayden looked off for a minute, probably trying to decide whether or not he was actually going to come early. He made sure to look all around the office before landing his eyes on Aiden. Aiden's gaze didn't waver. He was serious when he said he needed his twin there with him. Kayden was his lifeline.

"Ain't no way I'm winning and you ain't there with me."

Kayden sighed. "A'ight, man, damn."

Jessica was still seated on his lap, so she slapped him hard upside the back of his head. "You need to stop being like that. I told you ain't nothing wrong with you, and I'll slap anybody that thinks it is."

"I ain't being like nothing. I just want to make sure I'm looking out for my brother at all times. Even if that means keeping my black ass out of the way."

"Chile, Kayden ain't never played the victim in his life." Bronx giggled while pointing her thumb at him. "This nigga just wants somebody to beg his ass."

None of them could keep a straight face after that; the twins especially. The four of them stayed and chilled together for a couple more hours, even ordering lunch and eating together before they parted ways. It was funny how God knew what a person needed before they even knew.

From the time Aiden had awakened that morning, he had been on pins and needles about the results of his run. It wasn't until Kayden had sent him the gift of song, and had hung out with him, that he'd noticed just how tense he had been.

It was things like that that made Aiden wonder how people could not want to know Kayden. The nigga was really a very selfless and supportive individual who Aiden was lucky to have as a brother.

"Mr. Lattimore, it's time to head home and get dressed." Silvia's voice came over his office intercom.

"Headed out now, love. Thank you."

"Welcome."

Aiden stood to grab his suit jacket and everything else he assumed he would need for later, and exited his office and law firm. After getting settled in his car, he looked across the street at the small building where he'd held all of his campaign meetings, and would host his announcement party that night. He took a deep breath.

Prayerfully, all of his efforts in the city and in life would prove worthy tonight. If they didn't, he wasn't sure what he would do. He closed his eyes and sent up a quick prayer. Hopefully he wouldn't have to find out.

CHAPTER 4

"Hey, I made it!" Jessica yelled at the top of her lungs.

"I'm the world's greatest!" Bronx followed her up as they both jumped on Aiden screaming and singing while tears rolled down their faces.

"Congratulations, young nigga!" Kayden grabbed Aiden out of the grasps of the women. "I fucking knew it!" He hugged Aiden tighter than he'd ever hugged him before.

Aiden didn't even think he'd hugged him that tight at their parents' funeral, but then again, neither of them had ever accomplished something so massive in their entire lives. Aiden had graduated from college and law school, and had even won numerous cases that held clout in the city, but nothing seemed as big as him becoming the city's new mayor.

"I love you, man! Thank you for everything." Aiden squeezed Kayden's neck so tight, he was surprised he hadn't passed out yet.

"You deserve it, bruh." Kayden stepped back and hit Aiden in the chest with his fist. "You worked for this shit. It's yours. All of it . . . the city . . . the world, my nigga. It's yours."

Aiden nodded his head as he looked into the eyes that mirrored his. All of the passion, the pain, the struggles—everything that was in his eyes—were in Kayden's, and he could see it. Aiden could recognize it all, and was happy that he had someone that shared his every feeling without having to open his mouth and utter one word.

"Ours, twin . . . the world is ours!"

Kayden smiled at him before embracing him again. They hugged for only a few moments longer before Kayden released him to the press to give interviews and have his photo taken. Aiden watched as Kayden, Jessica, and Bronx all walked off to the side to watch him in his element without getting in the way.

They hadn't been away from him for any longer than a few seconds before he was being swarmed by the press. Cameras and microphones coming from every which way were stuck in his face. It was what he'd asked for, so he made the best of it.

The small room that had been neatly plastered with campaign posters, banners, and pictures of Aiden was now filled with flashing cameras, graffiti, and swarms of people there to celebrate his accomplishments. The energy in the room was exhilarating as the occupants screamed, hugged, and sipped from tall glasses of champagne.

Boisterous laughter and excited praise buzzed around the room as Aiden's friends and biggest supporters joined together to celebrate the biggest night of his life. Now that the moment they'd all been waiting for had arrived, it felt just as surreal as expected. To see continuous smiles and cheers in his honor brought great joy to Aiden, and he planned to bask in it for the rest of the night.

With a large smile on his face, Aiden posed for pictures pretty much the rest of the evening. He was over the moon with happiness once he noticed the reporters and cameras beginning to exit the room. It had been a long couple of hours already, and they had been in his face the entire time.

Aiden was famished and needed to sit down for a moment. He looked around the room in search of his family. They were in the corner near the front of the building, looking to be engaged in a playful argument of some sort. Jessica had just hit Kayden's arm, while Bronx's hand and mouth was going a mile a minute as she pointed at Kayden.

Aiden smiled at them all, happy to have them in his corner . . . literally and figuratively. After sending one of the waitresses to round them all up some champagne and shots, he headed in their direction. As soon as Kayden looked up and saw him coming, he threw his hands up in the hair and started clapping.

"It's about time that my backup got here. Bruh, get me away from these damn women. They haven't stopped talking yet."

"The hell y'all over here doing to my brother?" Aiden said to Jessica and Bronx. He looked around for a chair, but was stopped when Bronx stood up and told him he could have hers.

As soon as Aiden sat down, she made herself comfortable in his lap. Although he knew there was nothing to it, and they were all pretty much family, the drinks he'd been consuming that night had him feeling otherwise. Bronx was a bad little chick and could definitely get the business if she rubbed her li'l ass across his dick one more time.

"Damn, Bronx, get your ass out my brother's lap." Kayden frowned at her. "You ain't got no more manners than Jessica's ass." Kayden playfully pulled at her arm. "Didn't ask or nothing. Just plopped your happy ass down. Get up off that nigga."

Bronx looked over her shoulder at Aiden and smiled. "You want me to move, Aiden?"

Aiden's hands went up immediately. "You ain't bothering me none."

Kayden slapped his forehead just as the waitress walked up. "Ah, hell, nah, bruh. Don't let her do it to you. You know she ain't got no home training. You better get you one of these classy women up in here." Kayden shook his head. "Don't fool with Bronx's ghetto ass."

Aiden laughed at Kayden as he passed him and Bronx glasses of champagne and shots of clear liquor in short glasses. The Coke and plate of cheese the waitress extended was given to Jessica.

"Here, big girl, ain't no drinking for you tonight." Aiden laughed.

Jessica pouted. "Why you ain't have them bring me some wine? I can drink that as long as it's red."

Aiden looked to the waitress for an answer.

"I can check on that," the waitress said. "I'll be right back."

As the waitress walked away, Aiden raised his glass. "Let's make a toast." The others followed suit in raising their glasses. "To family."

"To family," the women said.

"And loyalty," Kayden added before they all took a drink from their glasses.

A few minutes later, the waitress returned with a glass of red wine for Jessica before leaving them to enjoy one another. As always, their night was filled with talking and laughter. Before long, a couple of hours had passed and the party had begun to thin out.

"Aye, my nigga. I think that's enough for you. You don't normally drink like this." Kayden took the glass of Patrón and pineapple juice out of Aiden's hand.

"I'm good. I ain't even drunk yet." Aiden tried to take it back but failed. His hand dropped from the glass and proved Kayden's point.

"Like hell you ain't. Your ass is tore up."

Aiden straightened his posture and washed his hands down his face. "All jokes aside. I'm good for real," he told them with a straight face. "I don't drink no more, but I'm straight right now."

Kayden and Jessica stared at him a little bit longer before accepting his answer and letting it go.

"How much longer you plan on being here, Aiden?" Jessica looked at him. "I'm getting sleepy as hell."

Aiden nudged Jessica's shoulder playfully. "I forgot your pregnant ass couldn't hang with the big dogs tonight. Y'all go ahead. I have to wrap a few more things up before I can go home, but I'll be right behind y'all."

Bronx and Jessica stood up with Aiden standing behind them, but Kayden didn't. "Bronx can take her home. I'll stay here and kick it with you."

Aiden looked at Kayden and saw right through him. He wasn't staying because he wanted to, he was staying because he thought Aiden was drunk.

"Man, Kay, I'm good. Go home with your girl. I'll be straight."

Kayden shook his head. "Nah, I'm good right here. I'ma make sure you get home first, then I'll get back with Jess."

"For real I'm good."

Kayden looked at Aiden as if he wasn't paying attention to a word he was saying, and though he knew Kayden was doing it out of love, it was annoying him.

"Kayden, take your ass home."

"Aiden, fuck no," he bellowed back with just as much feeling as Aiden had in his words.

The two men stood staring at each other in combative stances, neither of them shying away from the other.

"Kayden, how about you go ahead home and I'll stay with Aiden?" Bronx stepped between the brothers, turning her head so that she could look at them both. "I'll make sure he gets home. I can take care of him." The flirtatious way she'd said it gathered all of their attention. Especially Kayden's.

Aiden looked down at her and took a step closer to her so that his body touched hers. "You gon' take care of me, Bronx?"

She looked up at him and flashed a flirty smile. "Most definitely."

The two of them stared at each other for a few seconds, conveying their feelings through their eyes before Jessica interrupted them.

"Okay, baby, she said she's got him. Can we go now?" She grabbed Kayden's hand and pulled him from the chair he had been sitting in. "Maybe she'll give him some congratulatory pussy, too."

Bronx hit Jessica's arm playfully as the four of them shared a brief laugh.

"A'ight, but call me as soon as y'all get to Aiden's spot." He looked at Bronx then Aiden.

"I got you," Aiden told him before they dapped up and pulled each other into their thousandth hug for the night. "Thank you, man. I love you."

"Love you, too. I'm proud of you," Kayden told his brother. "Take your ass straight home, and let Bronx drive."

"Bruh, I said I got you."

"Yeah, whatever." Kayden pulled out of their embrace and grabbed Jessica's hand. "I'll hit y'all up once we make it to the house."

They all bid their goodbyes before parting ways. Aiden had a few more people to say goodbye to before leaving, so he instructed Bronx to wait for him at the door.

Agreeing, Bronx headed over to the door.

It took a little longer than he'd expected but after Aiden bid his goodbyes, he took a step back and looked around the room. He'd done it. He'd actually beat the odds of the little ghetto boy from the hood, and done it. The new mayor of Dallas County. He smiled to himself before going to grab his things.

"You taking off, Mr. Lattimore?" Silvia met him at the door.

"Indeed."

She leaned in for a hug before letting him go again. "Congratulations. I know you're going to do great things."

"Let us all hope." He winked at her before walking out of the door, stumbling a little along the way.

He knew he'd been telling Kayden all along that he was fine, but it was as if all of his drinks were hitting him at one time. His vision was a little off and so was his balance. He knew for a fact that he was walking, but for some reason he felt as if he was floating instead.

Because Aiden wasn't a heavy drinker, the few drinks he'd had were really taking a toll on his body. He looked around the parking lot for Bronx, but didn't see her. He squinted his eyes, looking everywhere, but she was nowhere in sight.

"Where the hell this girl done took her ass to?" he asked himself as he surveyed the parking lot for her.

He spent a few more seconds looking for her before assuming she must have left him. As he was on his way to the parking lot in search of his car, he heard his name being called. When he turned around, he noticed Bronx walking toward him.

"Nigga, I know you weren't about to leave me?"

Aiden pulled out his keys while giving her the same smile that had won the campaign for him. "I thought about it when I didn't see your ass."

Bronx shook her head and reached for his keys. "I can't believe you would do me like that." She shook her head. "I'll drive."

Aiden grabbed her by her hand and pulled her to him. "I'ma do you even worse when we get back to my house."

Bronx's brown skin seemed to glow when she smiled up at him. "You swear you're smooth, Aiden."

He kissed along her jaw. "I'm not trying to be smooth. I'm just trying to make you feel good."

She giggled the entire time that he kissed her face and neck.

"Man, come on. I'm not about to stand in the parking lot

and play with you all night." She backed out of his arms and snatched the keys out of his hand.

Aiden watched her hop into the driver's seat and close the door before he made his way to the passenger's side. The time he'd spent playing with her sobered him up a little and he was actually feeling like himself again.

"Put your seat belt on," she told him after sticking the key in the ignition.

Aiden followed her directions and then relaxed back in his seat.

"Oh, shit, Aiden," Bronx cursed.

He gave her a concerned look. "What?"

"I don't know how to drive a stick."

Aiden's face softened as he unbuckled his seat belt. "It's okay. I'm good to drive. Come on, let's switch."

Bronx looked defeated as she took the seat belt off and opened the door. Aiden laughed to himself as he observed how down she looked about something so small. To cheer her up, he tapped her butt lightly as they passed each other. Like he figured she would, Bronx simply snickered before sliding into the passenger side.

Once he'd scooted the seat back so that his legs could fit comfortably beneath the steering wheel, he looked over at her to make sure she was good. After confirming she was safely buckled, he pulled away. He could feel the effects of the liquor on him, but it wasn't to the point where he couldn't focus on what he was doing.

"You okay?" Bronx touched the gearshift.

Aiden rested his hand on top of hers. "I'm good. Stop worrying about me."

She laughed his comment off and looked out of the window, but turned right back around to face him. "So how do you feel? This is a big night for you. I know you've got to be excited."

The smile on Aiden's face reached both of his ears as he thought about his accomplishments. "I don't even know how I feel right now, honestly." He turned his head to look at her. "I was nervous as hell earlier for real until y'all came. Y'all really helped to make the day easier."

Bronx moved her hand and touched his arm. "You know me and Jess love you, but it was really Kayden that put it all together. That nigga loves you. He's been stressing all week trying to think of something special to do for you. He was happy as hell when he finally decided on those girls to sing for you."

Aiden's smile grew a little wider. "That's my best friend right there, man. People give him a hard time, but shit, they should count knowing him as a privilege. It don't get no realer than Kayden."

"Aww, it's so cute how much y'all love each other."

"We're all we got."

Bronx gave his arm a light squeeze. "That's not true. Y'all got me and Jess."

Aiden took his eyes off the road for a minute to look at her. She was gorgeous with a smile to kill for. Aiden enjoyed her appearance a few more seconds before looking back at the road. The rest of the ride was fairly quiet, both of them lost in their own thoughts just vibing to the music and enjoying the company of each other.

"Aiden! Look out!" Bronx yelled at the same time that he slammed headfirst into an oncoming car . . .

CHAPTER 5

The crash sounded loudly throughout the empty streets. Neither Aiden nor Bronx were given time to even think before the air bags popped out, pinning them to the seats. There was nothing that Aiden could think of or even feel for that moment when he looked over at Bronx, whose head was lying to the side with blood leaking from it.

"Bronx!" he screamed.

When she didn't answer, Aiden did everything he could to maneuver his way out of the car. Miraculously, he only sustained a few minor cuts and bruises. His legs were a little weak, but that was it. When he was finally all the way out of his car, he noticed just how much damage had been caused.

The floating feeling from the alcohol was still very present as he stumbled around the back of his car. He'd tried to go around the front, but there was no way for him to get around it without doing too much walking. The front of his car was smashed head-on into the front of the large black town car that he'd just hit.

Aiden's mind was all over the place as he thought about what he needed to do next. He didn't know whether to check on the person in the car, Bronx, or to call the police. Too afraid that Bronx as well as the people in the other car were dead, Aiden did the only thing his mind could think to do. He snatched his cell phone out and dialed the first and only person he wanted to talk to.

He answered on the first ring. "Y'all finally made it home?"

"Kayden!" Aiden yelled in a rush.

"What? What's wrong?"

Aiden could hear movement on the other end. "I hit somebody. You have to come. I don't know what to do."

"I'm already on the way. Tell me where you at?"

Aiden heard a car door slam on Kayden's end as he looked around to find out where he was. He hurried to tell it to Kayden before taking a seat on the sidewalk next to the smoking cars.

"Where's Bronx? Is she all right? Have you called the police?" Kayden asked in one breath. "Tell me where you are."

"I don't know . . . I'm afraid to check." Immediately after Aiden told Kayden where he was, he held his head down and began to cry. "I only called you. Her head is bleeding really badly," he told him through tears.

"Aiden, listen to me. Get yourself together. I'll be there in a minute. You hear me? I'm almost there."

Aiden could hear Kayden talking, but he was so overwhelmed with what had happened that he could barely think straight.

"I should have listened to you. I was way too drunk to be driving."

"We not gon' worry about that right now." Kayden cursed in the background.

Ten minutes of Kayden talking to Aiden passed before he was pulling his large blue truck up next to the back end of Aiden's car. He rushed to Aiden and pulled him from the ground before grabbing him into a hug.

"You gon' be straight, a'ight? We always make the best of

fucked-up shit." He held Aiden's head between both of his palms and made eye contact with him. "We gon' handle this shit the way we always do, you hear me?"

Aiden nodded but didn't say anything. When Kayden let him go, they walked to the passenger side of Aiden's car to check on Bronx. She was slumped over in the seat, drenched in blood. Her eyes were closed and her mouth hung open slightly.

Kayden was the first one to lean into the car. When he stood back up, Aiden's breath got stuck in his chest as he waited for Kayden to tell him whether she was dead or alive.

"She's alive. We need to call the police. She needs an ambulance."

Aiden's eyes grew wide.

"Chill right here for a minute. Let me go check on the other people."

Aiden grabbed his shoulders to stop him. "No. Stay here. Let the ambulance deal with that."

"Nigga, no, because if they're dead, we got some shit to figure out first." Kayden walked away, leaving Aiden standing there.

He watched feeling hopeless and pained. How had this happened so fast? One minute he had been talking and enjoying himself, and the next he could possibly be charged with a host of felonies.

"Ah, fuck." The disappointment in Kayden's voice told him everything he needed to know.

When he looked toward where Kayden had been standing, he noticed that he was now on his way back toward him. Kayden touched his shoulder, pushing him to the ground to sit down. He then took a knee in front of him.

"They're dead?"

Kayden nodded, and Aiden groaned inwardly as his head fell forward onto his knees.

"Aye, man, I don't know how this is going to play out, but this shit gets worse."

Aiden's head shot up. What could possibly be worse than him accidentally killing someone?

"It's that man-looking bitch that you was running against."

"Ahhhhhhh, damn, man!" Aiden's head fell forward again as his tears resurfaced.

Not only had he killed someone, he'd killed his opponent. She was married with three children and would be the perfect person to send him to jail for the rest of his life. Aiden killing her could provide one too many negative scenarios, leaving the courts nothing but space and opportunity to paint him as the bad guy.

"Like I said, I don't know how this is going to play out in the courts, but this shit is bad. I don't think you should do this."

"What do you mean? It's already done, Kay. There's nothing I can do about it."

Kayden's face held the most anguish and pain that Aiden had ever seen in all of their years. His eyes were drooping and his face held a solemn look. It was almost as if he was on the verge of tears. Kayden was biting his bottom lip as he looked at the ground.

"It's like this . . . I'm a known criminal, I can do this jail shit with my eyes closed. You can't."

Aiden already knew what his brother was suggesting, and he couldn't allow that to happen.

"No, Kayden. Man, no." He briskly shook his head from side to side. "You've been through enough. I won't let you do this."

"Twin, what choice do we have? You're a lawyer, you can get me out of this shit. You know the law. I don't know nothing but the cell. We have to work together to make it out just like we always do." Kayden's eyes watered as he looked at

Aiden. "We're all we got. It doesn't matter how much money I spend on a lawyer, nobody is going to go as hard for you as I would, and I know the same goes for you. So let's just do this. I got you, man. Always. I can do this shit."

Aiden could literally feel his heart breaking inside of his chest as he listened to his brother's scenario. Though it made good sense and was the most logical one, it still hurt him to even think about it.

"Is there a possibility that I could get off from this? Maybe do a few years and come home?" Kayden questioned.

Aiden nodded. "Vehicular homicide and involuntary manslaughter are both charges that don't carry much time. If I could get the judge to rule this accidental, you could possibly not do any time at all, but if not you might have to do a few years . . . maybe even a few months, and be right back home."

Kayden's face and attitude picked up as he took a few breaths and nodded his head. "You know I'm built for this. That's time I can serve without blinking."

The optimism in his voice gave Aiden hope, but the sick feeling in his stomach killed it two times over. Every time he thought about Kayden serving time for something that he'd done, he felt like passing out.

"Look, Aiden, you're going to have to get ahold of yourself if we're going to do this." Kayden's voice had taken on a stronger, undefeated tone. "I can't do this if you're going to be out here falling apart like a li'l bitch."

"This just ain't right, Kay."

"What ain't right is me letting you throw your whole life away over a few drinks. I've been in shit for years. Even if you do confess, they'll probably assume you're covering for me." He shrugged. "You're a fucking annihilator in that courtroom. You can beast in there and have me out in no time. Stop stressing."

Though Aiden still wasn't completely sold on the idea, he nodded his head anyway and stood with Kayden's help. They looked at each other with the love they had for each other radiating between them. Neither had to say anything for the other to already know that the bond they shared was about to be taken to another level.

"I love you," Kayden told him. "We got this."

"Nah, you got this. *You're* the world's greatest this time around, twin." Aiden grabbed his brother in a tight hug.

They held onto each other for another few minutes before pulling away for Aiden to call the police. Together they sat and waited for the inevitable. Even with both of them knowing how hard this was about to be, neither of them could have predicted what was yet to come.

Once the ambulance and police arrived and the ball began rolling, there was nothing they could do to stop it. Kayden, knowing his brother better than anyone, hurried to tell the police before his brother could stop him that he'd somehow lost control and had accidentally hit the other car.

The detectives handling the case allowed Kayden to have a seat on the curb while they finished investigating, which Aiden assumed was a courtesy to him, because they'd recognized him immediately. While some investigated the scene, others stopped near the twins to ask questions. After Kayden told them that he had driven Aiden's car home due to Aiden being a tad drunk, they seemed satisfied enough to move on, again probably on the strength of knowing who Aiden was and the position he held in the community.

"All right, Mr. Lattimore, as of now we're going to book your brother on one count of driving under the influence and possible vehicular homicide," a chubby detective in a white dress shirt told him. "I'm assuming you'll be representing him?"

Aiden's head felt like it weighed a thousand pounds as he nodded it up and down.

"Okay. You can follow us to the station if you'd like."

"Okay," Aiden said before asking to speak to Kayden first. The police granted Aiden's request.

"Make sure you put these damn girls on the same page as

us," Kayden told Aiden. "I don't have time for them to be fucking shit up for us." He chuckled. "And make sure Bronx is all right."

Aiden appreciated Kayden's comical attempt at making him feel better, but it hadn't worked.

"Do me one favor, twin," Kayden said.

"Anything," Aiden told him, and he meant it with every fiber of his being.

"Take care of Jess and my daughter. Look out for them until I come home, a'ight? I don't want her to have to do this alone."

Aiden grabbed the back of Kayden's neck and pressed his forehead against his. "I got you, man. I'll treat them like I know you would."

"Bet."

Kayden pulled away when the detective walked back to them and grabbed his arm.

"One more thing, twin." Kayden stood up from the ground with the assistance of the police.

Aiden raised his eyebrows in question.

"Make sure you get me out of this shit." He flashed him a bright smile and allowed the police to lead them to the back of the squad car and load him in.

Aiden tried as hard as he could not to pass out as he watched Bronx being loaded into the ambulance, his opponent being zipped up in the black bag, and his brother and best friend being driven away from the scene of a crime that he'd committed.

A cry loud enough to wake the dead escaped Aiden's mouth as he fell to the ground in the middle of the street. His entire world had just been flipped upside down, and there was nothing he could do about it. He cried for what felt like hours before pulling himself from the ground and going to Kayden's truck and getting in.

It took him a minute to gather his composure enough to put his seat belt on and crank up. Once he finally did, he looked around at the beat-up cars that had just been loaded onto the flatbed. All he could do was shake his head. He'd done all that he could to take care of Kayden since they'd been children, and now that the shoe was on the other foot, he didn't know how to handle it.

He wasn't used to being without his brother. What would he do if he couldn't get Kayden off? Would he allow him to spend unnecessary years of his life behind bars for something he didn't do? Or would he run to the courts throwing everything he'd worked for in the trash and confessing to his transgressions?

Aiden let out a delayed laugh at his last thought. That one probably wouldn't work, because as Kayden had said, they'd probably assume he was covering up for him anyway. Aiden laughed a while before his laughter turned back into cries.

It was nearing three o'clock in the morning when he finally pulled away and headed to Kayden's house to let Jessica know what had happened. It hadn't even been a full two hours and Aiden already felt like he was about to lose it. He couldn't fathom the thought of letting Kayden down.

Kayden was counting on Aiden, as he always did. And just like every other time, Aiden would do everything he could to make sure they both won. Though in their hearts they were both hoping this time would be like the rest, they had no idea just how fast their hopes would be shot to hell.

CHAPTER 6

"Damn, man. Look at my baby." Kayden stared at the picture of his daughter, Jayden.

He'd just finished reading the letter that Jessica had sent him, telling him all about her labor and how hard it had been without him. In the letter, she'd included three pictures. One of Jayden taken at the hospital, the other of her, Aiden, and Jayden at Jayden's one-week checkup. The last one was of her by herself in a nightgown.

That one had gotten the majority of his attention because it had been a little over two months since he'd been with her, and he was missing her like crazy. Aside from the fact that he hadn't had any pussy since then, he missed her touch. Being in jail was never easy, but for some reason, this time felt harder than all the others. Kayden didn't know if it was because he didn't know what was going to happen or because he was actually innocent this time. He didn't know what it was, but it seemed as if every day got harder than the last. Though he knew Aiden was actively working on his case to make sure when they went to court that they actually won, he was still a ball of nerves.

Even with Aiden visiting three times a week to check on him and update him on what they had going on, Kayden still felt like he was missing out. His daughter had been born a month ago, and though he'd seen plenty of pictures of her, not being able to hold her was eating him alive.

Being stuck in that dirty little cell every night, cuddled up with the paper-thin mattress and uncomfortably flat pillow, was torture. He was used to rolling around every night in his king-size bed on top of his pillow-top mattress with Jessica's ass resting in his lap.

Although the pictures that she'd been sending him of her and the baby eased his mind, nothing compared to being wrapped up in her love at any given moment. To have her thick thighs holding tightly onto him as he slept was the one thing he missed the most.

Being with Jessica was a part of his normal routine, so now that he had to live vicariously through Aiden, he was growing restless.

"That's your family?" His cellmate was looking down at the pictures Kayden had spread across his lap.

Kayden slid the picture of Jessica in her nightgown behind the rest of them before looking up and nodding his head. "Yeah."

"That's what's up. They're beautiful."

"Appreciate that."

"You're a lucky man. Make sure when you get out of here you sit down somewhere so that you can stay out and take care of them." The older man climbed onto his top bunk and made himself comfortable. "The world ain't made for women and children. They need their protector out there with them. You hear me?"

"Yes, sir. I hear you. That's the plan." Kayden shuffled the pictures around, stopping at the one of his girls with Aiden. "I've got my twin brother holding them down for me until I touch back down."

"Twin brother?"

"Yeah."

The old man grunted but didn't say anything. "You trust another man with your family?"

Kayden frowned as something in him was irritated by the old man's words. "Yeah. That's my fucking twin. After me, he's the best person for them to have in their corner."

"I hear you, young blood. Just do like I said and keep your head on straight when you get out."

"Um huh," Kayden mumbled as he lay back on his bed.

Though Kayden wasn't easily frazzled, the old man's words weren't sitting well with him. Never in his life had he tolerated anyone talking down about Aiden, especially insinuating something disrespectful. He didn't play that shit, but because he was already in enough trouble and didn't necessarily think the man was saying it in an insulting way, he would let his comment roll off. This time only.

"Lattimore. Visitation," the CO told him from the door.

Kayden sat up and stuffed his pictures under his pillow before walking out of the room and following the CO to the visitation room. Since Aiden was his lawyer, they didn't visit in the general visitation area. They were granted the lawyer-inmate room.

"You holding up pretty good?" the CO asked Kayden.

"You know it," Kayden told him.

It was no secret who Kayden was. Not only had he been in and out of jail for years, but his name rang bells in the streets, and with Aiden's new position in office, things only got better. It was only right that his street credibility carried over into the pen as well.

"You already know all you have to do is holla if you need me."

Kayden nodded as they stopped at the door of the visitation room. He could already see Aiden sitting there at the table looking over the papers scattered in front of him. The waves on the top of his head were spinning and on full display as he held his head down as he read.

The tailored gray suit and pink shirt fit every corner of his brother's rather large physique, making him look much bigger than he really was. Kayden smiled as he took in Aiden's full appearance. He looked like money, and that made Kayden feel like a proud father.

When the guard finally opened the door, Aiden's head shot up and he was out of his seat instantly. He moved quickly and smoothly across the floor until he was directly in front of Kayden. They hugged briefly before stepping back and looking at each other as if it hadn't only been two days since they'd last seen each other.

"Look at your li'l rich ass," Kayden joked with his twin.

Aiden flapped the lapels of his jacket before looking down at his shoes. "Don't act like you don't know how I do, young nigga."

They laughed before taking their seats. "You must have had court today?"

"Yeah. Just got out, but you know I had to come through before I headed to the house."

"You gon' pull up on Jess and Jayden?"

Aiden nodded his head. "You know it. Jessica hit me up earlier saying something about Jayden being constipated, so I got to stop by the store and grab her something."

"Ah, damn. I know her li'l stomach probably tore the fuck up. Drinking all that milk and can't even use the bathroom."

Aiden's smile reappeared. "Boy, you stupid as hell."

They laughed for a moment before Kayden brought up something that had been on his mind for the past few days. He'd avoided talking about it their last visit because Aiden hadn't been in good spirits. Every so often he would get into his feelings about their arrangement, and Kayden would have to do his best to cheer him back up. Luckily for him, that didn't seem to be the case today.

"Aye, so have they picked a court date yet?" Kayden asked.

"Yeah, it's set for February twelfth. That was the main reason for my visit today, to tell you about your court date. I've been pushing for an autopsy, but the family is doing everything they can to fight it. They're saying they don't want to cut her up and a bunch of other stuff, but I'm going to do my best to get it."

"Damn. That's in six months." Though it was a bit further off than Kayden had been hoping, it was better than nothing. He'd seen cats sit in jail for a year or more waiting to get a court date. "You think we gon' be ready by then? Especially with all the stuff the family is trying to pull right now?"

The thick hair above Aiden's eyebrows scrunched together as the lines in his nose appeared. The way he frowned at Kayden had him laughing before Aiden could even answer.

"Boy, fix your damn face. You look just like Daddy's ugly ass when you look like that."

Aiden unfrowned his face and tittered a little. "That's because I don't appreciate you trying me like that, li'l nigga. Talking about will we be ready? Hell, yeah, nigga. The fuck you mean? I stay ready and you . . . well . . . you know how you do."

The boisterous laughter of the twins filled the small visiting room as they continued to make light of their current situation and all of the things surrounding it.

"So what Jessica been up to? How's school for her? She ain't been stressed out with studying and the baby, has she?" Kayden leaned closer to his brother so he didn't have to talk so loud. "You know she'll lose her cool quick. Especially given the situation."

Though Aiden had set aside a few minutes before Kayden was booked for him to talk to Jessica and tell her everything, he had still been extremely worried about her. She hadn't handled that news well at all. Out of all the people they'd had to explain that night to, she had taken it the hardest. For days, she cried and wailed about Kayden being selfish and leaving her and the baby before letting it go and accepting what had to be done.

"She's cool. She was stressed out about taking some test the other week, but other than that, she seems okay. I try to help as much as I can with Jayden when I'm not working, or when Bronx can't keep her."

Bronx.

Kayden hadn't talked to her at all since the whole incident. After she'd been released from the hospital, she had been keeping her distance. Neither of the twins had given her the details on the switch-up, but Kayden didn't feel the need to. She was a smart girl. He was more than positive she already knew what had been done. The fact that she hadn't spoken on it to anyone was solid as hell in his eyes, and he was waiting for the right time to thank her for it.

"Cool, just keep an eye on her. Take her out to get some ice cream or something. She loves little shit like that. Just make her feel special for me. I know she's probably a little over-whelmed after the baby, so let her dress up and all that other shit women like, then take her somewhere. She thinks I don't pay enough attention to her, so make sure you listen to what-ever shit she be talking about. Act interested even if you ain't." Kayden maintained eye contact with Aiden to make sure he was listening as he spoke. "The last thing we need is for her to start acting like she ain't got no sense and get to running her mouth and shit."

Aiden nodded his understanding.

"What about li'l Bronx? She still ain't speaking to you?" A smirk accompanied Kayden's question.

"Hell, nah. She'll be right at Jessica's house with me and won't open her damn mouth." Aiden looked confused as he talked about Bronx. "She acts like the accident was on purpose or something."

"She'll be cool. She probably just don't know what to say. Give her some time. She'll probably warm back up to you."

"Hopefully. Because a nigga like me needs some pussy. I've been so busy seeing about your family for you, I haven't had any time for myself."

Kayden groaned loudly and leaned back in his chair. "Nigga, you? I'm used to being up in Jess's ass morning, noon, and night. Now I'm stuck on this hard-ass bed with all these stinking-ass niggas." Kayden shook his head and sighed. "At least you got ass to look at. I ain't got shit but a bunch of hard legs up in here."

"The only ass I got to look at belongs to you, so I'm still fucked."

Kayden sucked his teeth. "Man, please. Jessica has so much ass you can't help but to see that muthafucka, even when you ain't trying to."

Aiden and Kayden were laughing again as they dapped each other up.

"I ain't saying look at the shit, I'm just saying don't sit here and act like you don't see it." He ran his hand over his mouth. "Then Bronx's li'l sexy ass." He shook his head. "Boy, you good. You better get out here and get you some ass. Stop acting like you can't get bitches. Hell, that li'l secretary you got is fine as shit. I don't know how you ain't been tapped that."

"I don't mix business with pleasure. Women get too far in their feelings. I ain't got time for that shit. I just want to live a stress-free life with my girl and maybe have some kids." He smiled. "Jayden's li'l ass got me having baby fever and shit."

Kayden sighed as he looked off toward the wall behind Aiden's head. He wanted the same thing. Jessica, Jayden, and him. All under one roof living a happy life. Though he'd always been serious about Jessica, being away from her was bothering something inside of him. Not being able to touch her, hold her, kiss her . . . just be with her was killing him and bringing him back to life at the same time. He could finally see what was important.

"You straight, kid?" Aiden's voice brought him out of his thoughts.

When he looked at Aiden's face, for some reason, Kayden got emotional. His eyes felt like they wanted to water, but he held it back. One long, hard sniff and a quick swipe of his hand across his face, and he was back to himself.

"Yeah. Just thinking about the important stuff, you know? When I get out, I think I might have to straighten up a little. Try to do the right shit."

"You can do it." Aiden grabbed his brother's hand and squeezed it. "You will do it."

Kayden nodded and moved on to another topic. That one was too much for him, and he wasn't really in the mood to get too emotional and have to go right back to his cell. Too many eyes were on him at all times. He didn't want to give not one sign of weakness. The last thing he needed was to have a nigga try him and he have to beat their ass to sleep. More trouble equaled more time, and he wanted no parts of either.

When it was time for him to go back to his cell, he and Aiden stood and hugged again before Aiden told him that he would be back in a few days. Kayden expressed his gratitude for Aiden's hard work with the case and his family before they left each other to go back to their lives.

"Had a good visit?" Kayden's cellmate asked him as soon as he walked back in the cell.

"Yes, sir."

"Good. Good. They left you some mail down there."

Kayden saw the two envelopes with the purple flower stamp in the corner on his bed. He knew then that they were from Jessica. She had been using the same stamp on every letter she'd sent since he'd been locked up. Eager to see more pictures and read more of her sweet words, Kayden lay down on his stomach and picked them up.

He was shocked to see that only one of them was from Jessica. The other was from Bronx. That threw him for a loop, because he hadn't heard from her since that night. Judging by the way Aiden talked, she wasn't really fucking with either one of them like that.

Since he'd been hearing from Jessica, he chose to read Bronx's letter first. He admired her pretty handwriting before ripping the envelope open. As soon as he did, the smell of her perfume permeated the air. Kayden closed his eyes and smiled, because that was the closest he'd been to a woman in weeks, and though it was a small gesture, it was just what he'd needed.

> *Kay,*
>
> *What's going on, homie? I know you're probably like what the hell this bitch writing me for. Lol! I already know how you talk, so don't act like you wouldn't call me a bitch in your head. Lol! Anyways, it has taken me a minute to reach out to you because I honestly didn't know what I wanted to say. All of this is crazy, and I can hardly wrap my mind around any of it. I've always known the love you and Aiden had for each other was out of this world, but I had no idea it was this deep until now. Even though I don't know how you all are doing it, I respect it. It's real and I won't hate on you for it. What I will say is that you need to hurry home, because all Jess does is complain about you being selfish and leaving her and the baby and a bunch of other shit I know you don't want to hear. But I feel her. It's tough, you know? Just hurry home. I'm not sure if I'm on your visitation list or not, but if you need anything, hit me up. I've already put money on your books, so go get you some noodles and honeybuns, li'l nigga. Lol. I know your lame ass is smiling, too.*

Kayden looked away from the letter for a moment to wipe the smile off his face. Bronx swore she knew him. Once he'd made himself stop smiling, he went back to her letter.

It's hard out here for the people that love you the most, so while you're in there, make sure you keep your head up and handle things like the boss I know you are. I got Jess and Jayden's li'l cute butt, so don't stress about that. I want to kick Aiden in the face every time I see him, but I got his ass, too. Only because I know you would want me to look out for him too. *rolling eyes*! Let me know if you need anything, Kay. I'm here.

Love, B!

Kayden sat staring at the letter before reading it once again. He'd always known Bronx was solid, but if he hadn't known for real then, he knew it now. She knew their secret and had kept it to herself. He could definitely appreciate having a friend like her. Whether she agreed with them or not, she was rocking with it, and that was a lot more than he could say for Jessica.

Even with him understanding where she was coming from, Jessica hadn't given him anything other than grief every time she talked to him. No encouragement, no laughs, nothing that would give him the push he needed to carry this situation out. Kayden shook his head while looking at Bronx's letter again. He looked at Jessica's letter and decided to open it later. For now, he needed to write Bronx back.

CHAPTER 7

The water from the faucet dripped slowly, making just enough noise to ease Bronx's mind. She had been sitting in the same spot for the past twenty minutes trying to figure out what was next. She'd just finished reading Kayden's letter, and although she wanted to write him back, she didn't think she would.

He needed to sweat a little. She'd done her job by getting his interest; now all he needed was some time to miss her. After waiting to hear from her for a little while, whenever he finally did, he'd be ready for what she was ready for. The only way Bronx could get through to him was to rid his mind of Jessica's dumb ass, and as long as he didn't get a response from her, she'd be the one on his mind.

Judging from his letter, Bronx didn't have much waiting to do, because she was already there. In his letter he'd disclosed how appreciative he was for her loyalty and genuine concern about his well-being. He'd gone on to tell her how much he cared for her and valued the loving friendship that they shared.

In one part, he'd even mentioned how he'd contemplated on many occasions what it would be like if they were together.

That had sealed the deal. From that moment on, she'd been on cloud nine, because that had been exactly what she'd been hoping to hear.

She had been loving Kayden for pretty much his and Jessica's entire relationship, but had kept it to herself for obvious reasons. With him being in a committed relationship with her cousin, Bronx had hidden her feelings out of loyalty. But now that he was jammed up and Jessica did nothing but gripe and complain about it every day, it gave her a new outlook on things.

Jessica didn't care about Kayden's feelings, so why should Bronx care about hers? Fuck her. Cousin or not, Jessica's behavior had really been getting on Bronx's last nerve. One would think she'd never been in love with Kayden, or that she hadn't known he was a street nigga when she got involved with him. All day she talked negative, and Bronx was tired of it. Which was why, when and if the time ever came, she wouldn't hide her feelings for Kayden anymore.

"Hey, girl, why are you sitting in here like this?" Jessica's voice caught her attention.

Bronx jumped as Jessica's voice startled her. "Heffa, that key is for emergencies. Not for you to just waltz in here whenever you feel like it." Bronx stood up from the table with Kayden's letter in her hand and walked to the small table in the corner of the room. "I could have been in here fucking."

Jessica laughed as she sat Jayden's car seat on the floor. "Bitch, you ain't fucking no damn body. You need to be, but you ain't."

They laughed together as Bronx slid the letter into the small table drawer. "Don't worry about me and who I'm fucking. Worry about your dick-deprived ass."

"Girl." Jessica sucked her teeth and rolled her eyes. "Who are you telling? It's Kayden's fault with his stupid self. I should fuck off just because."

"Why would you do that, Jess? That's not right."

"What he did wasn't right. So"—she shrugged her shoulders—"we're even."

That remark caught Bronx's attention. "Hold on, what do you mean y'all are even? You been messing around with somebody else?"

Jessica smiled and shook her head as she patted Jayden's back. "Not yet, but I've thought about it. All these fine men at my school, then Aiden's sexy ass walking around me all day every day, it's just pure torture."

Thirsty ass.

Bronx looked away to keep herself from rolling her eyes at that bitch. She was starting to like Jessica a little less every day. Maybe it was because she was in love with Kayden, or maybe it was the loyalty that had been embedded in them growing up. Jessica may have forgotten about it, but she hadn't.

"Eww, Jess, you're such a thot."

Laughter erupted from Jessica's mouth as she shrugged her shoulders again. "I'll be that. Kayden is one, too, hell. He's probably got all kinds of bitches writing him while he's in there. Hoes probably been waiting on their chance to move in on his ass all along, and you know what?" She looked at Bronx. "I don't even care."

"Why not? That's your man. You're supposed to stay down for him through this, Jessica. If you don't, then it'll be easy for another one of those women to catch his attention, and keep it." Bronx thought about herself. She'd be the first woman in line to take him.

"You know what, B, when all of this first happened I was ready to ride, and be there for him. You know, all that girlfriend shit. But now? Kayden should have thought about me more than what he did, and since he didn't, I won't think about his ass, either."

"Jessica, that's not right. Kayden loves you. It would probably tear him up if he heard the shit you're saying right now. He's a street nigga, but he loves your mean ass."

When Jessica spun around and looked at Bronx, Bronx could see the fading feelings that she had for Kayden. It was all over her face and posture. She didn't look like she normally did when speaking about Kayden. Kayden's name alone used to make her face light up; it was dim as hell right then.

"Well, if you care so much about the nigga, you stay down for his ass then."

Trust me, I will. Bronx smirked while walking back to the table where she'd been sitting. "All right now, don't try me. I ain't had no dick in I don't know how long. I'll been done bust this pussy open for that nigga and give Jayden a sister-cousin."

Bronx watched Jessica laugh until tears rolled out of her eyes. Little did she know, Bronx wasn't joking. She was a real one, and Kayden would be lucky to have her. She'd love and treat him better than Jessica ever had.

"Well, if you do get that nigga, at least I'll know my baby will have a good stepmama."

"And I will. I'll be fucking the shit out of her daddy, and seeing about her at the same damn time." Bronx snickered. "You know I don't play."

"Good. Maybe if you get him, he won't give a fuck about me taking his brother."

Bronx stopped laughing and looked at her, because she had been making that same joke about Aiden for the longest time. Clearly that was something she thought about on the regular.

"You would really fuck his twin brother?"

Jessica looked at her like she was crazy. "Hell, yeah! If I thought he would fuck me back, I would have been hopped on that nigga."

"You're so dirty, Jess."

"Whatever. Kayden's ass is locked up; how would he ever know? I sure as hell wouldn't tell on myself."

Me either, bitch. Bronx smiled, before high fiving her cousin. She could most definitely relate to that. "I feel you on that one."

"For real, though, I think Kayden going to jail was the

mental break I had been praying for. I was getting kind of tired of him anyway. The shit he does is so not becoming of a father. I don't want Jayden around that."

Oh, see, this bitch is tripping. "Now, Jessica, you can leave that nigga, but you can't play with his baby. You're asking to get yourself hurt like that."

"So be it." She looked around the room. "Enough about him, though. You feel like watching Jayden for me?"

"Where you going?"

Jessica smiled mischievously. "Out."

Bronx nodded her head slowly as she squinted her eyes. "You dirty li'l heffa."

Bronx could tell by the way Jessica was laughing that she was up to no good, but that was her business. If she wanted to trick off, then that was on her. All it did was make Bronx feel even better about what she planned to do.

"Yeah, I got her. Go do your thing."

After she and Jessica talked for a little longer, Jessica handed her Jayden and got up to leave. Once she was gone, Bronx took the baby back into the dining room, so that she could grab Kayden's letter again. She sat on the sofa with a wide-awake Jayden and began reading the letter again. She was going to get Kayden when he got out, and she didn't care how anybody felt about it.

CHAPTER 8

The sun was shining brightly; a little too bright for the mood that Jessica was in, but what did that matter? She couldn't change the weather any more than she could change the unwanted stuff that was going on in her life right now. Even with it being her life, she had no control over almost anything happening in it. Jayden was the only thing that Jessica had full control over, and she was a helpless, tiny newborn. What did that matter?

Jessica huffed as she switched her backpack from one shoulder to the other. She'd just finished her final and was headed to the front of the building to wait on Aiden. He'd kept Jayden for her that morning and had promised to pick her up from class when she finished her test.

With Kayden gone, she appreciated everything Aiden was doing to help her, but she still felt some type of way. What kind of man would just forfeit being with his family to go to jail for another nigga? Even with her understanding Aiden and Kayden's relationship, she still felt that the choices they'd made were stupid and selfish.

Jessica sighed. Well, not really stupid. It was actually really smart and made perfectly good sense, whether she wanted to admit it or not. It was the only logical way for them to win, but she still didn't like it. Kayden should be out with her, but he wasn't. It wasn't fair that she'd had to give birth alone, wake up at nights with the baby alone, or go to doctor visits alone. None of it was fair.

Kayden was supposed to be there sharing all of that with her, but like he always did, he put himself and the things he wanted first, totally disregarding her feelings regarding the matter. At first, she'd tried to accept his choices and just make the best of it, but the more stuff she had to do alone, the more she hated that nigga and wanted to call it quits. It was going on two months, and with each passing day, she cared for Kayden and his selfishness less and less.

"Hey, boo, where you headed?" Amy walked up to Jessica and looped her arm through Jessica's.

The girls hopped down the stairs together.

"To the store," Jessica answered. "Jayden hasn't been feeling well, so I need to see if there's something I can give her."

Amy poked her lip out. "Aww. Poor thing. I hope she feels better."

"You? Girl, I'm tired of missing sleep because of her little ass."

"Why don't you ask your brother-in-law to stay over and help? I'm sure he wouldn't mind. He's supposed to be helping you out anyway, right?"

Jessica thought about what Amy was saying, but she didn't say anything. She, too, had been thinking about the same thing for a couple of weeks now, but she just figured that would be asking for too much. Aiden had a busy life. He was the mayor of the city, after all. He had an entire city to look out for, not just her and Jayden. She didn't want to become a burden.

He was already doing everything he could for them and for Kayden at the same time. The last thing she wanted to do was run off the little help he did give because it had become overwhelming.

"I'm just saying. They act like they love each other so

much, make that nigga show and prove," Amy said. "He wants to volunteer to pick up Kayden's slack, then let him." Amy shrugged before walking ahead of Jessica. "If you decide to take my advice and you get a free minute, let me know. Maybe we can hang out." She blew Jessica a kiss before walking away and leaving Jessica to her thoughts.

She was now at the front of the school and still thinking about the things Amy had said. Her friend was right. Aiden and Kayden had both told her that Aiden would do all that he could to help her with the baby, so maybe she should have him *really* pick up Kayden's slack. She'd been trying not to overload him, but fuck them. They'd overloaded her without thinking about it, so she would do the same. Starting right then.

Aiden was standing on the side of Kayden's truck with Jayden lying over his shoulder. His large hand was pressed against her back as his forearm rocked her up and down. He was so busy looking at her and talking that he didn't even see Jessica walking toward them.

She smiled at the sight because it was seriously the cutest thing she'd ever seen. It was the exact way she'd pictured Jayden and Kayden the entire time she was pregnant. With Aiden and Kayden being identical, one would never know that Jayden wasn't his. She looked exactly like him.

"Your mama needs to hurry her butt up, doesn't she?" Aiden kissed the side of Jayden's chubby face. "Got us out here in this sun. She knows we're both chocolate. We're going to melt soon, ain't that right, Jay? You're too sweet to melt." He held her up and kissed her nose before bringing her back to his chest as he heard Jessica's laughter.

"Nigga, don't be out here talking about me."

Aiden looked up at her and smiled. "Girl, bring your light-skinned ass on. Got me and this baby out here sweating and stuff." He pulled the door open for her to get in before closing it and walking to put Jayden back in her car seat.

Jessica admired him with a smile as he fastened the baby in

while talking to her the entire time. It was so sweet that it almost brought tears to her eyes. All she'd wanted was for Jayden to have a father in her life, and before she even had the chance to experience the presence of her father, he'd run his inconsiderate ass to jail for no good reason. Jessica's eyes rolled the more she thought about it. By the time Aiden got in the truck and pulled away, she'd developed a full-blown attitude again.

Aiden's hand on her thigh got her attention. "What you over there looking like a sad puppy for? Or should I say a pissed pup?" He chuckled, but it quickly faded once he realized Jessica didn't find any humor in his comment.

Jessica sat quietly, trying to decide whether she wanted to tell him the truth or not about how she was feeling. Aiden may have seemed cool, but he was Kayden's brother. Twin brother at that. There was no way he was going to be on her side. It didn't matter how much sense she made.

"Tell me what's wrong, Jess." His commanding tone made her stomach jump. "I know it's something, so don't lie." He looked over at her before looking back at the road. "You failed your test or something?"

"No," she responded quickly. "I passed that with flying colors."

A smile crossed his face at the same time he squeezed her leg. "That's big, girl. We need to go celebrate or something."

Jessica's mood picked up some upon seeing how excited he was about her accomplishments. Kayden was never excited for her like that. He would always buy her stuff, but that was typical. She wanted him to sound as happy as Aiden just had. She wanted him to care.

"You want to get ice cream?"

Jessica looked at Aiden's smiling face and nodded her head.

"Cool. Under one condition."

"What?"

"You have to go home, get dressed, do your hair, and put

on some of that li'l girly stuff women like to wear. Get all cute, and then we can go."

Jessica was jumping for joy on the inside as she sat in her seat trying to hold still. She didn't want him to see how excited she was and change his mind. It had been so long since she'd been out, she would hate to ruin it by seeming too eager. "Cool. Right now?"

Aiden nodded. "Yeah, now. Call Bronx and see if she can get li'l mama. That way you can get you a small break in the process."

Jessica's face lit up as she snatched her phone from the pocket of her backpack. She called Bronx as quickly as she could, praying the entire time that she would be able to keep Jayden. She breathed a sigh of relief when Bronx finally answered the phone.

"Hey, hoe, what's up?" She sounded chipper.

"Hey, my love. Can you keep Jayden for a little while for me? Aiden is about to take me out for ice cream for passing my final."

There was silence for a moment.

"Yeah, girl, I can get her. But damn, I passed mine, too. I can't get no ice cream?"

Jessica and Aiden both laughed at her.

"You got me on speaker phone?" Bronx sounded a little annoyed.

"Yeah, girl. We're just leaving the school."

"Well, tell that black-ass nigga he could have bought me some ice cream, too, but I guess I ain't that special."

Aiden leaned over the console. "I ain't think you was fooling with me like that no more."

"I'm not, but I still want a banana split."

Aiden and Jessica laughed briefly before Bronx told them that she was home and that they could bring the baby. After Jessica told her that she would drop her off on their way to the ice cream parlor, they ended their call. When Aiden finally pulled up at her and Kayden's house, she hopped out, not even bothering to grab the baby.

"I'll go drop her off and come back to scoop you. You should be ready by then."

Jessica told him that was fine as she let herself into the house. He beeped the horn at the same time she closed the door. It had been so long since she'd been out on a date, she was past excited. Even though this wasn't necessarily a date, she was still happy to be getting out and doing something other than being stuck in the house as she had been since having Jayden.

After hopping in the shower quickly to wipe away the remnants of her long day, she dressed in an ankle-length blue sundress. It was Kayden's favorite. It hugged her body in such a sinfully perfect way that she always ended up in some sort of weird place having sex. It never failed, anytime she wore it, Kayden acted as if he couldn't wait until they got home to be inside of her.

Thinking of him made her heart skip a beat. She missed his sex so much and wanted some of his dick more than anything. Jessica held her head down and could feel herself getting angry, so she hurried to dismiss him from her mind. After she'd gotten completely ready, she snapped a few pictures and sent them to Walgreens through the app on her phone.

There was no way she was going to wear Kayden's favorite dress and he not see it. He needed to see what he was missing. After their ice cream, she would have Aiden stop her by Walgreens to grab Kayden a card and to pick up her pictures to send to him as well.

Ten more minutes passed. She was spraying on her perfume when she heard a knock on the door. Jessica checked her appearance in the mirror before flipping off her bedroom light and grabbing her keys and purse. When she opened the door, she noticed Aiden had shed his suit jacket and rolled up the sleeves of his dress shirt, giving him a sexy, relaxed look.

He licked his lips before giving her the once-over. "Damn, Jess. You ain't come to play, did you?"

She began blushing immediately. His eyes hadn't left her body yet, and even though it wasn't supposed to feel good, it did.

"I like this." She touched the rolled-up sleeve of his shirt.

"Appreciate it. Come on, let me get you in these streets so you can show off this dress."

Jessica stepped out of the house and turned to lock the door. Maybe Aiden was too close to her. Maybe her ass was just too big. Either way it went, she bumped into him, putting her entire backside against his groin area.

"A'ight now, Jess. Don't be on no bullshit tonight now. Your ass been this big since I met you. You should know how to control it by now."

The humor in his voice had Jessica cracking up with laughter as she moved past him so that they could walk to the truck.

"Man, shut up and come on."

The ice cream shop Aiden chose to take Jessica to wasn't too far from her house, so it didn't take them long to get there. He helped her out of the truck and held the door for her as they went inside. Since it wasn't very crowded, they were able to sit right down. Aiden immediately began looking through their menu, trying to pick a flavor. Jessica visited there so much that she already knew what she wanted.

"You act like you're at a restaurant. Pick some ice cream, boy," Jessica told Aiden after having watched him flip through the little menu for the past few minutes.

He looked up at her and smiled. All she saw was Kayden. "I like to read what's all in each thing before I order something."

"It's just ice cream."

"It's just my mouth, and I don't put just anything in it," he told her in a stern yet humorous voice.

Jessica raised her eyebrows at him with a smile on her face. "I'm sure that's a lie."

"How you figure?"

"You eat pussy, don't you?"

Aiden smiled widely. "Why you all in my business, girl?"

Jessica giggled before pushing his forehead. "My point exactly, nigga. Now pick some damn ice cream." All of her teeth were showing as she snickered at him.

Aiden joined in on her laughter as he finally told her he would be getting the mint chocolate chip. "I guess if I'ma go by your logic, I'd might as well just pick anything. If I'm eating pussy, my mouth dirty anyway, huh?"

"Yep!"

Aiden sat back in his seat and stuck his hands in his pockets. "Well, it's been a minute, so my mouth probably super clean right now. Thanks to you and your baby."

Jessica's mouth fell open. "Me and my baby? What we got to do with you eating pussy? That ain't on us."

"Like hell it ain't. I be over there with y'all so much, my personal life is going down the drain."

Jessica's mood dropped after his admission. That was the one thing she hadn't wanted to happen: she and Jayden becoming a burden to him. That was why she hadn't asked him to spend more time over so that she could get some sleep or study longer than ten minutes a day. After hearing that, her feelings were shot to hell.

"I'm sorry. You can chill out some. You don't have to come that much anymore," Jessica told him, sounding a lot sadder than she'd intended to.

Apparently, her tone alarmed Aiden, because he was sitting up and grabbing her hand immediately. "I'm just talking, Jess. Y'all not bothering me. I vowed to be there for y'all, and that's what I meant. I don't care how long I have to go without tasting pussy, I got y'all." He chuckled at the end of his comment, and so did she.

She even hit him playfully. "You make me sick. You and Kayden's mouths are so crazy. Y'all will say anything."

Aiden smiled at her. "He's worse than me."

"Hell, yeah." Jessica laughed to keep herself from getting annoyed again. Her body warmed in anger as she looked up at Aiden. "I'm so mad at him for leaving me." She rolled her eyes. "It's like I understand why he did it, but I still feel like it was kind of selfish. He didn't think about me at all, but he's always like that. Kayden is going to think about Kayden before anything."

Aiden shook his head. "That's not true. This time it was me he was thinking about."

"No disrespect, but it should have been me, not you."

Aiden nodded but didn't say anything, nor did she. They ordered their ice cream and waited silently for it to come.

"So outside of Kayden, how's everything else been going?"

"Everything else is cool. I'm doing good in school. Jayden's little self is perfect. If I could just get a little more sleep, then I'd really be doing good."

"Why aren't you sleeping?"

"Jayden stays up a lot. Kayden used to promise he'd get up with her since I always have class, but . . . you see how that's going." The distaste was evident in her voice.

The table went quiet again.

"How about I stay over a few nights a week and help you out?" Aiden offered. "It's the least I can do since I'm technically the reason why he's not here. It may be late at night sometimes since I'll have a lot of business to handle during the day, but I will still come."

"You'd do that?"

"Hell, yeah, I would. I love y'all."

Jessica loved that last part of his statement, but she'd keep that to herself. To receive attention from another man, especially one as handsome and successful as Aiden, made her feel like she was on cloud nine. Since having the baby and being away from Kayden, she'd been feeling a little self-conscious, but Aiden's simple words had cured it. Even if it was just temporary.

"Cool. Well, you've got tonight. I'm going out with my friends for drinks."

Aiden smiled at her. "Damn, that's fast." He snickered. "It's cool, though. I got you."

Jessica smiled at him just as the waitress brought their ice cream. They stayed there together for another couple hours laughing and talking about any and everything. They ordered a banana split to go for Bronx and then left.

Once Jessica made sure Aiden and Jayden were good, she called Bronx, Amy, and Amelia and they hit the town. She'd been needing a mental break for a while, and she was finally getting one with the intention of taking full advantage of it.

Between hanging out with her girls and chugging down all the drinks she planned to have, Jessica was bound to have a night to remember, and it hadn't even started yet. Hopefully, whatever trouble she found herself getting into would be worth the trouble in the morning.

CHAPTER 9

"Shit!" Jessica mumbled as she stumbled into the house and hit her foot on the side of the sofa.

It was almost three o'clock in the morning and she and Bronx were just getting in from the little club they'd gone to.

"Bring me a cover, Jess." Bronx fell onto the sofa and snuggled against the pillow and closed her eyes. She was way too drunk to drive, and hadn't thought twice about crashing at Jessica's house.

Jessica wasn't as drunk as Bronx was. She was a little tipsy, though, and needed to lie down, so she hurried to grab Bronx a blanket. Still not fast enough for a drunken Bronx, because by the time she'd gotten back into the living room with the blanket, Bronx was already asleep.

Jessica spread the cover on top of her before padding down the hallway to her room. Assuming that Aiden was in the spare room where he always slept when he stayed over, Jessica pulled her dress over her head and tossed it onto the floor. Naked and sleepy as hell, she walked to her bed and got in.

"Oh, fuck," she said groggily when she bumped into Aiden's arm. "Aiden. Aiden, wake up. What you doing in my bed?"

She had to shake him a few times before he woke up enough to answer her. "The baby was crying."

Jessica sat up and noticed Jayden on the other side of him cradled in his arm. She smiled at how cute she looked cuddled up against Aiden's bare chest. Jessica swooned at the sight before getting out of bed so she could get Jayden to lay her in her crib. Even though it was arm's length from the bed, and Aiden could have done it, she decided to do it herself.

Apparently, Aiden had fallen back asleep, because when she reached to grab Jayden, his eyes popped open and he held her tighter against him. Jessica froze as he squinted, trying to focus his eyes. When he did, he let his arm fall from the baby, but his eyes remained on her. It took her a minute to realize why he was staring at her the way he was. She'd totally forgotten she was naked.

"I didn't know you were in here," she hurried to say.

"I shouldn't have been." He sat up in the bed and started moving the covers.

Jessica took that time to lay Jayden in her bed. When she walked back around the bed to get back in it, Aiden was sliding out to leave. His muscular, bare chest was out, and the briefs he wore did little to disguise the fact that he was indeed Kayden's twin. Instantly, her mind went left, thinking of Kayden and the bomb-ass love he made to her.

Jessica bit her bottom lip as the center of her core began to thump wildly. The liquor in her system only fueled the sexual feelings that were stirring inside of her.

"Let me get out of your way." Aiden stood from the bed and bumped into her in the process.

Both of them paused and looked at each other. His eyes were burning with the flame she felt in the pit of her stomach. The heat from their bodies intertwined as they stood in front of each other, deciding what their next move needed to be. Jessica didn't know about Aiden, but she was sex deprived, and being that close to him was killing her.

When she could no longer hold herself together, she took a step forward, pressing her body against his while simultaneously gripping the hardening bulge in his underwear. Aiden sucked air through his teeth while gripping her hips. His greedy hands slid all over her curves as hers did the same. Jessica stroked the length of his manhood as she placed kisses all over the front of his chest.

When he groaned in pleasure, Jessica took it a step further and pulled his undergarments from his body. It was over with after that. Aiden bent down and picked her up before turning and laying her back on the bed. His mouth covered hers and set her skin on fire. Jessica was so hot with need she could barely keep still.

Unlike Kayden, Aiden was gentle. He kissed and caressed her softly, making sure she felt him everywhere he touched her. The warm saliva from his mouth coated her nipples as he sucked and pulled them with his mouth. Jessica's back arched at the same time that her mouth fell open.

"Ummm," she moaned to him as he kissed his way down her body.

Jessica's hands covered her face when she felt his lips and tongue on the slippery folds of her love. Her thighs were being held firmly in the palms of his hands as he licked and slurped all over. Her eyes rolled with every flick of the thick pink tongue that slithered in and out of his mouth rapidly.

With her hands on the top of his head, Jessica worked her hips across his face and mouth until she felt like she was about to explode. Just when she felt as though she couldn't take any more, her body gave in to the pleasure she was feeling, and she creamed all over his mouth, nose, and chin.

With one orgasm out of the way, Aiden crawled his way to the top of the bed and pressed his lips to her ear. "I guess my mouth is dirty again, huh?"

Jessica smiled in the darkness as she recalled their conversation from earlier. "I guess it is."

Her smile faded as she circled his neck with her arms and pulled him to her. Aiden's hand went between them and grabbed his dick, placing it to her center before looking into her eyes. He pushed forward a tad before stopping and closing his eyes. Jessica waited to see what he had going on, but said nothing.

"I can't do this." He made eye contact with her. "This is so wrong, man," he gritted out with a frustrated sigh. "You're my brother's . . ." He stopped talking, which was a good thing since it sounded as if it pained him to even say the words he was trying to say. "You're my brother's girlfriend. He would be so angry if he found out."

"Well, we won't let him find out." Jessica scooted down some and thrust her hips upward so that his dick could slide in further.

Aiden's eyes closed again, but this time Jessica was almost certain that it was for a different reason. While she had him distracted from Kayden for a moment, she took control of the situation and sat up, pushing him off of her. As soon as he was on his back again, she straddled him and slid right back onto his dick.

Her warmth enveloped him, making him curse. Jessica smiled because she knew then that she had him right where she needed him to be. Like the sexually experienced grown woman she was, Jessica moved her body all over Aiden, pulling an array of moans and curse words from him.

Jessica smiled down at him because she knew she was the shit in the bedroom. The only man who had ever been able to match her was Kayden, and that was because he was a rough-ass nigga. It didn't matter how wild she got, he could and would get wilder.

"Oh, fuck, Jess." Aiden opened his eyes and grabbed her breasts in his hands as she rode him. "Your pussy feels good as hell."

"I know." Jessica squeezed her muscles before leaning over and sucking his neck. "Enjoy it, my baby. Enjoy it."

Her words coaxed him into another world, because he began moaning and singing her all types of praise. Jessica returned his energy by giving him all she had to give. By the time he was on the brink of his first orgasm, she was on her third. Aiden's dick was the bomb, and she didn't know if she would ever get enough.

"Oh, shit. I'm finna cum, Jess."

"Me too," she moaned.

Aiden was now behind her pounding her from the back. She could hardly breathe because of how far in her stomach he was.

"What you waiting on?" Aiden asked her sexily.

Hot and out of her mind with pleasure, Jessica moaned loudly as her body convulsed uncontrollably. Aiden held onto her hips, stroking her a few more times before snatching out of her and releasing himself all over her back.

He fell next to her breathlessly as she moved from the bed to grab his underwear from the floor. She had him wipe her back off before leaning over to clean him in return. When she was finished, she tossed the underwear to the floor and climbed back into bed with him.

His arm was stretched out, so she slid next to him and laid her head on his chest. She was a bit apprehensive at first, but once his arm curved around her, her mind eased a little.

"We ain't shit." Aiden's voice disturbed the silence.

"Ew, you sound just like Kayden." She rolled her eyes in disgust.

Aiden's chest moved when he laughed. "My fault. It's the truth, though." His voice lowered a little. "He would have never done no shit like this to me."

"For one, you don't know that. Two, you act like we're about to run out of here and tell the nigga. Don't nobody know this happened but me and you." She sat up and looked at him. "As long as you don't get to feeling guilty like you need to come clean and shit, then we're good."

Jessica hadn't set out to cheat on Kayden with Aiden, but it was done, so she wouldn't cry a river over it. They were all grown. Shit happens, especially to niggas like Kayden. There was no telling how many women he'd slept with on the side, so even though she probably should have felt guilty, she didn't. If she could go back and change who she'd cheated on him with, she would probably do that, but she would probably still cheat. Kayden had really hurt her by going to jail and leaving their family. She'd just chalk this up to her revenge.

"I would never tell him." Aiden shook his head. "I wouldn't even hurt him like that."

"Whatever helps you sleep at night," Jessica told him as she scooted back down in the bed. "I honestly don't care either way. You're here with us, he's not. You help me with the baby, he doesn't. Y'all are different. You have goals, ambition, and you want to live a good life. Kayden doesn't give a fuck. You can look at it however you want, but even this little thing y'all got going on right now was him not having a lick of sense. You did what was best for your life, because you want more. Kayden just took whatever because he doesn't desire to change anything about his life." Jessica sighed as she rubbed her hands over Aiden's abs. "I don't know if I can stay with anyone like that."

"Kayden has his reasons for doing what he did. You may not understand them, but he's not a bad person."

"Never said he was. I simply said he's content living the hood life, and there's a lot of things that he does that I don't necessarily care for. I love him, don't get me wrong, but I don't know if we'll be together much longer after this. This was kind of my breaking point. I keep trying to see the positive side of it, but it's hard. I understand it, but I don't like it." She shrugged.

"I feel you."

The room was quiet for a while, both of them lost in their own thoughts. The subtle cries from Jayden's crib had Aiden sitting up. He reached to grab her, and Jessica sat up to watch them. She was in awe at how good Aiden was with her. In her mind, she liked to think that Kayden would have been the same way, but she wasn't sure.

"Get some rest. I've got her." Aiden looked at her over his shoulder.

Just like that, Jessica was back in awe. She didn't know what it was in that moment that she was feeling, but it was something. To watch Aiden with Jayden was a joy all in itself, but to see him with Jayden at four o'clock in the morning after he'd just fucked her mother into oblivion was something totally different. Jessica knew it was farfetched and would probably never be, but she lay back enjoying the thought of Aiden replacing Kayden as the third member of their family. It was wrong, but it wasn't impossible.

CHAPTER 10

The tag in the back of her shirt was really starting to irritate her. On any other normal day when she'd worn it, she'd never even known it was there. But today—today of all days—it wanted to rub against the skin on her back every time she moved. She was positive that the people she'd been in the waiting room with had probably figured she was either infested with something or was suffering from a really bad rash, neither being less embarrassing than the other.

Thankfully for her, Kayden obviously had some sort of clout in jail as well because she hadn't been taken with the other visitors. She'd been led by one of the guards to the little room in the back where she anxiously waited.

"B, what's good, baby?" Kayden swaggered in, commanding the entire space she'd been occupying for the past ten minutes.

Bronx smiled as her eyes tracked up and down his tall, lean frame. Every inch of his chocolaty goodness appealed to her senses. Even the parts of him that were covered by the jail uniform's top and bottoms. Never in all of her life had Bronx seen an inmate as sexy and cool as Kayden.

To be honest, he didn't even look like he was in jail. The way his clothes hung on his body was stylish and neat, which was the exact same way he'd dressed on the outside. Other than the color of their uniforms, nothing about him looked similar to the other inmates she'd seen, and even that was simply because of the colors of their matching garb. Kayden's looked new, like he'd taken it out of the pack before coming to visitation.

His hair was freshly cut, his big, round eyes were bright, and judging from the puffiness in the front of his shirt, he even looked like he'd gained weight. His chest sat out a little higher, making the center of his shirt dip in, while the muscles in his arms strained the sleeves of his shirt. Overall, Bronx was satisfied. She'd expected him to look depressed and dirty like the inmates she watched on TV shows. But that certainly wasn't the case.

"Kay." She smiled and stood up from her seat and walked to him, but stopped short to wait for the guard to finish uncuffing his hands and feet.

"Look at you." His pretty smile brightened up the dimly lit room as he stood admiring her. "All grown up and shit."

Giggles erupted from her throat immediately as she covered her face with her hands. "Boy, I've been grown."

"Yeah, you have." He stepped over the chains as the guard stepped out of the way. "But you ain't been this grown." He opened his arms for her to walk into them and squeezed her to his chest, wrapping his arms snugly around her body. "I've been gone too long if Bronx got hips and ass. Turn around and let me look at it for a minute."

Bronx was so happy that her face was in his chest, which prevented him from seeing the way she was blushing from embarrassment. "I really hate you." She pulled away from him. "I really do."

Kayden's hands slid slowly from her body, grazing her back

and the top of her butt before falling back to his sides. He looked down at her and winked. "Let's sit down."

Bronx followed him back to the little table that she had been sitting at, and he took the seat across from her. Once they were comfortable, he rested his hands on the table as she held hers in her lap. For some reason, she was nervous and had no idea why. Kayden was her homey. They'd been cool for years.

"Pigs must be out there flying all over the sky if you up in here."

Bronx pushed his hand softly. "Shut up. I told you I was coming."

"Yeah, you did . . . three months ago."

Bronx held her head down because he was right. It had been almost four months since she'd last contacted him, and she'd been feeling bad about it every day since. Although she'd had her own little plan to make him crave her as she did him, she still felt kind of bad for blowing him off. She'd tried to talk herself into visiting him plenty of times, but every time she would think about their life together and punk out. Being in love with her cousin's man was a hard pill to swallow, so to re-place her time, she used her money and kept his books stacked. Clearly that wasn't enough.

"Listen, it's cool. I ain't tripping. I got two months left, then I'll be on my way home hopefully. If everything goes right in court." He shrugged. "If my record wasn't so fucked up to begin with, I probably wouldn't be here anyway. They denied bail on all my shit just because of my past charges."

Bronx looked at him with her eyebrows raised in question. "How long has it been?"

"Six months."

Bronx's chest sank at that revelation. She'd known it had been a while, but to better cope with it all, she'd blocked him out of her mind and spent all of her time at school and work. Kayden had been a big part of her life for a while, and to have him snatched away so suddenly was really bothering her.

Kayden's hand on top of hers got her attention. "What you been up to, B? You must got a li'l man or something? Good dick is the only thing that'll have women acting brand-new."

Bronx squealed in laughter. "You would know, wouldn't you? Been serving bitches that dope dick for years, huh?"

Kayden was laughing when he shrugged his shoulders. "I can't help a nigga is blessed." He leaned on the table. "But I ain't been serving shit these last few months." He shook his head. "I feel like my damn dick about to bust."

"Sounds painful."

"Man, shut your ass up." They both laughed before settling down again. "For real, though, what you been up to? Jess told me you don't really be at the house no more."

Surely damn don't. Bronx thought about her cousin's scandalous ways.

Bronx leaned her head to the side and bit the inside of her cheek. "Nah, I been too busy with school and work. I don't really be having time for nothing no more. Especially Jessica's dramatic ass."

"You ain't lying. That's my baby, but she's been extra dramatic lately. Every time I talk to her she's wilding on me. I know it's because I ain't at home. Your cousin needs some dick, B." He cheesed at her. "She's acting just like a woman that ain't getting laid."

If you think that.

Bronx smiled to hide her true feelings. If only Kayden knew that was the least of Jessica's worries, he wouldn't be smiling or calling Jessica's cheating ass his baby. Not after that heffa had slept with his damn twin brother. It had taken everything in Bronx not to go off on them the next morning after hearing them have sex. The only thing that stopped her was hurting Kayden. She already knew their guilty asses would probably try to tell on themselves before she could and end up hurting him in the process. Even after all the talking Jessica did, she still hadn't thought she would actually go through with sleeping with Aiden, but she had. Though Bronx was disgusted by her cousin, she was happy, too. Now she was really in the clear to be with Kayden.

"Well, I don't know what to say about all of that, but she definitely needs something, and I ain't the one to give it to her. I've got my own stuff to worry about." Bronx waved her hand dismissively as she rolled her eyes.

"What you got to worry about, B? You claim you ain't got no man, even though I know you do. What's good?" Kayden linked his fingers together and leaned across the table so that their faces were closer to each other. "What's stressing you?"

"I'm just talking for real. I'm good."

"You sure? You know you can talk to me, right?" Sincerity accompanied his words.

It was on the tip of her tongue to tell Kayden how his brother had practically moved into his spot and taken over his life, but not only was it not her place, but she didn't want to hurt Kayden like that. The person he was doing all of that jail shit for was the main one doing him dirty.

"I know, but I'm good. Tell me what's going on with you? How you holding up?"

Kayden sighed. "I'm as good as can be expected. You know this jail shit ain't nothing to me. I'm just nervous about Aiden really getting me off. He told me yesterday that they'd finally gotten the autopsy back and proved that the lady had drugs in her system. If they can prove that the drugs are what killed her, then I'm a free man." He smiled, and Bronx leaped from her chair and across the table.

Her arms went around his neck immediately. "Oh, my God! That's so good, Kay. I'm so happy for you. It's time for you to come home." She spoke loudly.

Kayden was laughing as he stood and wrapped his arms around her, picking her up off the ground. His face was buried in her neck as he took one deep breath after the next. Bronx could feel his chest rising and falling against hers as he held her. When she tried to pull away, he wouldn't let her.

"What's wrong, Kay?" She rubbed the back of his head.

"Jess wasn't even that happy when I told her."

Bronx's body relaxed in his arms as she sighed deeply and closed her eyes. "Jess just has a lot going on right now."

When he finally let her go, he sat back down on the table and pulled her to him so that she was standing between his legs with his arms draped loosely around her waist.

"That's what I left Aiden for. That nigga is supposed to be helping her so she doesn't get loaded down. Every time I talk to him, I'm telling him stuff to do for her, say to her, you know? Just little shit to keep her happy."

"He's there." Bronx looked up into Kayden's eyes. "Doing everything you're telling him to, which is probably not helping your case any."

His face frowned. "What you mean?"

"I mean you're basically telling another man, brother or not, how to keep your woman happy. With you being gone, that only makes him look like everything that you're not." Bronx shrugged. "I'm just saying with women any time a man shows us a little affection, does one thing more than what our man does, treats us like we matter, we fall for them. I don't even want to get on how good he is with Jayden." Bronx gave a half smile. "You know bitches love when a nigga is good with her kids."

Bronx laughed to dumb down the truth she was telling, but judging by the look on Kayden's face, it wasn't working.

"So, you think she's wanting Aiden more than me now?" He stretched one of his legs out in front of him. "I mean since he's basically being her man?"

Bronx probably would have found his bewilderment a little cute if his baby mama wasn't really fucking his twin brother. She just might have thought it was cute how his lips poked out and his eyes sagged in the corners if she didn't know he was only looking that way because he'd just realized how big a mistake he'd been making.

"Listen, Kay, I don't know how Jessica is feeling, I'm just telling you what I think about the situation."

Kayden sat there in thought for a moment. "What you think I should do now?"

"I think you should focus on yourself and doing better when you get out of here. Jessica's little trifling ass ain't going nowhere."

"I don't know, B. When I talked to her the other day she hit me with some shit about paying child support when I get out." He scratched his head. "Why would I need to pay child support if I'ma be there with her and the baby?"

Bronx looked away and rolled her eyes. She hated women like Jessica: the ones who cheated then started doing the nigga they're cheating on wrong like it's his fault. Then to make matters worse, that hoe didn't even know how to cover her tracks. She was so busy with her head up Aiden's ass, she probably hadn't even realized she was telling on her own self.

Kayden used his pointer finger to turn Bronx's head toward him. "B, tell me what's good, baby? I know you know something. Am I holding on to false hope here? Did Jessica tell you she's going to leave me?"

Bronx's heart broke for him as she listened to how wounded he sounded. As much as she wanted to make him feel better, she wanted to save him from future pain more.

"In so many words . . . yes,"

His head fell forward before he lifted it back up and nodded it up and down. "So, I should just let her go?"

Bronx nodded.

"Cool." He cleared his throat and grabbed her hand. "Thank you for telling me."

"You my boy. You know I got you." She smiled at him and picked off the piece of eyelash that was sitting on his cheek.

When she went to move her hand, he caught it and placed a kiss in the center of her palm. "Thank you."

"It's nothing, for real."

He kissed her hand a few more times before making eye contact with her. "To me it is. Loyalty is everything to me."

"Well, one thing you never have to question is my loyalty to you."

"If that's the case, tell me about this li'l nigga you trying to hide." A smile crept across his face as he pushed her hair over her shoulder.

Bronx snickered and fell into his shoulder. "He cool."

"Man, you ain't shit. I knew you had a man."

She shrugged her shoulders and tried to step out of his grasp, but he locked his arms around the back of her thighs.

"Nah stay your li'l ass right here. Tell me about this nigga."

Bronx tapped her chin with her pointer finger as if she was thinking. "Well, he's sexy as hell first of all. The nigga's swag is on hundred. I'm talking about he can pull off anything he puts on." She smiled at him as he sat in front of her smirking. "He's really sweet, kind of misunderstood, but sweet nonetheless. I think his heart is good; it's just hidden behind a bunch of rugged shit. Kind of like a diamond in the rough."

Kayden pushed her face playfully. "Man, this nigga must be gay, you calling him a diamond in the rough and shit."

"See, that's why I started not to tell you. You play too much."

Kayden pulled her back to him and held her close to him again. "Dang, this nigga must be special to you. Got you getting mad at me and shit."

"He really is, and I don't call him a diamond in the rough because he's gay. I compared him to that because his beauty is hidden by layers of dirty stuff, and people expect him to stay that way. But I know he can be better. I can change him. I think I can make him shine . . . you know?"

Kayden's face was serious as he nodded his head. "Yeah, I

know. You basically want to show him real love? All that other shit you said was sweet, but in my opinion, the only way you can change a man is if you give him the kind of love he can't deny." He bit his bottom lip. "It's some stuff in life you can't run from, and love is one."

"Aww, look at you being all deep."

He chuckled in embarrassment. "See, this why I can't be real. Everybody always thinking I'm a joke."

He was smiling, but Bronx knew he was serious, so she stopped smiling and wrapped her arms around his neck, leaning her body against his and kissing the side of his mouth. Kayden sat still, letting her kiss him for a minute before pushing her backward a little.

"Wasn't you the same one just sitting here telling me about your man?"

"Yeah, so?"

"Don't do that man like this. If you really like him like that, he doesn't deserve a woman that's sprung off another man's dick. Because I promise you, if I fuck you, you gon' be sprung."

Bronx fell all over him laughing as he did the same. The two of them cut up for a little while longer before gaining their composure again.

"But nah, for real. If you got a nigga that make you feel like that, give him a chance. It's hard to find real love out here. You see the boat I'm in."

They were still holding on to each other when Bronx leaned in and kissed the side of his mouth again before moving over and kissing his lips. Like she'd known he would, he welcomed her touch. His arms tightened, pulling her further between his long legs as his mouth captured hers in an intense session of tongue play. They were both lips and moans as they shared the passion they had for each other.

"B, you're a hot li'l joint. You know that?"

She nodded with a smile on her face.

"You gon' let me meet your nigga?"

"Hell, no. You don't know how to act."

"Man, I ain't gon' say nothing to that man."

Bronx pulled out of his grasp as the guard opened the door. Kayden looked over toward the door and told him to give him two more minutes. When the guard nodded and closed the door, Bronx was amazed.

"You got it like that?"

"You must have forgot who you're talking to," he said. "I know you ain't think this was the way regular visitations go."

Bronx looked around lost before nodding her head.

"Girl, fuck no. This room is for lawyers and inmates only. I just told them I ain't want to see you through no glass. I wanted to be able to feel on you and shit."

"You don't have no sense at all."

"I really do. People just don't know it. I guess I'm a diamond in the rough like your boyfriend." He shrugged nonchalantly while standing and towering over her easily.

Bronx watched with stars in her eyes as he stretched his long limbs. She'd always been in love with Kayden, but had been prepared to ignore it until Jessica started messing around on the boy. He was hers for the taking now, and she planned to do exactly that: take him.

His chest bumped into her as he stretched a little more before grabbing both of her hands and looking down at her. "Thank you for coming to see me."

"You don't have to thank me, I wanted to come."

They walked hand in hand to the door and stopped again for him to hug her. Kayden's body felt so right. He was tall and strong and loyal. A big beautiful man who she would make hers before it was all over with.

Moments passed before the guard came back in and began cuffing Kayden again. They stood in front of each other communicating with their eyes, neither opening their mouths to say anything. Kayden waited until he was completely cuffed and on his way out of the door before stopping and calling her name. Bronx looked at him with anticipation heavy in her chest.

"You think I'm a diamond in the rough, too?" he asked.

She gave him a big smile. "How could I not when you are *my* diamond in the rough?"

His smile matched hers as he winked. "I knew it."

"Know it when you touch down." Bronx blew him kisses until she could no longer see him.

"I love you B!" Kayden's voice traveled from the hallway to where she was standing.

Her heart smiled when she heard him yell it. That was something they both had always known and kept to themselves, but now that they'd vocalized it, Bronx would never hide it again.

CHAPTER 11

"What do you mean you can't be with me?" Jessica stood in front of him with her hands on her hips yelling.

Aiden rubbed his temples and blew out a frustrated breath as he tried to soothe the headache that he felt coming on. He hadn't been at Jessica's house any longer than fifteen minutes, and she was already acting a fool. That was something she'd begun to do more often. It was like having sex with her pushed some sort of control button on or something.

From the first time they'd had sex—over four months ago—until now, she'd been practically painting the perfect family with him in her head. Though it was wrong, and had been since the first time, Aiden had been indulging in sex with Jessica almost every night. Her pussy was seriously like some form of addiction he couldn't shake.

The way she worked it on him made him want to cry sometimes. That's how he'd known it was good. However, had he known it would come with all the drama that she put him through on a daily basis, he would have never gone there with her.

"Exactly what I said, Jessica. We had no business doing this from the beginning. I'm most definitely not about to live my life with you like we're some big, happy family." Aiden shook his head as he frowned. "Once my brother gets out, this shit is dead."

Her light-colored face turned bright red as she stood in front of him flabbergasted at his admission. "Are you serious?"

"Yes, Jess. It was fun, and I love you and Jayden, but not like a wife and daughter. I love y'all like a sister and niece. If the sex led you to believe more, I apologize. I just thought we had a mutual understanding that it was *just* sex."

"I cannot believe you're sitting here playing me like I'm some quick fuck that doesn't mean anything to you."

Aiden wanted to tell her that's exactly what she was, but he didn't think that would be the smartest thing to do at that very moment.

"Oh, Lord," he mumbled when he looked up and saw that she'd started to cry.

That was definitely nothing he wanted to be a part of. Aiden stood and grabbed his suit jacket before kissing the top of Jayden's head as she sat on Jessica's hip.

"I have to go see Kayden. I'll holla at you." Aiden walked past Jessica and out of the door.

He took the stairs to the driveway and headed for his car. He didn't have the time for Jessica and her drama. She was too old to not have known the sex that they had would lead to nothing. He shouldn't have had to spell that out for her. His brother was doing a bid for him. He wasn't going to have him come out to find that he'd taken over his life.

Aiden cranked up the engine and headed for the jailhouse. His mind had been heavy since Bronx had left earlier after seeing the baby. She'd talked about how she'd gone to visit Kayden and that he was doing well. She mentioned a host of other things that had Jessica heated. Aiden didn't know if she was mad Bronx had gone to visit, or if she was just annoyed by Kayden and the situation all together. Either way it went, her attitude had been on ten from then to now.

For the life of him, Aiden couldn't understand how Jessica was mad with Bronx for going to see Kayden when she was standing in the living room of her and Kayden's living room crying about starting a family with his twin brother. He shook his head in disgust. Jessica had turned out to be a lot more than he'd bargained for, and he regretted crossing his brother for her every day.

In his heart, Aiden wanted to tell Kayden about him and Jessica, but his mind just wouldn't let him. If it came to losing the relationship he had with his brother or living with a lie, he'd take it to his grave without batting an eye, no matter how much it tore him up on the inside.

He loved Kayden too much to lose him over a woman. Although they'd passed around a few hoes in the past, with Jessica, he still felt like he'd crossed the line. Every night he prayed that if Kayden happened to find out, that they'd be able to move past it. If he did find out and couldn't accept it, Aiden didn't know what he would do. Thankfully the ringing of his cell phone brought him out of that mental scenario.

"Aiden Lattimore."

"Hey, Mr. Lattimore. It's Silvia. The lab called and the official cause of death was a heart attack induced by the drugs in her system. She was dead before your brother ever hit her," Silvia relayed excitedly.

"Yeah!" Aiden hit his steering wheel.

"I've already called the judge. They're going to sentence your brother to time served on the DUI charge and release him. You should probably head on over to the jail."

"Thank you, Silvia." Aiden ended the call with tears in his eyes.

They'd done it. He'd been worried sick waiting on the reports to come back and everything had finally come through. Though that outcome was something that the court system could have handled a lot faster had her family been more cooperative, he was still grateful. All that mattered now was that his brother was coming home.

Now in a hurry, Aiden sped all the way to the county jail. After parking, he hurried into the building and did all of the necessary things to get upstairs to meet with Kayden. Since it would take some time to get him released, he was sure they had enough time for him to sit him down and tell him the good news himself.

Aiden waited on pins and needles in the same little room they always met in as the guards went to get Kayden. The dingy yellow walls and the cold steel table were all about to be a thing of the past, and Aiden was glad. He was so excited he could hardly sit still, so he stood up and paced around the room. When he heard the locks clicking, he turned to see the door being opened for Kayden to walk in.

As usual, he looked good. Fresh haircut, clean uniform, and that silly-ass smile. "What's good, twin?"

Aiden rushed to him and hugged his brother before the guard even had the chance to remove the chains. He could tell the way Kayden was laughing that he was shocked by his burst of excitement.

"Damn, Aiden, you hugging me like I'm your damn mama or something."

Aiden stood up laughing. "I ain't hugging your stupid ass like you're my mama. I'm hugging you like you're a free man."

Kayden's face grew serious as his eyes got big. "Say what now?"

"She was dead before the accident happened. They're giving you time served on the DUI charge," Aiden hurried to get out.

Kayden's smile reappeared as he used his now free hands to hug his brother. He had moved in such a rush that he tripped over the guard, who was still unlocking his legs. Had Aiden not been in front of him, he probably would have hit the ground. They stood hugging each other for a few minutes before pulling away.

"I knew you could do it." Kayden held his hand out to dap him up.

"I'm glad one of us did. You know how hard it is to run a city, run your house, and do lawyer shit?" Aiden took his suit jacket off. "I'm glad your ass is out. Now I can be the mayor and that's it. You can have all this other stuff back."

"Jessica's pussy must be getting old to you now?"

Aiden stopped moving and looked at Kayden. His face was void of any emotion as he stared silently. Aiden wanted so badly to say something in his defense, but not only did he not know what to say, his mouth probably wouldn't have moved even if he did.

How in the hell had Kayden found out about him and Jessica? He stood tall staring at his twin brother as his heart beat rapidly in his chest. Aiden strained for air as he battled with whether to tell the truth or tell a lie.

"Kay—" Aiden started.

Kayden shook his head and waved Aiden off. "Don't say nothing. It ain't shit to say."

"I didn't mean for it to happen."

"Yeah, niggas never mean to fuck your girl until after that last nut." Kayden walked past him and sat on the small table in the center of the room. "You know something, I actually gave you more credit than that. Here I am giving you tips and shit on how to look out for my girl, so that the next nigga didn't scoop her up. I was just helping *you* take my girl from me." Kayden laughed casually.

"She ain't mean nothing, though."

"I'm sure she didn't, since she was my woman, but that's actually the worst part of it all. She ain't mean shit to you, but she meant everything to me."

"Kayden, I'm sorry, man."

"I know you are." He looked at Aiden. "Now that I've found out." He stood up again. "So what y'all plan to do now? Raise my baby and live happily ever after?"

"Nah, man. That's that shit Jessica's on. I was just fucking. Nothing more."

Aiden leaned against the wall watching his brother stare at him in disappointment. He wanted to say more, or do more, but he couldn't think of anywhere to start. He didn't know whether to plead his case or go balls to the wall and let his brother be mad at him until he felt better. He was even open to fighting Kayden if that's what would make him get it out of his system and forgive him.

"I appreciate you for helping me get out of here."

"It's my fault you were here in the first place."

Kayden nodded his head. "Yeah, you're right, it is." He looked at Aiden a little longer while standing. "Clearly it was for the best, though. I may have never known you and Jessica were snakes lurking in my grass. You feel me? Now I know." He walked to Aiden and stopped in front of him. "Thank you for that, brother."

"Kayden, let me fix this, man."

"I'm good. I'll find a way home once they release me." Kayden turned away. He looked at Aiden over his shoulder once more before walking out of the door, leaving Aiden there to sulk in his deceit.

Kayden took the long walk back to his cell in chains for the last time. His eyes scanned over the entire pod as he moved slowly. He was surrounded by convicts, some accused of some of the most heinous crimes in the state of Texas, and not one of them had hurt him as bad as his brother had.

He had been thinking about everything Bronx had told him the day she visited him, but none of it made sense. Then all of a sudden everything that had been confusing him made sense. Jessica had been acting out and giving him her butt to kiss because she had a new man. What else would explain her going from being in love with him to expressing her hate for him almost every time they talked?

As bad as he hadn't wanted to believe it, it was right there plain as day. Bronx hadn't come right out and said it, probably trying to spare his feelings, but her words had painted a clear enough picture. The part that sealed it all for him was Bronx openly expressing her feelings for him. The only way she would have felt safe enough to do something like that was if she'd known he and her cousin was over for sure.

Maybe she'd known all along that once he'd found out, he was going to be done with her. Kayden had been cutthroat from the time he'd met her. Bronx had done a good job at keeping it to herself, but she'd known what was up the whole time. He had to give her credit, though, she never folded. Even when he asked her on the phone the night before, she'd danced around the question. Further answering his question.

"What's on your mind, young blood?" Kayden's cellmate interrupted his thoughts as soon as he walked into the room.

"They're letting me out of here." He smiled up at the old man.

He had a large, genuine smile on his face as he held his hand over the side of the bed for Kayden to shake. Kayden shook it and began clearing out his things.

"Was it true?" The man's voice stopped his movement.

Kayden nodded his head. He had told his cellmate about his thoughts on Jessica and Aiden possibly sleeping together as well. He wanted to make sure he was going at the situation from all angles before approaching Aiden. He would have hated to approach him on some false bullshit and ruined their relationship. Had he known it was going to be ruined anyway, he probably would have kept his business to himself.

"What you plan to do about it?"

"I don't even know. In my mind, I'm like, fuck both of them, but my heart is fucked up behind the shit. That nigga is my family. He's really all I've got besides my baby."

"Didn't you just tell me you really like the little girl that had our room smelled up with her perfumed letter?"

Kayden smiled and nodded as he thought about Bronx.

"Well, my advice for you is to just let it go. Forgive your brother, forgive your daughter's mother, and move on with your new lady. Life's too short to hold on to grudges. God has blessed you with a second chance; get out of here and make the best of it." He scooted to the edge of his bed. "Don't waste your time hurting over something you have the power to change. You understand?"

"I hear you, but I still just don't know. They betrayed me in the worst way. Everybody that knows me knows I'm big on loyalty, and those two showed none. They showed me absolutely NO LOYALTY!" Kayden yelled the last part as he grew angry at the thought of their transgressions.

"Nah, they didn't. But what did you expect? Out of sight means out of mind. You were in here, they were out there. They did what anybody else would have done. Your brother is a man. A young man at that. You sent him to your house to do your job, and now that he's done it, you're mad?"

Kayden plopped down on his bed with his arms folded across his chest and his mouth poked out.

"I've seen the picture of that woman. That's too much behind for any man to pass up. I don't care how you look at it. I probably would have dipped in it, too, if she would have let me. I probably wouldn't have lasted long, but I still would have did a little dip in it."

Kayden couldn't even keep a straight face after that. The more he thought about it, the harder he laughed, his cellmate laughing along with him. The two of them were laughing so hard that Kayden almost missed the knock on their door. When he looked up and saw the guard with some papers and an empty laundry bag, he stood up and looked up at his cellmate.

"I'm gon' miss your old ass."

"Well, miss me with your wallet and keep that commissary full. I know you got it."

Kayden nodded and held his hand out for a handshake. "I got you, old timer."

They talked for a few more minutes until it was time for Kayden to exit the premises. He looked around the room, taking nothing but the pictures of his baby. There was nothing in there that he wanted to take home with him, not even the pictures of Jessica. He left those to his cellmate to do whatever he pleased. Jessica was no longer a concern of his. Even if he did forgive her, he would never fuck with her again, and that was on his baby girl's life.

CHAPTER 12

"What the fuck you doing here?" Kayden turned his nose up at Jessica.

She rushed to him with her hands outstretched toward him. "Kayden, just listen to me."

Kayden looked all around the parking lot for Bronx's car. There was no way in hell she had really sent Jessica to pick him up from jail. This had to be some kind of a joke.

"Jessica, get your ass on away from me." He walked past her, and she grabbed his arm.

Before she had the chance to brace herself, Kayden pushed her backward. Jessica stumbled a few feet but caught her footing. As soon as she was steady on her feet again, she was running back to him. This time she was mindful of her hands and kept them to herself.

"Kayden, I promise we never meant for this to happen. I was just so lonely, I felt like I was starting to lose my mind."

"And let me guess, you found it on my brother's dick, huh?" Kayden watched her look away, and he scoffed. "Dirty bitch."

Her head shot up with a look of surprise on her face. Even had he not been able to look at her face and tell, he knew she was shocked by his verbiage. As long as they'd been together, Kayden had never called her out of her name. He'd done nothing but treat her with respect, and she couldn't even handle that.

"Really, Kayden?" she yelled as he walked farther away from her.

Kayden didn't even bother to turn around. Instead he continued to walk toward the red Lexus he'd bought her. He hated the fact that she'd finagled her way in as his ride home, but that didn't mean he wasn't going to take it. He was so ready to get away from that damn jailhouse, he'd do whatever he had to, including riding with Jessica, to get away from there.

"Give me the keys."

"Not until you talk to me," she had the audacity to tell him.

With his nose turned up on one side, Kayden saw her as the scandalous fool that she was and crossed his arms over his chest. After leaning back on the side of Jessica's car, he gave her his attention.

"Talk about what, Jessica? What the fuck do you want to talk to me about?"

Jessica cleared her throat and walked closer to him. She was staring at him with a look of despair in her eyes. Pleading for some sort of forgiveness, or hope. Too bad, he didn't have any to give.

"I never meant for this to happen. It was just so hard for me after you left." She fumbled with her clothing. "Aiden was there to fill the void, but I didn't love him. I love you." The crocodile tears on her face moved nothing in Kayden.

"Jessica, kill this bullshit. You're probably out here begging because Aiden doesn't want your ass anymore."

Jessica's eyes darted away quickly as she bit her bottom lip. Kayden didn't have to be told that was the reasoning behind her drama right then, because he'd already known. He'd been in love with Jessica for years; he knew her. Even if she thought he didn't.

"That's not true, Kayden."

"Yes, the fuck it is, and quite frankly, I don't have time to hear the shit." He held his open palm out toward her. "Give me the keys to my car."

"Your car?" she asked in disbelief.

"Yeah, bitch, mine. Now give me the keys."

"You can't take my car."

"Like hell I can't. I paid for this shit. Hell, I paid for everything in your life, and that still wasn't good enough for your hoe ass. You had to take the one thing that was important to me." Kayden ran up on her so that he was in her face. "The one thing that was off limits, you just had to get that, too." Kayden slapped his chest. "I gave you everything!"

More tears fell from Jessica's eyes as she grabbed at his clothes. Kayden snatched away and pushed her off him.

"It was a mistake," she told him.

"Fuck all that. The mistake was me picking you over your cousin, that was the mistake."

Her face dropped in shock. "My cousin?"

Kayden smiled and nodded his head. "Hell, yeah, Bronx's li'l ass held me down better than you. Now guess what?" He leaned forward to make fun of her. "I'm about to be with her and give her all the shit I tried to give you. She recognized a real one when saw me, so she kept my ass. Now the world is hers."

Kayden stepped back away from her with his face now frowning. "You better not ask me for shit, and I'm getting custody of my baby, too. Now hop on the reality of that shit, like you hopped on my brother's dick."

"You stupid son of a bitch!" Jessica screamed. "How you gon' be mad at me when you fucking my damn cousin? We're two and the same, dirty dick-ass nigga."

Kayden looked at her long and hard. He didn't recognize her. Jessica had truly turned into another person since he'd been gone. Never in his life had he thought his girl, his love, the mother of his child, would turn into the person in front of him. That was some serious shit there. So serious, Kayden couldn't do anything but laugh.

"We're two and the same, huh?"

Jessica crossed her arms over her chest. "Damn right."

"Nah, I don't think we are, because the person that I dipped on you for actually wants me back." Kayden smirked. "Aiden ain't thinking about your ass."

Jessica stood there looking dumbfounded, like he'd known she would.

"Oh, you thought he would pick you?" Kayden burst out laughing again. "Wrong, bitch. Me and that nigga been running through bitches since we were kids. I thought you was different, but I was wrong as fuck. It's cool, though. What's done is done. Let's dip." Kayden winked at her before snatching the keys from her hand.

As soon as he hit the locks, Jessica took off toward the passenger seat. Kayden laughed because she'd been right to do that. Just as sure as his name was Kayden Lattimore, had she not gotten her ass in, he was going to pull off and leave her.

Kayden drove toward his old block, as Jessica sat in the seat trying to explain her case. It was too late for that, though; she was never getting another chance with him. If it didn't have anything to do with Jayden, he wasn't fucking with her.

"Get your ass out." Kayden told her as he parked at their house and got out.

He walked ahead of her toward the door. When he reached it, it was already open. As soon as he walked in, he noticed Bronx sitting on the sofa with Jayden in her arms. She smiled upon seeing his face, but it dropped immediately.

"She begged me to come, I'm sorry."

"You know better than that shit, B."

She stood up. "I know, but I wasn't sure how you wanted to deal with us right now."

Kayden's brows knitted together. "What you mean how I wanted to deal with us? You're with me, ain't you?"

Bronx nodded.

"A'ight then. Fuck the rest. Don't worry about Jessica's fucked-up ass. You're my baby, so don't hide that shit."

Bronx's smile made all of his troubles worth it. Including the shit Jessica was about to get started.

"Y'all ain't shit," she said as she walked in past him. "Bitch, give me my damn baby." Jessica snatched Jayden from her, but Kayden intervened.

"Jessica, if you hurt my baby, I'ma kill your ass." He pulled Jayden out of her arms and handed her back to Bronx. "This my house, and Bronx is my girl. You don't get no say-so around this muthafucka no more." He fumed. "Matter of fact, get your ass back there and pack your shit. You're getting up out of here today."

"What?" Jessica screamed.

"Just go get your shit." He pointed toward the back of their house with his thumb.

Kayden watched Jessica rant and rave until he'd had enough. When he couldn't take it anymore, he went through the house snatching all of her things and throwing them outside into the yard. He was moving so quickly and carelessly that he'd even broken a few things, but he didn't give two fucks. Her time was up.

"Kayden! Stop!" she yelled as he pushed past her with some more of her shoes.

"I'm tired now, so that's all you get. You lucky you got that much, now get the fuck out," he told her before looking over at Bronx, who was rocking a crying Jayden.

Jessica was in tears as she shook her head from side to side in protest. "I won't leave. This is my house. You can take your bitch, leave my damn baby, and y'all can get out."

"Girl, kill all that noise, and get your ass out." Kayden grabbed Jessica from the living room sofa and picked her up.

Though she kicked and screamed the entire way, he pushed her out of the door with the rest of her things.

"Kayden, how could you do me like this?" She fell to her knees and cried at the same time Bronx walked up next to him with Jayden in her arms.

"The same way you did it to him, cousin." Bronx smiled mischievously. "I told you there would be women ready to fill your shoes; you didn't listen."

"Fuck her, don't explain." Kayden looked down at Bronx and kissed her forehead. "She did this shit to herself."

With nothing left to be said, Kayden looked down at Jessica before slamming the door closed in her tearstained face. She could cry until her tears turned into blood for all he cared. He'd done it before and survived; she could, too.

EPILOGUE

Jayden's First Birthday

Bronx looked around her living room trying to make sure everything was in place before Kayden got home. He'd gone out to run, and she'd used that time to finish cleaning. She'd had a long and very busy work week so her house had been a mess, and that was something she could not tolerate.

Though she and Kayden had known each other for years, being his full-time girlfriend was something totally different. They'd been in a real, exciting, passionate, and loving relationship since he'd come home from jail, and Bronx loved it.

The way Kayden loved her was like no other. He was always so sweet and genuine with her. Even when he was being obnoxiously goofy and mean, he treated her with nothing but respect. Nothing like the way he'd been doing Jessica.

After the stunt she'd pulled, Bronx couldn't blame him, but she still felt sorry for her cousin sometimes. Kayden had done his best to be cordial with her for Jayden's sake, but that was as far as he took it.

The moment she'd tried to come at him and Bronx sideways about them caring for her daughter, Kayden would put his foot right back on her neck until she learned how to act. Being that Jessica had nothing without him, it was a cakewalk getting custody of Jayden. Especially since Aiden had fought as hard as he could for them.

With Kayden not speaking a single word to Aiden the entire time, the case had been a tad difficult, but they'd come out victorious. Bronx was sure it had a lot to do with Aiden wanting to rebuild his and Kayden's relationship, but it hadn't worked. Kayden didn't want anything to do with that nigga. Had Bronx not pleaded on his behalf, he probably would have hired a totally different lawyer. Luckily, she'd been very persuasive, and he'd followed her lead. Although Bronx couldn't care less if he ever forgave Jessica, she at least wanted him to consider forgiving Aiden. Even though that looked like a long shot.

Bronx was busy fixing the pillows on her sofa when Kayden finally walked in the front door. His muscular, bare chest was out and glistening from sweat, while his arms flexed every time he moved them. The red gym shorts hung loosely off his waist, dipping a little lower in the front than anywhere else, outlining the extra-large package she'd been waiting to open since he'd gotten out of bed that morning.

"What you got this music up so loud for? You know I hate that shit," he fussed.

Bronx had been cleaning since he'd left to go running, and when she cleaned, she liked loud music, but that was the least of her worries right then. The only thing on her mind was him, those shorts, and the sweat dripping from his chocolate body.

Bronx bit her top lip and pulled her shirt over her head. She dropped it to the floor and pushed her shorts from her waist immediately afterward. She smiled when she looked up and noticed Kayden had joined her in the removal of his clothes.

He'd kicked off both shoes and was pushing his shorts and boxers to the ground. Bronx finished before him and wasted no time jumping on him. With her arms around his neck, her body dangled against him.

"Wrap your legs around my waist and hold on tight." His husky voice in her ear made her shiver.

Bronx did as she was told, and he held her up by her butt as he walked them back to the bedroom. She busied herself kissing and licking all over his neck until she felt her back pressed against the bed. She released her limbs from him immediately and pushed him away from her.

"Wait, not yet." She slid to the floor in front of him. "I've been waiting to do this all day."

Kayden looked down at her and smiled. "I don't know why, since you just topped me off this morning. Plus, I just got done running; let me take a shower first."

Bronx smiled and shook her head no. "I like you smelling like this. Plus, getting your dick sucked puts you in a good mood, and I want you to be in one." She smiled up at him.

"As long as I got you with me, I'ma stay in a good mood."

Bronx's heart beat wildly in her chest as she listened to the love of her life speak so deeply for her, but she didn't let his words deter her.

"It better stay that way." Bronx didn't give him any time to say anything else before her mouth was covering the head of his penis.

His head fell backward simultaneously with his hand grabbing the back of her head. He pumped his hips forward, pushing more of himself into her mouth. Bronx looked up and watched him unravel beneath her touch as she pulled out her best tricks to please him. She felt like patting herself on the back when he snatched her from the floor in a hurry, shoving himself inside of her.

"I was about to nut." He kissed her mouth gently. "I know you ain't want that."

Bronx moved to give herself room to adjust to his girth. "I was gon' be mad as hell."

Kayden gave her a lazy smile before kissing her mouth again. "Get mad on this dick then."

Bronx pulled him to her before lifting the bottom of her body up to meet his thrusts. When he caught her rhythm, he matched her stroke for stroke until she was moaning and shaking beneath him.

"You love to act tough until you get my dick up in you."

Bronx licked her lips and moaned as he taunted and stroked her at the same time. Deeply in love and happier than she'd ever been before, Bronx wrapped her arms and legs around Kayden, making sure he was close to her. Skin to skin, heart to heart, she enjoyed the passion from her man, best friend, and soon to be father of her child.

She'd taken a test a couple of days ago and planned to tell him the positive results later. That was one of the main reasons for her oral sex session. He hadn't been too keen on baby mamas since Jessica, and though she understood his feelings, she didn't like it.

"Why you so wet?" He pecked her nose. "Huh? Why your pussy so wet, Bronx?"

Bronx stared at him trying to figure out whether that was a real question, or was it sex talk? When she couldn't figure it out, she just ignored him, and what did she do that for? He tore her little ass up until they both climaxed before he slapped his hand hard across her butt.

"Next time, answer me when I talk to you."

"Yes, sir." She rolled from the bed and grabbed his hands, pulling him with her. "Get up. We have somewhere to be."

"Where?"

"Jayden's birthday party."

Kayden's face dropped as he looked at her.

"A good mood, remember?"

"I'm straight. I just don't understand why you're so bent

on her having a party. She has us, that's all she needs." He ran his hand over his face. "She's a damn baby, she doesn't know anything about a party anyway."

"She needs to be around all of her family."

"What family? I know you aren't talking about Jessica and Aiden? Fuck them!"

"Why do you talk like that about your brother?"

Kayden exhaled a frustrated breath. "Why won't you just leave it alone, B?"

"Because he's your brother and best friend, Kayden. Stop being a butthole. You did time for the damn boy. Surely you can forgive him for getting his dick wet." Bronx rolled her eyes. Kayden hadn't talked to Aiden since the day he'd been released from jail, and in her opinion that was too long. She'd felt like she was suffocating through the entire custody case being stuck between the three of them. It was time for the madness to stop.

"It ain't about him getting his dick wet, it's about who he let wet it."

Bronx rolled her eyes and walked out of the room. Kayden acted a fool every time she tried to get him to talk to Aiden, and she was getting tired of it. Aiden had made a mistake, and it was time for him to forgive him.

"I know you hear me talking to you," Kayden walked in the bathroom and told her while she was in the shower.

"What?" she yelled from inside of the shower.

"I said Aiden at the door."

Bronx snickered. "Why you ain't let him in?"

"Because that nigga ain't welcome here," Kayden told her nonchalantly as Bronx got out of the shower and grabbed her towel. "I'ma kill your li'l sneaky ass." He leaned on the sink and watched her.

When she'd finished patting her body dry, she got dressed and followed him from the bathroom and up the hallway. When she got into the living room, she went to the door and let Aiden in. He looked skeptical, but walked inside anyway.

"Hey, Aiden. Sorry about that."

He nodded. "It's cool."

Bronx turned around to find out that Kayden hadn't followed her. "Kayden!" she screamed for him. "Come here, real quick."

It took a minute before he walked up the hallway and looked at her. He didn't even bother to look at Aiden. He gave only her his attention.

"What's good?"

"Come talk to your brother."

"I'm straight. Is that all you wanted?"

Bronx's face softened as she looked at him before looking back at Aiden. "I'm sorry. I really did try."

"It's cool," Aiden told her with a half-smile.

It was all over his face, how sad and wounded he was, but sadly, he'd done this to himself. Much like Jessica had. They had truly hurt Kayden, and there was only so much she could do. The forgiveness would have to come when he was ready to give it; until then, they'd just have to suffer the consequences of their actions.

"I still love you, and I truly am sorry. It was poor judgment on my part." Aiden looked at Kayden, who was looking down at his phone screen, tapping away. "I'll be here whenever you're ready to talk," he said before walking to the door.

"That ain't happening, so do me a favor and don't show up at my spot no more. Better yet,"—Kayden walked toward him—"I don't want you talking to Bronx no more, either. I'd hate for you to have poor judgment when it comes to her, too."

Bronx died on the inside for Aiden.

"I deserve that," Aiden responded.

"You deserve more than that, but I don't even care about your ass enough to give it to you. Get up out my house."

The twins stared at each other for a long time before Aiden let himself out of the house. Once the door was closed, Bronx looked at him, ready to go off, but Kayden wasn't trying to hear it. He held his hand up to silence her before she could even get a word out.

"I don't want to hear it. You shouldn't have done that shit."

"I just want to help."

"That nigga don't need no help. He's grown as hell. He knows what he did was wrong. Fuck him."

Bronx nodded her understanding and went to him. With her arms around his neck, she kissed his mouth.

"You need your family, baby."

"Nah, what I need is you." Kayden dug in his pocket before pushing her away from him and kneeling in front of her.

Bronx grabbed both sides of her face and gasped before her hands went to her mouth, covering it in surprise. Kayden was smiling as he reached up and pulled her hand from her mouth.

"Marry me and let me be your diamond in the rough forever, baby."

Bronx felt like she was going to pass out as she looked at him in shock.

"Oh, hell, yeah, Kay!" She fell over on top of him. "Hell fucking yeah!" She laughed as he stood to his feet and slid the ring onto her finger.

He laughed with her before getting off the floor. "I love you."

"I love you, too." Bronx held her hand out so that she could see her ring. "How much you spent on this ring?"

"Why?"

"Because, you need to be saving your coins for all these kids you got."

Kayden looked at her, confused.

"I'm pregnant. Hopefully with twins that are as close as you and Aiden."

His smile faded. "Why you ruin the moment like that?"

"Because I want you to give him another chance for real, baby."

Kayden rubbed his hand over his head before looking down at her. "Maybe I'll forgive the nigga one day, but not now."

Bronx smiled. That was enough for her. All she'd wanted was for him to consider forgiving Aiden, so that he would have unconditional love surrounding him, even if there was no loyalty. Kayden was selfless and loving; he deserved a happy life. Now that she knew he would eventually give it a try, she could marry him, have all of his babies, and live happily ever after.

Connect with Us

Visit us online at
KensingtonBooks.com
to read more from your favorite authors, see books
by series, view reading group guides, and more.

Tell us what you think!

To share your thoughts, submit a review,
or sign up for our eNewsletters, please visit:
KensingtonBooks.com/TellUs.